Praise for Andreas Eschbach

"This is a novel of ideas that evokes complex emotions through the working out of an intricate and ultimately satisfying plot, with echoes of Gene Wolfe, Ursula K. Le Guin, and Isaac Asimov."

—*The New York Times Book Review*

"A world-class SF voice."

—*Locus*

"*The Carpet Makers* will blow you away. . . . [Eschbach] is clever, insightful, entertaining, and satisfying."

—*Analog*

"Effective writers of science fiction find in their alternative realities an emotional, spiritual, or cognitive consistency with the world we live in, and use fantasy not as a gimmick but as a tool to connect with readers. German author Andreas Eschbach is just such a science fiction writer."

—*The Intelligencer-Journal* (Lancaster, Pennsylvania)

TOR®

A Tom Doherty Associates Book

NEW YORK

ANDREAS ESCHBACH

The Carpet Makers

TRANSLATED BY DORYL JENSEN

THE CARPET MAKERS

Copyright © 1995 by Franz Schneekluth Verlag, München

English translation copyright © 2005 by Doryl Jensen

Originally published as *Die Haarteppichknüpfer* in 1995 by Franz Schneekluth Verlag in Munich, Germany.

A Tor Book
Published by Tom Doherty Associates, LLC
175 Fifth Avenue
New York, NY 10010

www.tor.com

Tor® is a registered trademark of Tom Doherty Associates, LLC.

Library of Congress Cataloging-in-Publication Data

Eschbach, Andreas, 1959–
    [Haarteppichknüpfer. English]
    The carpet makers / Andreas Eschbach; translated by Doryl Jensen; [with a foreword by Orson Scott Card].
        p. cm.
    ISBN 0-765-31490-8
    EAN 978-0-765-31490-1
    I. Title.

PT2665.S34H313 2005
833'.914—dc22   2004058866

First Hardcover Edition: April 2005
First Trade Paperback Edition: March 2006

Printed in the United States of America

0 9 8 7 6 5 4 3 2 1

Acknowledgments

It was Orson Scott Card who first introduced me to Andreas Eschbach's books, and then to Andreas himself. I was delighted to find that I not only enjoyed reading the novels and short stories, but that I liked Andreas very much as well: he is a man of charm and intelligence. So I am grateful to Scott for that introduction, and also for the years of friendship that he and Kristine have extended to my family and to me.

Das Europäische Übersetzer-Kollegium in Straelen, Germany, also deserves my special gratitude. I spent very productive weeks there while working on *The Carpet Makers*. Their reference library is superb, but the real pleasure of working there is the interaction with the staff and with the ever-changing coterie of other translators. I have seldom been in the company of more literate, intelligent, and helpful colleagues and friends.

Of course, I am always thankful to my four daughters—J.R., Emily, Kathryn, and Amanda—for their support and love, for their occasional reading of my translated texts, and for their willingness to offer insightful suggestions.

Doryl Jensen
Greensboro, NC

About The Carpet Makers . . .

I was at a science fiction convention in Poitiers, France, and all that anybody could talk about was this fantastic German writer, Andreas Eschbach. He wasn't the best new German writer, or even the best new European writer. He was, in their estimation, the most exciting new writer in the world.

I met him there, and found him a gentle, funny, wise young man without pretension or visible ego. I wanted very much to read his fiction, but I don't read German. And while there's plenty of translation from English into the languages of Europe—which is why I had been invited to the convention in the first place—there is very little translation into English.

I did, however, have a very good friend, Doryl Jensen, who not only speaks German fluently, but is also a fine writer and poet. "Do you have something short?" I asked Andreas. "Something I could take home and ask a friend to translate for me?"

It turned out that the first chapter of Eschbach's most noted novel had existed first as a short story. So I took that, and his synopsis of the rest of the plot, to Doryl, and asked him to translate it for me.

The result was a story that blew me away. Not only did Doryl assure me that Andreas was a superb writer in German, but he was as enthusiastic as I was about trying to get a Doryl Jensen translation of the entire novel published in English.

I was delighted when my own publisher, Tor, agreed that this was a book that transcended boundaries. Doryl's translation doesn't feel translated; it's so good that it seems as though the novel were originally written in English. Thus, Andreas Eschbach's novel has a good chance of meaning as much to American readers as it has to readers in Europe.

I know what it means to me. Eschbach is a novelist with vision, with compassion, and with a sense of tragedy, of character, of spectacle, and of human possibility, and also human inevitability. Sometimes, when I read a good book by someone else, I find myself wishing I had written it . . . but with *The Carpet Makers*, I was delighted that I did *not* write it, because I far preferred being able to discover it page by page, like any other reader.

I'm proud to have had the small role of bringing author, publisher, and translator together. But now my job is done. It's your journey now, into the pages of this unforgettable, beautiful, perpetually entertaining novel.

Orson Scott Card
Greensboro, NC
31 August 2004

The Carpet Makers

I

The Carpet Makers

KNOT AFTER KNOT, DAY IN, day out, for an entire lifetime, always the same hand movements, always looping the same knots in the fine hair, so fine and so tiny that with time, the fingers trembled and the eyes became weak from strain—and still the progress was hardly noticeable. On a day he made good headway, there was a new piece of his carpet perhaps as big as his fingernail. So he squatted before the creaking carpet frame where his father and his father before him had sat, each with the same stooped posture and with the old, filmy magnifying lens before his eyes, his arms propped against the worn breastboard, moving the knotting needle with only the tips of his fingers. Thus he tied knot upon knot as it had been passed down to him for generations until he slipped into a trance in which he felt whole; his back ceased to hurt and he no longer felt the age in his bones. He listened to the many different sounds of the house, which had been built by the grandfather of his great-grandfather—the wind, which always slipped over the roof in the same way and was caught in the open windows, the rattling of dishes and the talking of his wives and daughters below in the kitchen. Every sound was familiar. He picked out the voice of the Wise Woman who had been staying in the house the past few days in anticipation of the confinement of one of his wives, Garliad. He heard the muted doorbell clang; then the entry door opened and there was excitement in the murmuring of the voices. That was probably the peddler woman who was supposed to bring food supplies, textiles, and other things today.

Then heavy footfalls creaked up the stairs to the carpet-knotting room. That must be one of the women bringing him his midday meal. Below they would be inviting the peddler woman to the table to learn the latest gossip and to let themselves be talked into buying some bauble or other. He sighed, tightened the knot on which he was working, removed the magnifying lens, and turned around.

Garliad stood there with her enormous belly and with a steaming plate in her hand, waiting to come in when he gave permission with an impatient gesture.

"What are the other women thinking, letting you work in your condition?" he growled. "Do you want to deliver my daughter on the stairs?"

"I feel very well today, Ostvan," Garliad responded.

"Where's my son?"

She hesitated. "I don't know."

"Then I can imagine where he is," snorted Ostvan. "In the city! In that school! Reading books until his eyes ache and having his head filled with nonsense."

"He tried to repair the heating and left to get some sort of part. . . . That's what he said."

Ostvan hoisted himself up from his stool and took the plate from her hands. "I curse the day I allowed him go to that school in the city. Was I not blessed by God until then? Didn't he first give me five daughters and then one son, so that I didn't have to kill any of my children? And don't my daughters and wives have hair of all colors so that I don't have to dye the hair, and I can tie a carpet that will be worthy of the Emperor one day? Why can't I succeed in making a good carpet maker of my son, so that someday I can take my place beside God to help him tie the great carpet of life?"

"You're quarreling with fate, Ostvan."

"Should I not quarrel—with such a son? I know why his mother didn't bring me my food."

"I'm supposed to ask you for money to pay the peddler," said Garliad.

"Money, always money!" Ostvan put down the plate on the windowsill and shuffled over to a chest with steel fittings. It was decorated with a photograph of the carpet his father had tied and contained the money left over from the sale of that carpet, packed in individual boxes, labeled by year. He took out a coin. "Take it. But remember that this must last us for the rest of our lives."

"Yes, Ostvan."

"And when Abron returns, send him to me immediately."

"Yes, Ostvan." She left.

What kind of life was this, nothing but worry and aggravation! Ostvan pulled a chair up to the window and sat down to eat. His gaze became lost in the rocky, infertile desert. He used to go out occasionally, to look for certain minerals needed to make the secret compounds. He was even in the city several times to buy chemicals or tools. In the meantime, he had accumulated everything he would ever need for his carpet. He probably would not go out again. He was no longer young; his carpet would soon be finished, and then it would be time to think about dying.

Later, in the afternoon, quick steps on the stairs interrupted his work. It was Abron.

"You wanted to speak to me, Father?"

"Were you in the city?"

"I bought sootbrick for the heating."

"We still have sootbrick in the cellar, enough for generations."

"I didn't know."

"You could have asked me. But any excuse to go into the city is good enough for you."

Unbidden, Abron came closer. "I know it displeases you that I'm in the city so often and read books. But I can't help it, Father. It's so interesting . . . these other worlds. . . . There's so much to learn—so many different ways for people to live."

"I want to hear nothing of it. For you there is only one way to live. You have learned from me everything a hair-carpet maker must know; that is enough. You can tie all the knots, you have been instructed in soaking and dyeing techniques, and you know the traditional patterns. When you have designed your carpet, you will take a wife and have many daughters with different colored hair. And for your wedding, I will cut my carpet from the frame, bind it, and present it to you, and you will sell it in the city to the Imperial trader. That's what I did with the carpet of my father, and he did the same before me with the carpet of his father, and he with the carpet of his father, my great-grandfather; that is the way it has been from generation to generation for thousands of years. And just as I pay off my debt to you, you will pay off your debt to your son, and he to his son, and so on. It was always this way, and it will always be so."

Abron gave a tortured sigh. "Yes, of course, Father, but I'm not happy with this idea. I would rather not be a hair-carpet maker at all."

"I am a carpet maker, and therefore you will also be a carpet maker." With an agitated gesture, Ostvan pointed to the uncompleted carpet in the knotting frame. "For my whole life, I've worked on tying this carpet—my whole life—and from the profit, you will one day eat for your entire life. You have a debt to me, Abron, and I require that you pay off that debt to your own son. And God grant that he will not cause you as much sorrow as you have caused me!"

Abron did not dare look at his father as he replied, "There are rumors in the city about a rebellion, and rumors that the Emperor must abdicate. . . . Who will be able to pay for the hair carpets if the Emperor is gone?"

"The glory of the Emperor will outlast the light of the stars!" Ostvan said threateningly. "Didn't I teach you that phrase when you could barely sit up next to me at the carpet frame? Do you imagine that just anybody can come along and change the order of things, which was set by God?"

"No, Father," mumbled Abron, "of course not."

Ostvan watched him. "Now go to work on your carpet design."

"Yes, Father."

Late in the evening, Garliad's birth pangs began. The women accompanied her into the prepared birth room; Ostvan and Abron stayed in the kitchen.

Ostvan got two cups and a bottle of wine, and they drank silently. Sometimes they heard Garliad crying out or moaning in the birth room; then again there was nothing for a while. It was going to be a long night.

When his father fetched a second bottle of wine, Abron asked, "And if it's a boy?"

"You know as well as I do," Ostvan responded dully.

"Then what will you do?"

"The law has always said that a carpet maker may have only one son, because a carpet can support only one family." Ostvan pointed to an old, rust-flecked sword hanging on the wall. "With that, my grandfather killed my two brothers on the day of their birth."

Abron was silent. "You said that this is God's law," he finally erupted. "That must be a cruel God, don't you think?"

"Abron!" Ostvan thundered.

"I want to have nothing to do with your God!" screamed Abron, and flung himself out of the kitchen.

"Abron! Stay here!"

But Abron tore up the stairs to the bedchambers and did not return.

So Ostvan waited alone, but he did not drink any more. The hours passed, and his thoughts became more gloomy. Finally the first cries of a child were mixed among the cries of the mother, and Ostvan heard the women lamenting and sobbing. He stood up heavily as though every movement were painful; he took the sword from the wall and laid it on the table. Then he stood there and waited with somber patience until the Wise Woman came from the birth room with the newborn in her arms.

"It's a boy," she said calmly. "Will you kill him, sir?"

Ostvan looked at the rosy, wrinkled face of the child. "No," he said. "He will live. I want him to be named Ostvan after me. I will teach him the craft of a hair-carpet maker, and should I not live long enough, someone else will complete his training. Take him back to his mother, and tell her what I've said."

"Yes, sir," said the Wise Woman, and bore the child out.

Ostvan, however, took the sword from the table, went with it up to the bedchambers, and killed his son Abron.

II

The Hair-Carpet Trader

YAHANNOCHIA WAS GEARING UP for the annual arrival of the hair-carpet trader. It was like an awakening for the city that would lie motionless under the searing sun for the rest of the year. It began with garlands that appeared here and there under the low roofs, and with meager sprays of flowers that tried to cover up the stained walls of the houses. Day after day, there were more colorful pennants fluttering in the wind that swept, as it always did, over the ridges of the rooftops. And the smells from the cooking pots in the dark kitchens settled heavily into the narrow streets. Everyone knew it was important to be ready for the Great Festival. The women brushed their hair, and that of their mature daughters, for hours. The men finally patched their shoes. To the constant chatter of excited voices everywhere came the dissonant blaring of trumpets rehearsing their fanfares. The children, who usually played quietly and somberly in the alleyways, ran about yelling and wearing their best clothes. It was a colorful whirl, a feast for the senses, a feverish anticipation of the Great Day.

And then the day arrived. The riders who had been sent out returned and dashed through the streets trumpeting the news: "The trader is coming!"

"Who is it?" a thousand voices shouted.

"The carts bear the colors of the trader Moarkan," the scouts reported, then spurred their mounts and galloped on. And the thousand voices passed the name of the trader along through every house and hut, and everybody had something to say. "Moarkan!" They remembered when Moarkan had last been in Yahannochia and what goods he had had to offer from distant cities. "Moarkan!" They speculated where he might be coming from and from which cities he was bringing news and maybe even letters. "Moarkan is coming! . . ."

But it still took two whole days before the trader's enormous caravan entered the city.

First came the foot soldiers, marching ahead of the train of wagons. From a distance, they had seemed like a single, gigantic caterpillar with glittering spines on its back, creeping along the trade route toward Yahannochia. As they got closer, it was possible to distinguish the men in leather armor carrying their spears pointed skyward, so that the polished spear points caught the gleam of the sunlight. Tired, they trudged along, their faces crusted with dust and sweat, their eyes dull and clouded with exhaustion. All of them wore the colored insignia of the trader on their backs, like a brand.

Behind them rode the trader's mounted soldiers. Barely keeping their snorting mounts in check, they rode up the trail, armed with swords, maces, heavy whips, and knives. Some proudly bore old, scratched rayguns on their belts, and all of them looked down with disdain on the city folk lining the road. There was trouble for anyone who came too close to the procession! Whips responded immediately, and with the loud crack of leather, the riders opened a wide ford for the carts that followed them through the stream of curious onlookers.

These wagons were pulled by large, shaggy baraq buffalo with matted pelts; they stank as only baraq buffalo can stink. The carts came creaking, rattling, and jolting along, their uneven, iron-rimmed wheels grinding dry furrows into the road. Everyone knew that these wagons were laden with costly items from distant places—that they were packed full of bags of exotic spices, bolts of fine material, barrels of expensive delicacies, loads of luxurious woods, and strongboxes filled to the brim with priceless gems. The buffalo plodded along good-naturedly, but the carters, sitting on their coach-boxes with grim expressions, drove them forward to keep them from stopping when confronted with the unusual excitement all around.

Magnificently decorated and pulled by sixteen baraqs, the great cart, in which the trader and his family lived, came next. Every neck craned in the hope of catching a glimpse of Moarkan, but the merchant didn't show himself. The windows were curtained, and only two gruff carters were sitting on the coach-box.

Then finally, the hair-carpet wagon arrived. A murmur passed through the crowd at the roadside. There were no fewer than eighty-two buffalo pulling the steel colossus. The armored cart appeared to have no windows or openings, except for a single door to which the trader alone had a key. The eight broad wheels of the multiton monster dug into the road with loud crunching noises, and the driver had to constantly sting the backs of the buffalo with his whip to keep them moving ahead. The cart was accompanied by mounted soldiers, who scanned about suspiciously, as though they feared attack and plunder by superior forces at any moment. Everyone knew that the hair carpets the trader had already bought on his route were transported in this cart, along with the money—vast amounts of money—for the carpets he would still buy.

Other carts followed: the wagons in which the more important of the trader's servants lived, provision wagons for the soldiers, and wagons for the transport of tents and all sorts of equipment needed by such a mighty caravan. And behind the procession ran the children of the city, hollering, whistling, and shouting with enthusiasm for the exciting spectacle.

The caravan rolled into the large market square to the sound of fanfare. Flags and standards fluttered on tall masts, and the city craftsmen were giving the final touches to the stands they had erected in one corner of the big market to display their wares in the hope of doing good business with the trader's buyers. When the wagons of the caravan train came to a stop, the trader's servants immediately began setting up their own stands and sales tents. The square echoed with a babble of voices, with shouts and laughter, and with the clatter of tools and poles. At the fringes of the square, the residents of Yahannochia pressed in timidly, because the merchant's mounted soldiers were urging their proud steeds through the busy tumult, reaching threateningly for the whips at their belts whenever one of the city folk became too bold.

The city elders appeared, clothed in their most magnificent robes, escorted by city soldiers. The people from the trader's company made room for them and opened up a path through which they strode toward Moarkan's cart. They waited there patiently, until one small window was opened from the inside and the merchant peered out. He exchanged a few words with the dignitaries and then signaled to one of his servants.

This man, the trader's crier, scurried as nimbly as a lizard up to the roof of the trader's wagon, where he stood with his legs apart and his arms extended wide. He shouted, "Yahannochia! The market is open!"

. . . .

"We've been hearing strange rumors here about the Emperor for some time," one of the city elders said to Moarkan, while the tumult of the market's opening swirled around them. "Do you know anything more?"

Moarkan's crafty little eyes narrowed. "What rumors do you mean, sir?"

"The rumor is going around that the Emperor has abdicated."

"The Emperor? Is it possible for the Emperor to abdicate? Can the sun shine without him? Would the stars in the night sky not be extinguished without him?" The merchant shook his fat head. "And why do the Imperial Shipsmen buy the hair carpets from me just as they've always done for as long as anyone can remember? I've heard these rumors, too, but I know nothing about such things."

. . . .

In the meantime, on a large, decorated platform, the final preparations were being completed for the ritual, which was the real reason for the arrival of the trader: the presentation of the hair carpets.

"Citizens of Yahannochia, come and behold!" the master of ceremonies called out; he was a white-bearded giant of a man, robed in brown, black, red, and gold, the colors of the Guild of the Hair-Carpet Makers. The people paused, looked toward the stage, and slowly approached.

There were thirteen carpet makers who had finished their hair carpets this year and were now ready to present them to their sons. The carpets were attached to large frames and draped with gray cloth. Twelve of the carpet makers were present in person—old, bowed men who were able to stand only with difficulty and who glanced around with half-blind eyes. Only one of the carpet makers had already died and was represented by a younger member of the guild. On the other side of the platform stood thirteen young men, the sons of the old carpet makers.

"Citizens of Yahannochia, cast your eyes on the carpets that will beautify the Palace of the Emperor!" As happened every year, a reverent whispering went through the crowd when the carpet makers then unveiled their hair carpets—their life's work.

But this year there was already a skeptical undertone in the harmony of appreciative voices. "What's the meaning of the rumor that the Emperor has abdicated?" some voices asked.

The photographer who traveled with the merchant's train walked onto the platform and offered his services. As was the tradition, each hair carpet was photographed separately, and, with trembling fingers, each of the carpet makers accepted the image the photographer had created with his shabby, ancient apparatus.

Then the master of ceremonies spread wide his arms in a sweeping gesture that demanded silence; he closed his eyes and waited until quiet had settled over the large square, where everyone now paused and followed the events on the stage, spellbound. All conversation stopped, the craftsmen at their stands put aside their tools and other implements, everyone stood where he was, and stillness descended— so complete that every rustle of clothing and the wind lamenting in the beams of the large houses could be heard.

"We give thanks to the Emperor with all we have and with all we are," he solemnly intoned the traditional prayer. "We offer our life's work in gratitude to the One through whom we live and without whom we would be nothing. Just as every world in the Empire contributes its best to the beauty of the Emperor's Palace, we praise our good fortune that we may gratify the Emperor's eye with our art. He who created the brightest stars in the heavens and the darkness between them grants us the favor of placing his foot on the work of our hands. May he be praised now and forevermore."

"May he be praised," the people mumbled across the great square and bowed their heads.

The master of ceremonies gave a signal and a gong sounded. "The hour has come," he called out as he turned to the young men, "when the eternal covenant of the makers of hair carpets is renewed. Every generation takes on a debt to the previous one, and pays off its debt to its own children. Are you willing to keep this covenant?"

"We are willing," the sons responded in chorus.

"So you shall receive the work of your fathers and become indebted to them," the master of ceremonies concluded the ritual formula and gave the signal for the second striking of the gong.

The old carpet makers took out their knives and carefully severed the bands holding their carpets in the knotting frame. Cutting the carpet from the frame was a symbolic act closing out their life's work. One after the other, the sons approached their fathers, who carefully rolled up their carpets and—many with tears in their eyes—laid them in the arms of their sons.

Applause surged up when the last carpet had been presented, music began to play, and, as though a dam had been breached, the loud bustle of the market began again and turned into a festival.

. . . .

Dirilja, the trader's beautiful daughter, had watched the presentation ritual from her window, and when she heard the music ring out, she had tears in her eyes, too—but they were tears of pain. Crying, she lowered her head against the windowpane and dug her fingers into her long, reddish-blond hair.

Moarkan stood before the mirror and busied himself with giving just the right cast to the folds of his radiantly glittering robe; he snorted angrily, "It's been more than three years, Dirilja! He has surely found someone else, and all the tears in the world won't change that."

"But he promised to wait for me!" the girl sobbed.

"Pah! That's easy to say when you're in love," the merchant replied. "And just as quickly forgotten. A hot-blooded young man makes that promise at least every three days to someone else."

"That's not true. I'll never believe that. We swore to love one another forever—until we die—and it was an oath as sacred as the covenant oath of the carpet makers."

Moarkan observed his daughter silently for a while and shook his head with a sigh. "You hardly knew him, Dirilja. And believe me: someday you'll be happy that everything worked out this way. Why would you want to be the wife of a hair-carpet maker? You can't comb your hair without someone standing behind you to pluck every one of the strands from your brush. You have to share him with two or three wives or more. And if you bear him a child, you have to assume that it will be taken from you. On the other hand, with Buarati—"

"I don't want to become the wife of a fat, oily trader, even if he pays my weight in hair carpets!" Dirilja screamed in rage.

"As you wish," Moarkan responded. He turned to the mirror again and put on the heavy silver chain, the symbol of his status. "I have to go now." He opened the door, and the noise of the market flooded in. "But it seems to me," he said as he went out, "that fate is on my side— thank the Emperor!"

. . . .

Accompanied by the guildmaster of the carpet makers, the trader stepped onto the stage to appraise the carpets and to buy them. With dignified bearing, Moarkan approached the first heir and had the young man's hair carpet displayed to him. He tested the density of the knots with his fleshy fingers and thoroughly inspected the pattern before naming a price. The music played on without interruption; observers could only see the merchant's gestures and the carpet makers' reactions when he made his offer. The words that were spoken were hopelessly lost in the tumult of the market.

Usually the young men simply nodded with pale but composed expressions. Then the trader signaled to a servant who had been waiting a few steps away and gave him some brief instructions. In turn, with the help of several soldiers, the servant took care of the remaining business—bringing and counting out the money and transferring the hair carpet to the armored wagon—while Moarkan went on to the next carpet.

The guildmaster intervened when the price named by the trader seemed unjustifiably low to him. Heated discussions sometimes ensued, in which, however, the trader had the upper hand. The carpet makers could only choose to sell to him or to wait a year in the hope that the next trader would make a better offer.

One of the old carpet makers collapsed suddenly when Moarkan named his price, and he died a few moments later. The merchant waited until the man had been carried from the stage and then continued on without emotion. The crowd hardly took note of it. Something like that happened nearly every year, and the carpet makers considered such a death especially honorable. The music didn't even stop playing.

. . . .

Dirilja opened one of the windows on the side of the wagon toward the stage and extended her head. Her beautiful, long hair caused a stir, and whenever she saw someone looking in her direction, she waved him over and asked, "Do you know Abron?"

To most, the name meant nothing, but some of them knew him. "Abron? You mean the carpet maker's son?"

"Yes, do you know him?"

"For a while, he was often at the school, but I heard his father was against it."

"And now? What's he doing now?"

"I don't know. Nobody's seen him for a long time, for a very long time...."

Although it cut her to the heart, when she found an old woman who knew Abron, she overcame her reluctance and asked, "Have you heard if he has married?"

"Married? Abron? No . . . ," said the old woman. "That would have had to be last year or the year before at the Festival, and I would know about that. You see, I live right here on Market Square, in a little room under the roof of that house over there. . . ."

. . . .

In the meantime, preparations for the Courting had begun. While the last hair carpets were being sold, fathers brought their daughters of marriageable age to the edge of the platform. And when the hair-carpet trader and the guildmaster left the stage, the band switched over to lively dance tunes. With seductive movements, the girls began to dance slowly toward the young carpet makers, who were standing in the middle of the platform with their money chests. There, somewhat embarrassed, they watched the performance being played out for them.

Now the city folk gathered closer around the stage and clapped encouragement. The girls swirled their skirts as they tossed their heads, so that their long hair flew through the air and, in the setting sun, looked like the colorful flames of will-o'-the-wisps. In this manner, each one danced toward the young man who attracted her, touched him fleetingly on the chest or on the cheek, and leapt away again. They lured and teased, laughed and batted their eyes; sometimes they even raised their skirts above their knees for just a moment or traced the curves of their bodies with their hands.

The crowd cheered when the first of the young men stepped out of the circle and followed one of the girls. She tossed him promising glances while seeming to fall back in mock shyness, and she ran the tip of her tongue slowly over her half-opened lips to keep her advantage over the other girls now also trying their luck with this fellow. She lured him over to her father to ask for her hand with the ritual words. As usual, the father requested a glance into the carpet maker's money chest, and they walked back together through the wild hubbub to the circle at the center of the stage, from which other young men were now separating themselves to choose their own headwives. There the young carpet maker opened the lid of his chest, and if the father was satisfied with what he saw inside, he gave his consent. Then it was up to the guildmaster to examine the woman's hair and, if he had no objections, to perform the ceremony and record the marriage in the guildbook.

. . . .

Dirilja stared at the platform without really seeing what was going on there. The Courting of the carpet makers seemed sillier and more trivial to her than any children's game. Once again, she relived the hours together with Abron—back then, three years ago, when her father's trading caravan last made a stop in Yahannochia. She saw his face before her; again she felt the kisses they had exchanged, felt his soft hands on her body and the fear of being found together in a situation that had gone far beyond the boundaries of what was appropriate for young unmarried people. She heard his voice and felt again the certainty of that day, that this was real.

Suddenly she knew she could no longer live without learning about Abron's fate. She might try to forget Abron, but the price she would pay would be the loss of faith in herself. She would never know again whether she could trust her feelings. It was not a question of wounded honor or of painful jealousy. If it was the nature of the world, that such certainty as she had felt could be an illusion, then she didn't want to live in this world anymore.

She looked out through all the cart's windows and couldn't see her father anywhere. He was probably sitting with the city elders, swapping news and making secret deals.

In the marketplace, the first torches were being lit as Dirilja began to pack articles of clothing and other personal effects into a small shoulder bag.

. . . .

The music had stopped. Many stands were already being dismantled, the wares packed into wagons, and the money counted. Many of the city folk had already gone home.

After the marriage ceremonies of the young carpet makers to their headwives, the platform had become the scene for another market—for carpet makers seeking other wives, their subwives. The podium was illuminated by the flickering light of the torches. Men stood there expectantly with their young or not-so-young daughters. Several older carpet makers, most of them accompanied by their wives, shuttled their critical gazes from one girl to another, felt their splendid hair with trained fingers and, here and there, began serious discussions. No special ceremony was necessary to take a subwife; it was sufficient for the father to release her and for her to follow the carpet maker home.

. . . .

The next morning, the departure of the caravan was delayed. The wagons were ready to move, the buffalo snorted in agitation and shuffled their hooves, and the foot soldiers stood waiting in a large circle around the train of wagons. The sun rose higher and higher without the trumpets blaring out the departure. The gossip was that Dirilja, the trader's daughter, had disappeared. But, of course, no one dared to ask.

Finally, the sound of express riders galloping through the city streets was heard. A trusted servant of the trader hurried to his wagon and knocked on the windowpanes. Moarkan opened the door and stepped outside, decked out in his most splendid robes and decorated with all the insignia of his rank. He awaited the report from the scouts with a stony expression.

"We've looked everywhere, in the city and on all the roads leading out to the fortifications," the commander of the mounted soldiers reported, "but we've found no trace of your daughter anywhere."

"She is no longer my daughter," said Moarkan darkly, and issued his order: "Signal the departure! And make a note on the maps: we never intend to return to Yahannochia again."

. . . .

The merchant's caravan began to move slowly, but as unstoppably as a landslide. Now, as the train moved out of the city, only the children lined the roadside. In a cloud of dust, the monstrous parade of carts, animals, and people surged ahead, leaving behind deep wheel ruts and hoofprints that would not be covered over by the wind for many weeks.

Dirilja waited in her hiding place at the edge of the city until the caravan had disappeared beyond the horizon—then still one more day— before she dared emerge. Most of the people didn't know her, and the few who did recognize her reacted with nothing more than disapproving glances.

She managed to ask unobtrusively for directions to the house of the carpet maker Ostvan. Outfitted with some provisions, a water bottle, and a gray cloak for protection from the sun and dust, she started on her way.

The road was long and difficult without a mount. Enviously, she eyed a peddler coming toward her, a small woman, as old as the hills, riding on a yuk mule and leading behind her two others packed high with bundles of fabric, baskets, and leather purses. Although Dirilja had enough money to buy any animal in the city, nobody would have sold even a lame yuk mule to her, a young woman traveling alone.

When the stony path led uphill, she often had to stop, and while the sun was high in the sky, she crept into the shadow of an overhanging ledge and rested until her strength returned. In this way, it took her almost the entire day to reach her destination.

The house squatted there, sun-bleached and weathered like the skull of an old animal. The black caverns of its windows seemed to stare inquisitively at the young woman standing exhausted in the clean-swept yard, looking about indecisively.

Abruptly, a door opened and a small child came toddling out on unsure legs, followed by a slender woman with long curly hair.

A cramp gripped Dirilja's heart when she recognized that the child was a boy.

"Excuse me, is this the house of Ostvan?" she asked with effort.

"Yes," said the woman, and looked her over curiously from head to toe. "And who are you?"

"My name is Dirilja. I'm looking for Abron."

A shadow darkened the woman's face. "Why are you looking for him?"

"He was . . . I mean, we had . . . I'm the daughter of the hair-carpet trader Moarkan. Abron and I had promised one another . . . but he didn't come and . . ." Her speech faltered when the woman stepped up at these words and embraced her.

"My name is Garliad," she said. "Dirilja, Abron is dead."

. . . .

They led her inside—Garliad and Mera, Ostvan's headwife. They sat her down on a chair and gave her a glass of water. Dirilja told her story, and Mera, Abron's mother, told hers.

And when everything had been said, they were silent.

"What should I do now?" Dirilja asked quietly. "I left my father without his permission; he will be forced to reject me, and if I should ever meet him again, he will have to kill me. I can't go back."

Garliad took her hand. "You can stay here. Ostvan will take you as a subwife if we speak with him and explain everything."

"Here you'll be safe—that, at least," said Mera, and added, "Ostvan is old and won't be able to lie with you, Dirilja."

Dirilja nodded slowly. She looked down at the small boy sitting on the floor, playing with a little wooden carpet-knotting frame; she turned to the door that stood wide open and looked out into the distance across the rocky peaks and valleys, across the dusty, unfruitful desert land known only to the wind and to the merciless sun. Then she opened her bundle and began to unpack her things.

III

The Hair-Carpet Preacher

A SUDDEN GUST OF WIND tousled his hair and blew strands of it across his face. He pushed it back with an irritated sweep of the hand and then looked sullenly at the white hairs that had come out between his fingers. He was annoyed by every reminder that he was steadily getting older. He shook the strands of hair from his hand as though he were trying to rid himself of this thought.

He had tarried too long in all those houses, had tried too often to enlighten those recalcitrant patriarchs. A lifetime of experience should have told him he was just wasting his time. Now the evening winds were already tugging at his worn, gray cloak, and it was starting to get cool. The long, lonely roads between the remote houses of the carpet makers seemed more arduous to him each year. He decided to make only one more stop and then head home. Besides, the house of Ostvan was on his way.

Still, age did have one advantage that softened his mood from time to time: it gave him authority and dignity in people's eyes in a way that the poorly respected office of teacher had never afforded him. It happened less and less frequently that he had to argue about the necessity of children attending school or that a father refused to pay school fees for the next year. And more and more often, a stern look was sufficient to nip such objections in the bud.

But all that, he thought as he shambled, panting, along the stone path, all that wouldn't be reason enough to get old if I had a choice. He had made it his habit to get a head start on the calendar and collect the school fees somewhat earlier than usual, so that he could make his rounds during the cold season. Especially the visits to the carpet makers, who all lived far outside the city and to whom—as befitted their status—one had to go in person with any request . . . those were always strenuous days. He no longer wanted to attempt these treks in the glare of the sun at the end of the year.

Finally he reached the terrace in front of the house. He allowed himself several minutes to catch his breath while studying Ostvan's home. It was quite old, as were most of the homes of the hair-carpet makers. The teacher's sharp eye recognized a joining technique in the stone wall that had been commonly used in the last century. Some building additions were recognizably more recent, even though they appeared equally old.

Who was still interested in such things nowadays? he thought unhappily. That was the sort of knowledge that would disappear with him. He knocked on the door and glanced down quickly to be sure that his teacher's robe was properly draped. It was important to present a correct appearance, especially here.

An old woman opened the door for him. He recognized her. It was Ostvan's mother.

"My greetings to you, Garliad," he said. "I have come about the school tuition for your granddaughter Taroa."

"Parnag," she replied simply. "Come in."

He propped his staff against the wall outside and entered, gathering his robe about him. She offered him a seat and a cup of water; then she retreated to the rear of the house to inform her son. Through the open door, Parnag could hear the way she shuffled up the stairs to the carpet-knotting room.

He took a swallow. It felt good to sit down. He scrutinized the room he knew from earlier visits—the bare white walls, the rusty sword on a hook on the wall, the row of wine bottles on a high shelf. Through a crack in the door, he caught a glimpse of one of the carpet maker's other womenfolk, who was engaged in folding laundry in the next room. Then he heard steps again; this time they were young, resilient steps.

A young man with a narrow, hard-bitten face walked through the door. Ostvan the Younger. He was known to be very abrupt and offensive in his dealings with people and, in person, he gave the impression he was constantly trying to prove something. Parnag found Ostvan disagreeable, but he knew that Ostvan held him in high regard. *Maybe he senses that he has me to thank for his life,* Parnag thought bitterly.

They greeted one another formally, and Parnag reported the progress the carpet maker's daughter Taroa had made in the past year. Ostvan nodded at everything without seeming overly interested.

"Surely you're training her in obedience and in love for the Emperor, aren't you?" he wanted to know.

"Of course," said Parnag.

"Good." Ostvan nodded and pulled out a few coins to pay for the school fees.

Parnag departed, lost deep in thought. Every visit here stirred up something inside him: memories of times long past when he was young and full of energy and had believed he could concern himself with the whole universe—of times when he had felt strong enough to force the world to give up its secrets and its truths.

Parnag snorted in irritation. All long past that was. Today he was nothing more than a peculiar old man who suffered from too great a capacity for remembering. And besides, the sun already hung hazy red just above the horizon, and its rays were not strong enough to give any warmth. He had better hurry if he wanted to be home before nightfall.

A shadow that was moving along caught Parnag's attention. When he followed it with his eyes, he perceived the silhouette of a rider on the horizon. Bent over as though asleep, a large figure sat on a poor little mount that was plodding laboriously onward.

Parnag couldn't have said why, but this image elicited a sense of approaching doom in him. He stopped and squinted, but could see no better than before. A sleeping rider at dusk—that was surely nothing unusual.

. . . .

When he arrived home, he discovered to his dismay that he had forgotten to close the window to his schoolroom. The tireless north wind had had the entire day to blow fine sandy dust in from the desert and distribute it in every corner of the room. Aggravated, Parnag fetched his ragged straw broom from the cabinet where he also kept his small hoard of teaching supplies. He even had to sweep some sand out of the window frame in order to close it. He lit the earthen oil lamp and went to work in its warm, flickering light, dusting off the table and chairs, cleaning the shelves against the wall and the tattered books on them, and finally sweeping up the sand on the floor.

Afterward, he sat down exhausted on one of the chairs and stared into space. The unsteady light and this room at night—these things also stirred up memories, which had been awakened by the visit to Ostvan. It was here that they had often sat, had read to one another out of books. Filled with passionate intensity, they had discussed those words, sentence by sentence, until—more than once—night had turned into morning. But without warning, he had suddenly dissolved the little group. And since then, he had always avoided being in this room at night.

He still had the books. They were lying in a dark corner of the attic, bound up in a worn-out old sack and hidden beneath firewood. He was absolutely determined never in his lifetime to bring them out again; he would leave it up to his successor to find them . . . or never to find them at all.

Misfortune will befall whoever begins to doubt the Emperor.

Odd. He remembered suddenly that—even as a child—this doctrine had troubled him more than any other. Doubt was probably a sickness he was born with, and fighting against it was his lot in life . . . and learning to trust. Trust! He was very far from being trusting. In truth, he thought bitterly, I am satisfied just to stay away from the whole subject.

Misfortune will befall whoever begins to doubt the Emperor. And he will bring misfortune on all who associate with him.

Back then, purchasing these books had been a victory. He was able to convince a friend making a trip to the Port City to buy them for him, and the following year, he took possession of them with an unmatched feeling of triumph. He had paid an unbelievable sum of money for them, but it had been worth it to him. He would have given his right arm to own these books—books that came from other planets in the Empire.

But, without him realizing it, this act had planted the seeds of his doubt in fruitful ground.

To his boundless astonishment, he found references to makers of hair carpets in these books from three different worlds. Sometimes he came across words and expressions whose meanings were unclear to him, but the descriptions of this highest of all castes identified them clearly enough: they were men who spend their entire lives tying a single carpet for the Emperor's Palace out of the hair of their wives and daughters.

He still remembered the moment he stopped reading, looked up with furrowed brow, and stared at the sooty flame of the oil lamp while questions began to form in his mind that would never leave him from that moment on.

He began to make calculations. Most of his pupils never achieved any significant proficiency in dealing with large numbers, but arithmetic was one of his greatest strengths; even so, he soon found himself having difficulty. About three hundred carpet makers lived in the region of Yahannochia. And how many other such cities could there be? He wasn't sure, but even with cautious estimates, he came up with a breathtaking quantity of hair carpets, which the traders brought annually to the Port City for transfer to the spacecraft of the Imperial Shipsmen. And a hair carpet wasn't exactly small—about as long as a man was tall and as broad as his reach: that was considered to be the ideal size.

What were the words in the covenant oath of the carpet makers? *Every province of the Empire does its part to beautify the Palace of the Emperor, and it is our honor to tie the most precious carpets in the universe.* How big was this palace if the production of an entire planet wasn't sufficient to lay it with carpets?

He had had the sensation that he was dreaming. He could have done these calculations at any time in the past, but the idea wouldn't have occurred to him; before that moment, such number games would have seemed pure blasphemy to him. But now he owned these books telling him about makers of hair carpets on three other planets. . . . And who knew how many others there might be?

Now after so much time had passed, it wasn't easy for him to reconstruct the reasons for what he did then: he organized a little circle that met regularly in the evening, several men about his age who thought that continuing their learning was a worthy goal. Among them were the healer, several craftsmen, and one of the wealthy herdsmen.

It was a time-consuming and tiring business. He was trying to do nothing less than train them to become the conversation partners he was seeking. There was so much they had to learn before it made any sense to discuss the questions that were on his mind. Like most people, they had only the haziest concepts about the nature of the world they lived in. The Emperor lived "in a palace in the stars"—they knew that much—but they had no idea what that meant. So, he began by teaching them what he knew about stars and planets. That stars in the night sky are simply distant suns, many of them with their own planets, on which other people lived. That, of course, all these planets belonged to the Empire, and that, on one planet immeasurably far away in the heart of the Empire, stood the Star Palace. He had to teach them how to calculate area and how to deal with large numbers. And only then was he able to begin cautiously acquainting them with his heretical thoughts.

But . . . misfortune will befall whoever begins to doubt the Emperor. And he will bring misfortune on all who associate with him. Doubt starts at one point and then spreads like a consuming fire. . . .

. . . .

His memories pursued him even the following day while he was teaching. As usual, the little room was filled to the last chair and to the last available seat on the floor, and today it took great effort to keep the horde of lively children in check. The class read in unison while Parnag followed the text absentmindedly in his own book and tried to recognize the individual voices of those who were reading poorly or slowly. Usually, he was capable of that, but today he heard the voices of people who weren't there at all.

"There's a preacher speaking on Market Square," one of the older boys, the son of a cloth merchant, called out. "My father told me to go there after class."

"We can all go together," Parnag replied. He made it a point to appear especially zealous in religious matters.

That hadn't always been the case. In his younger years, he had been more open, had shared his thoughts and feelings without hesitation. When he felt low, he asked his pupils' pardon, and when a problem occupied him, he even made comments about it in class from time to time. Even when those books cast him into deep doubt and confusion, he tried to explain the situation to his pupils.

But he had looked into the uncomprehending eyes of the children and had changed the subject. Only one of his pupils, a curious, unusually intelligent boy named Abron, reacted differently.

To his amazement, Parnag found in this skinny, little boy the conversation partner he had been seeking without success among the adults. Abron knew so little, but what he knew was a foundation for surprisingly independent thoughts. He could look at you with his unfathomable, dark eyes, and with the simple, straightforward intelligence of a child, he could see through flawed conclusions and ask questions that got to the heart of the matter. Parnag was fascinated, and without a second thought, he invited the boy to participate in his evening discussion group.

Abron came, and he sat there with wide eyes, not saying a word. His father, Ostvan the Elder, a carpet maker, subsequently forbade him to attend school at all.

The teacher, however, invited Abron to come to see him whenever and as often as he wanted, to read all his books, and to ask anything that interested him. So Abron became a regular guest in Parnag's house. Again and again, he found excuses to slip into town to spend hours and then entire afternoons poring over the teacher's books. Parnag made him tea from the best herbs and answered all the boy's questions as best he could.

Looking back, Parnag realized with emotion that these had been the happiest hours of his life. He had come to love Abron as though he were his own son, and he tried with almost fatherly tenderness to satisfy the boy's unquenchable thirst for knowledge.

That was the reason Abron was present when Parnag unexpectedly received a visit from his friend who had returned from a second trip to the Port City, with a package of books—and an unbelievable rumor.

"Are you sure?" Parnag had to assure himself that he had heard correctly.

"I heard it from several of the foreign traders. And I can't imagine how they could have cooked it up together."

"A rebellion."

"Yes. A rebellion against the Emperor."

"Is that even possible?"

"They say the Emperor had to abdicate."

After that evening, Abron never returned. Sometime later, after exacting a promise of silence, someone informed Parnag that Abron was no longer alive. He had apparently made heretical, blasphemous statements at home, following which his father had killed him in favor of a newborn son.

At that moment, Parnag recognized the scope of his crime. He had allowed his doubt to destroy a promising young life. He had sown misfortune. Without a word of explanation, he dissolved the discussion group and refused ever afterward to talk about the questions that had been posed there.

. . . .

Now, as he trotted toward Market Square, surrounded by his pupils, a feeling of depression came over him. It was a cool, sunny day, but he felt as though he were walking through a valley engulfed in the black of night. He sank down into his memories as though they were quicksand. At the edge of his consciousness, he watched himself make several indecisive efforts to keep the band of children together, but he didn't really care, so he allowed them to do as they wished.

The preacher sat on one of the stone pedestals between which the stage was erected for festivals. A crowd of people of every age and social standing had gathered and was listening to his words.

"In my wanderings far and wide, I meet people in every city who say they are miserable; they are suffering, be it from hunger or poverty or at the hands of their fellow men," he shouted in the psalmodic intonation of itinerant preachers, which carried his voice a considerable distance. "They tell me this because they hope I can help them—perhaps with good counsel, perhaps with a miracle. But I can perform no miracles. I also have no good counsel, at least none you couldn't better give yourselves. All I do is to remind you of something you may have forgotten—namely, that you do not belong to yourselves, but to the Emperor, our Lord, and that you can only live if you live through him!"

Somebody brought him a piece of fruit as an offering, and he interrupted his sermon to accept the gift with a thin-lipped smile and to place it with the other things he had piled up next to him.

"And if you are suffering," he continued in an imploring tone, "you are suffering for only one reason: because you have forgotten that truth. Then, you try to think for yourselves, and the misfortune begins. Oh!" He raised his right hand in a sign of warning. "It is so easy to forget that you are the Emperor's. And it is such a difficult job, to remind you of it over and over again."

Strangely gaunt, his arm protruded up out of the sleeve of his ragged habit toward the sky. Parnag watched the scene with a somber gaze. He couldn't rid himself of the feeling that he had made a mess of his life.

"Why do you think that everywhere on this world we expend so much effort and are engaged in nothing but the tying of hair carpets? Do we do that just so the Emperor doesn't have to place his foot on bare stone? There must surely be other, easier solutions. No, all this—all the rituals—are nothing but the merciful gifts of our Emperor to us; they are his means of helping us, of preventing us from becoming lost to him and running headlong to our destruction. That is the sole purpose. With every hair the carpet maker picks up and knots, he is thinking, I belong to the Emperor. And the rest of you, you herdsmen and farmers and craftsmen, you are the ones who enable the carpet maker to do his duty. As you perform each of your chores, you have precisely the same right to repeat that thought: I belong to the Emperor. I am doing this for the Emperor. And as for me," he continued, folding his hands in a meek gesture across his chest, "when I wander from place to place and shout 'Remember!' to all I meet, I am only another humble tool of his will."

Parnag felt uneasy. He thought of the long list of houses he still had to visit to collect tuition, and it seemed a waste of time to stand around here. But he couldn't very well just leave.

The preacher looked about him, his eyes glistening with passion. "And therefore I must also speak of the unbelievers, of the doubters and heretics, and I must warn you who are true believers about them. The unbeliever is like someone with a contagious disease. He isn't like you who occasionally forget the truth—that is human, and it only takes a reminder to revive your faith. The unbeliever has not simply forgotten the truth, but rather, he knows it well and willfully ignores it."

A flush of heat rose in Parnag. It took effort to maintain a neutral expression. It seemed as though the haggard, bearded man were suddenly speaking to him alone.

"He does that because he expects some advantage from it, and he devises all kinds of cunning doubts and arguments to justify himself. And these doubts are like poison for the heart of a simple man, who can be led astray and in whom the unbeliever sows the seeds of doubt and, therefore, of destruction. I say unto you, if you suffer an unbeliever in your community, then you are acting like one whose house is burning and who sits calmly next to the fire."

Parnag had the feeling that some of the city folk were looking over at him, inspecting him suspiciously. His seditious questions had still not been forgotten, even after twenty years. Surely some of them were remembering now and wondering.

And they were right. The doubts were still inside him, like a seed waiting to bring forth destruction, and he was incapable of ripping it out. He had seen the way he had sent others tumbling into disaster, and he himself was persisting in a life of shapeless, gray days strung together one after another. Once doubts arose, they couldn't be made to disappear again. He was no longer able to think with the performance of each of his duties: I am doing this for the Emperor. He could only think, Does the Emperor even exist?

Who had ever seen the Emperor? They didn't even know where he lived—just that it had to be on a very distant planet. Naturally, there were the photographs, and the face of the Emperor was more familiar to everyone than the faces of his own parents. But, as far as Parnag knew, the Emperor had never yet set foot on this planet. It was said that the Emperor was immortal, that he had lived since the beginning of time and that he ruled all human beings. . . . So much was said and so little was known. Once you started doubting, it became an evil inner drive to continue.

"Be forewarned against the voices that preach doubt and unbelief. Be forewarned against lending your ears to heretical talk. Be forewarned against anyone who tries to convince you that you must find out the truth for yourselves. Nothing could be more false! The truth is much too big to be comprehended by a single, weak, mortal human being! No, only through love for and obedience to the Emperor can we partake of the truth and be guided safely—"

The preacher paused and scrutinized Parnag. Parnag returned his stare, and like a sudden bolt of lightning, the realization shot through him that he knew this face! He knew the preacher from somewhere and from so long ago that he couldn't at the moment recollect where. Then the sudden recognition was mutual; Parnag sensed that the other man recognized him, and he saw something like panic flash in the other man's eyes. But only for an instant, and then the eyes burned with a fanatical hate, with thirst for revenge.

Parnag felt sick. What might the ragged preacher be remembering? He felt his heart race, heard the blood rushing in his ears. He was only indistinctly aware that the preacher was continuing to speak. Was he challenging the crowd to stone him? He couldn't understand a thing.

He had doubted the Emperor and had brought misfortune down on others. Was it his turn now? Was his destiny catching up with him, despite all his regret and repentance?

Parnag fled. He heard himself say something to his senior pupil, probably that he should see that all the children got home, and then he left, felt the stones crunching underfoot and heard the sound echoing from the walls of the houses as his steps got faster and faster. The corner of the first house was like a lifesaver. Just disappear, get out of sight!

But then he suddenly remembered from where he knew the man. He stopped abruptly and let out an inarticulate sound of surprise. Could that be possible? This man he had known—a preacher? Although he knew deep inside that he was right, he had to turn around and return to be sure of himself. He stopped behind the corner of the building that had just served as his escape and peered out into Market Square.

There was no possible doubt. This man sitting in the circle of a reverently attentive crowd, dressed in the hair shirt of a holy wanderer, was no other than the man with whom he had directed the school in Kerkeema when he was young. He recognized the way he moved and now he recognized the facial features again. Brakart. That was his name.

Relieved, Parnag exhaled and only now did he sense how mortal fear had constricted his chest as though with steel bands. He had been afraid the man had identified him as a doubter, an atheist. He had run away because he was afraid of being stoned as a heretic. But he had nothing to fear. The other man had recognized him and had seen that Parnag knew who he was—so he realized he had come across someone who knew his secret. His dirty secret.

It had been almost forty years ago: Kerkeema, the city on the rim of the dormant volcano crater—with the long view across the plain and the bizarre shadows cast by every sunset. They had run the school in the city together, two young teachers; and while Parnag was thought of as friendly and sociable, Brakart soon had a reputation for strictness and severity. Hardly an evening went by when he didn't keep someone after class for individual instruction, and most of them were girls; he said they were less attentive in class than the boys.

The years passed until one day a case of illness, many tears, and a confession revealed that Brakart had used one of his female pupils for lascivious purposes, and that this had been the real reason for his rigid discipline. He fled headlong in the middle of the night before the enraged citizens could do anything to him, and Parnag then had to endure so many unpleasant hearings that he finally left Kerkeema, as well. That was the reason he had come to Yahannochia.

And now they had met again. Parnag suddenly felt miserable. Part of him was exulting that he was safe and that he had the other man in his power, but another part of him found it depressing: Would he really get off so easily? He had doubted and with that doubt he had killed a young man. He was hopelessly addicted to doubt, and the man who could have avenged that guilt was now in his power. It was a cheap victory without honor. No, not a victory—just an escape. His skin had been saved, but his honor was lost.

. . . .

On this afternoon he stayed home. The stingy carpet makers would not be sorry to keep their money one day longer. He paced back and forth in the house, randomly cleaned one thing or another, and remained lost in his thoughts. Gray. Everything was gray and desolate.

He stood for a long time in front of the leather satchel that hung on a hook in the entryway, lost completely in the sight of it. The satchel had once belonged to Abron. On his last visit, the boy had hung it there, and forgot it when he left. It had hung there ever since.

Later he had a sudden impulse to sing. With a cracking, untrained voice, he tried to start a song that had impressed him as a child. It began with the words: "I submit my all to you, my Emperor. . . ." But he couldn't remember the rest of the text and finally gave up.

Sometime later there was furious knocking at the door. He went to open it. It was Garubad, the herdsman, a short, gray-haired fellow in weathered leather garb. Twenty years ago, Garubad had also been a member of his discussion circle.

"Garubad . . ."

"My greetings to you, Parnag!" The bullish herdsman seemed to be in a fine mood, almost cheery. "I know it has been forever since we last spoke, but I absolutely have to tell you something. May I come in?"

"Of course." Parnag stepped aside and let him enter. He was oddly touched that this man would show up just now. They had had nothing to do with one another for years, actually since the herdsman's daughter had graduated from school.

"You'll never guess what happened to me," Garubad rattled on without a pause. "I just had to come to tell you about it. You remember those discussion evenings we had here at your place—when we were all still young? And all the things we talked about, right? I still remember it well; you taught us everything about planets and moons, and that the stars are very distant suns. . . ."

What's going on? thought Parnag. Why is everything from that time surrounding me today at every turn?

"Well, first I have to explain that I have come directly to your door from a rather long drive with my herds. Somebody, I think it was one of the itinerant peddler women, told me that for several weeks there had been water flowing in the old riverbed. Since things don't look good at the moment around the city, I drove my keppo sheep down there in the hope of finding grazing land and so on, you understand, right? Well, it was a trip of three days driving the sheep down there, and one day back alone."

Parnag fortified himself with patience. Garubad loved to hear himself talk, and he seldom got to the point without long detours.

"And here's the good part: On the way back, I made a side-jaunt to Schabrat Rock—after all, I was in the area anyway—just to see if I could pick up a few of those crystals people sometimes find there. And I am just starting to search, when he comes out of the cave!"

"Who?" Parnag asked, somewhat irritated.

"I don't know. A foreigner. He wore very odd clothing, and the way he talked! I don't know where he comes from, but it must be quite far away. Anyway, he comes up to me and asks who I am and what I do and where the closest city is and lots of other things like that. And then he tells me a bunch of the strangest things you can imagine, and finally he explains to me that he's a rebel."

Parnag had the distinct feeling his heart had skipped a beat. "A rebel?"

"Don't ask me what he meant by that, I didn't understand everything he said. He said something about being a rebel and that they had deposed the Emperor." Garubad giggled. "Imagine . . . he said that very seriously. Well, then I had to think about you, you know, and about your friend who came that afternoon and talked about rumors in the Port City—"

"Who else did you tell about this?" Parnag asked with a voice he hardly recognized as his own.

"Nobody yet. I just thought it would interest you. I just got back to the city—" He was already getting impatient; he had lost control of his story and wanted to continue. "By the way, what's going on here right now? The whole city is out and about."

"Probably because of the preacher who's been in town since yesterday evening," Parnag answered. He felt tired, confused, and overwhelmed by the things of the world. On a sudden impulse, he told Garubad that he knew the preacher and from where. "He's probably going around as a holy wanderer to free himself from his sins."

When he saw Garubad's face, he knew he should have kept all that to himself. Apparently it had touched a nerve with the herdsman, whose joviality changed suddenly, with no transition, into frosty politeness.

"I don't want to contradict your memory, Parnag," he responded stiffly, "but I think you should look again more closely. I'm almost certain that you must be wrong."

"Oh, that may be," the teacher backed off carefully.

. . . .

After Garubad left, Parnag stood for a long time in the entryway and stared straight ahead. It felt as though someone had pierced him with a big iron hook to stir everything up inside him—a thick sediment of repressed memories and feelings and an overpowering flood of images. The words of the cattle breeder echoed inside him like the sound of steps in a great cave.

A rebel? What might that mean? Was it even possible to depose the Emperor? He understood the words, but the idea seemed absurd and contradictory to Parnag.

But there were those books he kept hidden under stacks of dry wood and baraq dung. The other planets where hair carpets were knotted. That rumor that had reached him twenty years ago from the Port City.

Now he had to decide—what was the right thing to do? Something that required courage. Something that was frightening, because the unknown was lying in wait on the other side.

He suddenly felt how his hands were cramped and his fingers were digging into his own flesh. There was not much time for reflection. Nobody could know how long the foreigner might stay at Schabrat Rock. If he missed him, he would someday come to the end of his life with still-unanswered questions.

He met only a few old women on his way out of the city, and they didn't even bother to look at him. When he had left the city gates behind him, he could feel that the disquiet of the past few hours had disappeared. He was filled with calm clarity.

The horizon had become a molten, fire-red band and the first stars were appearing in the blue-black sky when he arrived at his destination. The cave-filled rocks rose up against the twilight like gloomy domes. He could see no one.

"Hello?" Parnag called finally, cautiously and quietly at first. Then, when he got no answer, louder: "Hello?!"

"He's not here anymore, the foreigner," intoned a voice, sharp as a knife.

Parnag twirled around. The preacher was standing there as though by magic. Brakart, the preacher. Brakart, the holy wanderer. Brakart, who had abused little girls. And now even more men came out from their hiding places behind the rocks.

Parnag saw that all of them carried stones in their hands. A hot wave rose from his belly and crashed in his head. He knew that they would kill him.

"What do you want from me, Brakart?" he asked with pretended indignation.

The preacher's eyes gleamed maliciously. "Don't call me by a name! I am a holy wanderer, and I no longer have a name."

Parnag was silent.

"It has been reported to me, Parnag," the preacher began slowly, "that many years ago you made heretical statements, and that you even tried to seduce your fellow men."

At that moment, Parnag discovered Garubad among the men who had made a large circle around him. "You?"

The herdsman raised his hands as though to defend himself. He was the only one not carrying a stone. "I didn't tell him anything except what I told you, Parnag."

"When Garubad told me about his chance meeting this afternoon, and also that you were the first one to learn of it, I thought the time had come to test your faithfulness," the holy wanderer continued. With naked triumph in his eyes, he added, "And you didn't pass the test!"

Parnag said nothing. There was nothing more to say. His guilt had finally caught up with him.

"I don't know who or what Garubad met. Maybe someone was playing a bad joke on him. Maybe he ran into an insane man. Maybe he imagined the whole thing—it doesn't matter. The only thing that matters is that you came. It proves that you think it's possible that there could be a rebellion against the Emperor. Maybe you even think it's possible—although a delusion of that magnitude goes beyond my imagination—that somebody could depose the Emperor. However that may be, your mere presence here proves that you are not a believing, god-fearing man. It proves the opposite. You're a doubter, and you probably have been all your life. And who knows how much misery you have brought on your fellow men?"

"Heretic," screamed one of the men.

The first stone struck Parnag near his temple and knocked him to the ground. He saw the sky . . . the wide, empty sky. I submit to you, my Emperor, he thought. The stones rained down on him now. Yes, I confess. I doubted you. I confess. I gave doubt a place in my heart, and I didn't repent. I confess. In your righteousness, my Emperor, you will destroy me, and I will be lost. I confess, and I submit to your judgment. . . .

IV

The Lost Hair Carpet

LATER, HE COULDN'T REMEMBER what had awakened him, whether it had been the smell of fire or the rustling of the flames or something else. He jumped up from his bed and screamed with only one thought—the carpet!

He screamed, screamed as loud as he could, screamed out against the raging crackle of the fire, filled the whole big house with the sound of his voice.

"Fire! Fire!"

He saw nothing but the licking tongues of flame, the scornfully flickering orange-red reflection on the walls and doors, the soot trails ascending like ghosts, and the smoke swirling and boiling at the ceiling. He shook off the hands trying to hold him back; he didn't hear the voices calling his name. He saw only the fire that would destroy his life's work.

"Borlon, stop! Save yourself! . . ."

He dashed ahead, without a thought for his wives. The smoke enveloped him and launched a stinging attack: it filled his eyes with tears and burned his lungs. Borlon grabbed a tatter of fabric and pressed it to his face. A clay pot burst on the floor; he stumbled over the shards and ran on. The carpet. He had to save the carpet. He had to save the carpet or die.

The fire roared through the house with unimaginable violence, like a raging storm; it looked for a worthy opponent and found none. Half-suffocated, Borlon reached the foot of the stairway leading up to the carpet-knotting room just as the wooden steps, charred black and spraying sparks, collapsed. His uncomprehending eyes watched as tongues of flame leapt up in a wild ballet to the balustrade where his knotting frame stood, and his ears heard the sound of the supporting beams slowly beginning to give way—it sounded like the terrified scream of a child. Then something inside him, which understood that it was too late, took over and allowed him to retreat.

When he reached his family standing outside at a safe distance, everything happened very fast. They took him between them— Karvita, his headwife, and Narana, his subwife—and he watched with a stony expression and without feeling as the fire ate its way through the ancient house, as it shattered the windowpanes and then flickered through them as though offering a derisive greeting, and as the roof suddenly began to glow, became more and more translucent, and finally collapsed, sending a cloud of sparks spiraling toward the sky. They hung there in the darkness like gently dancing stars and went out one after another while the fuel for the fire ran out below; in the end, there were hardly enough embers to send a bit of light into the night.

"How could that happen?" he wanted to ask, but he couldn't. He could only stare at the walls, charred black, and his mind refused to grasp the enormity of the event.

He would have stood there, motionless, until dawn, not knowing what to do. It was Karvita who found the charred remains of the money chest and put the sooty coins into her scarf, and it was Karvita who led the three of them along the difficult footpath through the bitter cold night to the house of her parents on the edge of the city.

. . . .

"It's my fault." He said it without looking at anyone, his tortured eyes staring off into an uncertain distance. A nameless pain swirled inside his chest, and something within him hoped to bring just punishment more quickly and painlessly down on his head by indicting himself and declaring his own guilt.

"Nonsense," his wife responded firmly. "Nobody knows whose fault it is. And you should finally have something to eat."

The sound of her voice pained him. He took a quick, sidelong glance at her and tried to find in her again that girl with the breathtakingly long, black hair he had fallen in love with. She was always so cool, so unapproachable, and in all the years, he had never succeeded in melting the ice. It was his own heart that had been frostbitten.

Without a word, Narana pushed a plate of grain mush across the table to him. Then, almost frightened that she had overstepped her bounds, she retreated to her chair. The delicate, blond subwife, who could have been the daughter of the other two, ate silently and quietly, bent over her plate as though she wanted to make herself invisible.

Borlon knew that Narana believed Karvita hated her, and she was probably right. Whenever the three of them were in a room together, there was tension in the air. Karvita never let it be seen in her cool mien, but Borlon was sure that she was jealous of the young subwife, because he slept with her.

Should he have forgone the pleasure? Narana was the only woman from whose bed he ever rose with a happy heart. She was young and shy and troubled, and originally he had only taken her to wife because of her glorious white-blond hair, which formed an unbelievably effective contrast to Karvita's hair. And she had lived untouched in their household for several years before he slept with her for the first time . . . at Karvita's suggestion.

When he was alone with her, she could be wonderfully relaxed, passionate, and filled with grateful tenderness. She was the ray of light in his life. But since that time, Karvita's heart had become inaccessible to him—permanently, it seemed—and he felt responsible for that.

He watched from the corner of his eye as Karvita ran her fingers through her hair, and out of pure habit, he extended his hand to receive the hairs that had come out in her fingers. In the middle of this gesture, he realized what he was doing, and he stopped himself. There was no carpet anymore on which he could continue his work. He sensed the memory of it like a burning ache in his chest.

"It does no good to blame yourself," Karvita said when she noticed the movement of his hand. "It won't bring back the carpet . . . or the house. There could be any number of causes: a spark from the cooking fire, embers in the ashes, anything."

"But what should I do now?" Borlon asked helplessly.

"First we have to rebuild the house. Then you'll start a new carpet."

Borlon raised his hands and looked at his fingertips, grooved from years of work with the knotting needle. "What did I do to bring this on me? I'm not young enough to finish a carpet of regulation size.

I have two wives with the most wondrous hair ever seen in the Emperor's realm, and—instead of tying a carpet—I will only be able to complete a narrow, little rug—"

"Borlon, please stop complaining. You could have died in the flames, then you couldn't have accomplished anything in your life." Now she was really annoyed. That's probably why she added, "Besides, you still don't have an heir, so the size of the carpet isn't very important."

Yes, Borlon thought bitterly. I haven't managed to do that either. A man with two wives, who still had no children, had nobody to blame but himself.

. . . .

Borlon thought he could see a hint of disapproval, even disgust, in the eyes of his mother-in-law when the little old woman let in the guild-master of the carpet maker's guild.

"I can't tell you how sorry I am, Borlon," said the guildmaster. "I was deeply shocked when your wife reported to me. . . . Such a misfor-tune hasn't occurred for as long as anyone can remember!"

Was he trying to humiliate him? To rub his nose into it, to show him what a failure he, Borlon, was? He scrutinized the tall, gaunt fig-ure of the guildmaster; the old carpet maker's gray-flecked hair was more disheveled than Borlon had ever seen it.

It sounded honest. The old man, otherwise always businesslike and serious, was really deeply moved and filled with empathy.

"When did it happen? Last night?" he asked as he sat down. "No one has heard about it in the city—"

"I don't want people to talk," Borlon said with effort.

"But why not? You can use all the help you can get—"

"I don't want it," Borlon insisted.

The guildmaster observed him for a while and then nodded his understanding. "Well, yes. At least you're informing me. And you're asking for my advice."

Borlon stared down at his hand lying large and heavy on the unfinished wood of the tabletop. The veins on the back of his hand pulsed almost unnoticeably, but continuously. When he began to speak, he had the feeling he was not speaking at all; he listened to himself and thought he could hear Karvita speaking in his voice. Hesitantly at first, then, after he got started, more and more fluently, he repeated what she had drilled into him.

"It's about my house, Guildmaster. It has to be rebuilt, I need a new knotting frame, new tools—I don't have enough money for all that. My father got a very bad price for his carpet, back then." My father was a failure, too, he thought. He tied a wonderful carpet and gave it away for a lousy starvation wage. But at least, he *finished* a carpet—the son of the failure, on the other hand . . .

"I know."

"And?"

"You're asking for a long-term loan."

"Yes."

The old carpet maker opened his hands slowly in a gesture of regret. "Borlon, please don't put me in a bind. You know the guild regulations. If you don't have a son, you can't get credit."

Borlon had to fight the feeling that he was sinking into a bottomless black hole. "I have no son. I have two wives and neither will bear me a son—"

"Then it probably isn't the fault of the women."

Oh yes. Of course not.

He stared at the guildmaster. There was something he was supposed to say now, but he had forgotten it. Or maybe there was nothing he could say.

"Look, Borlon, this sort of credit would have a term of a hundred twenty or a hundred sixty years. The children of your children would still have to pay on it. You can't make such a decision lightly. And naturally, the guild treasury needs some sort of security. If it appears that you might have no heirs, we can't give you long-term credit. That's the purpose of the regulation. And even so, we would be taking on a big risk, because who knows whether your son would have a son himself?"

"And short-term credit?" Borlon asked.

"With what do you intend to pay it back?" the guildmaster asked tersely.

"I'll tie another carpet," Borlon assured him hastily. "If I should have no heir, I can pay back the loan with it, and if I actually do have a son, then the credit could be changed over to a long-term loan. . . ."

The old man sighed. "I'm sorry, Borlon. I'm really sorry for you, because I have always valued you, and I loved the carpet you were making. But I am responsible to my office, and at the moment, I think I have a more realistic view of things than you do. First, you're no longer very young, Borlon. How large a carpet can you make, even if you work until you're blind? And a carpet that doesn't reach the prescribed dimensions will draw an extremely low price, as you know. In most cases, one would have to be satisfied if the trader took it at all. And second, you'd have to do your work on a new carpet frame whose wood still has to settle and which hasn't yet been under tension for decades. Everyone knows—and you know it, too—that you can't achieve the same quality on a new frame as on an old one. And you want to build a house, you have to live—I can't see how you could accomplish all that."

Borlon listened in disbelief while the guildmaster, whom he had considered a friend in good times and from whom he had hoped for help, delivered blow after blow without mercy.

"But . . . what should I do, then?"

The guildmaster looked at the floor and said quietly, "It happens from time to time that a carpet maker's line comes to an end. Some die young or without heirs—that's always been the case. Then, the guild looks for somebody who wants to fill the vacant position and found a new line, and we take care of his training and so on."

"And give him credit."

"If he has a son, yes."

Borlon hesitated. "One of my wives . . . Narana . . . she may be pregnant. . . ."

It was a lie and they both knew it.

"If she bears you a son, the credit will be no problem, I promise you," the guildmaster said, and stood up.

At the door, he turned around again. "We've talked a lot about money, Borlon, and very little about the meaning of our work. In this difficult time, I think you should try to renew your faith. There's a preacher in the city, I've heard. Maybe it would be a good idea for you to look him up."

. . . .

Borlon sat motionless after the guildmaster had gone and brooded in numb silence. Soon Karvita entered and asked about the outcome of the discussion. He just shook his head angrily.

"They don't want to give me a loan, because I have no son," he finally explained when she persisted.

"Then let's try," she responded immediately. "I'm not too old yet to have children." Reluctantly, she added, "And Narana's not nearly too old."

Why was everything the way it was? Why did everything have to be this way? You spend your entire life on one single carpet . . .

"And what if it still doesn't work? Karvita, why have we been together for so long and still don't have any children?"

She looked him over while her hands played with a lock of her blue-black hair. "Your son," she said cautiously, "just has to be borne by one of your wives. But it isn't really necessary that . . . you also father him!"

What was she daring to suggest to him? Penniless and battered by fate—now he was supposed to let himself be dishonored?

"It would naturally have to be done with the greatest discretion . . . ," his wife continued her thoughts.

"Karvita!"

She looked into his eyes and stopped in fright. "Pardon me, it was just an idea. Nothing more."

"Do you have any more ideas like that?"

She was silent. After a while—after she gave him a cautious glance—she said, "If the guild won't help you, maybe you have friends who will give you a loan. We can ask some of the more well-to-do carpet makers. Benegoran, for example. He must have much more money than he and his family can ever spend.

"Benegoran won't give me anything. That's why he's so rich—because he doesn't give anything away."

"I know one of his wives well. I could make a casual inquiry through her."

Borlon looked at her as she stood there in the doorway, and suddenly he could see the young girl in her again, and he remembered another late afternoon many years ago when she had stood in this doorway, exactly like this. The memory sent a sharp pain through his heart. She had always been a good companion to him, and he hated himself for all the times he had done wrong by her or treated her badly.

He stood up, actually intending to take her in his arms, but then he turned away and walked to the window.

"All right," he said. "But I don't want the whole city to hear about it."

"Sooner or later, we won't be able to keep it a secret."

Borlon thought about the isolated homes of the carpet makers in the mountain gorges and valleys all around the city. There was probably no spot in the whole region from which you could see two of these country estates at the same time. If all of them had succumbed to flames, it would have taken a long time before it was noticed in the city.

It would probably be the itinerant peddler women who would find the charred ruins and pass the news along.

"If so, then I prefer later. After we know how we'll get on with our lives."

The sun was low on the horizon again. Borlon could see the city gate and a few old women who stood chatting beneath it. An older man hurried out of the city; Borlon thought he looked familiar, but couldn't place him at the moment. Only after he was out of sight did it occur to him that it had been the teacher. In the past, he had come occasionally to ask about children, but he hadn't come for many years now, and in the meantime, Borlon had even forgotten his name.

I don't know the people in the city anymore, he thought. I had already reached the point in a carpet maker's life when he no longer leaves the house. Among all the feelings coursing through him at that moment was a powerful disillusionment: the boundless disillusionment of a man who has taken on a great and arduous enterprise and has failed shortly before reaching his goal.

He felt the strain and stress of the day—physically now, as well: the long march in the night and the few short hours of fitful sleep from which he had repeatedly awakened with a start; the forenoon when they had all tramped back out there to pace around the burned-out skeleton of the house, to rescue a few household articles from the ashes and to estimate the damage. Borlon reached for a bottle of wine and two cups. Suddenly, the acrid smell of the ashes was in his nose again, and he thought he could taste the smoke on his tongue.

He set down a cup for Karvita and one for himself. Then he opened the bottle. "Come," he said. "Drink with me."

. . . .

He was up early the next morning and was drawn out into the city streets. For the first time in his life he had lain with both his wives in one night, and also for the first time in his life, he had not been able to successfully complete this marital act—neither time.

My life is crumbling away beneath me, he thought. One piece after another is disappearing, failure is rippling out in all directions, and in the end, I will sink down and disappear, too.

No one paid him any heed, and he preferred that. It felt good to be invisible—not to be seen and to leave no traces behind. He had feared that the rumor might already have gotten around and that they would stare at him and whisper behind his back. But there were other things on the minds of the city folk. From what he gathered of their conversations in passing, a heretic had been stoned the previous evening on the order of a holy wanderer who had been in the city for two days.

Borlon recalled the advice of the guildmaster and turned his steps toward Market Square. Maybe it really was a question of his faith. He had not thought about the Emperor for a long time now; he had been concerned with nothing but his carpet and his own petty worries. He had lost his vision of great things, of the whole picture, and he would probably have continued along the same path until the end of his life, if nothing had happened.

Maybe the fire was his punishment for that. I don't want your carpet, if you don't tie your heart's blood and your love for me into it, the Emperor seemed to be telling him.

Oddly enough, these trains of thought comforted him. Everything seemed to have an explanation: at least there was that. He had sinned and, as a result, had deserved to be punished. The verdict was not up to him; whatever had happened was just, and it was his duty to accept it without complaint.

Market Square was almost empty of people. A few women sat at the edge of the market offering some vegetables they had spread out on tattered cloths, and since hardly anyone wanted to buy, they killed time with chatter. Borlon approached one of them and could tell by her eyes that she didn't recognize him. He inquired about the holy wanderer.

"The preacher? He already moved on early this morning," she responded.

"His words were so moving," interrupted one of the others, a fat woman missing her lower incisors. "Too bad he was here only one day."

"Strange, isn't it?" opined a third in an unpleasant, yapping voice. "I mean, usually you can't get rid of these holy men. I think it's odd that he's already taken off."

"That's true," nodded the fat woman with the gaps in her teeth. "I heard his sermon yesterday morning, and he listed all the subjects he wanted to preach to us about."

"You want to buy something, sir?" the first woman asked Borlon. "I have wonderfully fresh karaqui . . . or the bandroot here, great price—"

"No." Borlon shook his head. "Thanks. I just wanted to ask . . . about the preacher. . . ."

Everything was black and gloomy. The court of judgment was gathering around him, and there was no chance that he could sneak off and evade his culpability.

The dark windows of the houses around Market Square stared back at him like curious black eyes. He stood motionless for a while and sought out the feeling within himself, the feeling that he was falling without ever reaching the bottom, condemned to tumble eternally without striking solid earth and finding relief. Abruptly, he turned around and headed back.

In front of the house, he encountered Karvita's father, a little old man who was a weaver by trade and who, like all weavers, felt pious reverence for carpet makers. He had always approached his son-in-law in an almost subservient manner—but now Borlon also discovered the seeds of contempt in his eyes.

They merely nodded to one another. Borlon rushed into the house and up the stairs into Narana's room. She was sitting on a chair at the window, quiet and shy as always and looking much smaller and younger than she actually was. She was sewing. He took the needle and thread from her hand and lifted her onto the bed; without a word, he threw up her skirt, unbuttoned his trousers, and immediately forced himself into her with hard, quick thrusts of total despair. Then he fell down next to her on the bed and, gasping, he stared at the ceiling.

She left her skirt turned up, but pressed both hands between her legs. "You hurt me," she said quietly.

"I'm sorry."

"You've never hurt me before, Borlon." She spoke almost in amazement. "I didn't even know that it could hurt."

He said nothing; he just lay there and stared into space. After a while, she turned toward him, studied him with her large pensive eyes and began to stroke him gently. He knew that he didn't deserve it, but he let her continue while he desperately tried to understand what was going wrong.

"You are so terribly worried, Borlon," she whispered. "And all the while . . . think about it . . . we had enough money for the rest of our lives before the house burned down. Now we don't have a house anymore, but we still have the money. So what can happen to us?"

He closed his eyes and felt his heart pounding. It just wasn't that simple. "The carpet," he muttered. "I don't have a carpet anymore."

She didn't stop caressing his face with her fingers. "Borlon . . . Maybe you'll never have a son—so why do you need a carpet? If you die without an heir, the proceeds from the carpet will revert to the guild anyway . . . the guild that doesn't want to help you now."

"But the Emperor—"

"The Emperor gets so many hair carpets; he surely doesn't even know where to put them all. It can't be important whether there's one more or one less."

He sat straight up. "You don't understand. If I die without completing a carpet, then my life will have had no purpose."

He stood up, straightened his clothing, and went to the door. Narana was still lying on the bed with one hand between her naked legs, and in her eyes was the look of a wounded animal. He wanted to say something, he wanted to say how sorry he was and that he was ashamed, he wanted to talk about the pain tearing at his heart, but he couldn't find the words. "I'm sorry," he said, and he left.

If he only knew what was going wrong. There seemed to be no escape from all the guilt that was piling up higher and higher around him. With each heavy, awkward step he took down the stairs, he expected to fall down and to shatter like a clay pot.

Nobody was in the kitchen. The wine bottle was there and next to it, the cups from yesterday evening. He poured the wine without bothering to wash out the cup and began to drink.

. . . .

"I spoke with Benegoran," Karvita reported. "He'll lend you the money for a new house and a new knotting frame."

Borlon, who had sat the entire afternoon silently at the kitchen window watching the slow progress of the shadows until the sun had finally set, didn't move. The words barely penetrated his mind; they reached his consciousness as distant sounds devoid of meaning.

"However, he did set one condition."

Finally, he managed to turn his head and look at her. "A condition?"

"In return, he wants Narana," Karvita said.

He felt the bubbling beginnings of a laugh rising from his belly and stopping somewhere between his heart and his throat. "No."

He watched as she curled her hands into fists and struck them against her hips in a gesture of helplessness. "I don't know why I do all this," she exploded. "I've been on my feet all day long, I humiliate myself, I plead and beg and swallow the dust of the desert, and you dismiss it all with one word."

She reached for the wine bottle and looked inside. "And all you contribute to the effort is to get drunk and feel sorry for yourself. Do you think that's a solution?"

He understood dully that she wanted an answer—the way she was standing there and looking at him.

"No," he said.

"And what sort of solution do you have in mind?"

He shrugged his shoulders helplessly.

"Borlon, I know that Narana is important to you, probably more important than I am," she said bitterly. "But I implore you, at least think about it. At least, it's a possibility. And we don't have many possibilities."

There were so many things he had always wanted to tell her and so many things he wanted to tell her now that he didn't know where he should begin. Above all, he needed to make her understand that he loved her, that she had an unassailable place in his heart, and that it pained him that she didn't want to fill that place. And . . . that none of these things had anything to do with Narana. . . .

"You could at least speak with Benegoran yourself," she insisted.

That was useless. He knew that it was useless. Everything was useless.

"Then what will you do?" she asked.

He didn't know that either. He was silent. Silent, awaiting the sentence of the court. Silent, waiting for the towers of guilt all around him to collapse and bury him beneath them.

"Borlon? What's the matter?"

The words had again forfeited their meaning and become part of the background noise of the night. He turned back to the window and looked out at the dark sky. The small moon was there—it could be seen moving quickly across the firmament toward the big moon, which moved slowly toward it in the opposite direction. Tonight the small moon would pass directly across the bright face of the big moon.

He heard someone speaking, but he understood nothing, and understanding wasn't even important. Only the moons were important. He had to stay here and wait until they met one another and touched. A bang, like the slamming of a door, but that, too, was meaningless.

He sat motionless while the small moon moved. When he sat this way and waited, he could see how the stars in the lesser moon's path seemed to move closer and closer to the little oval ring of light until they were finally overwhelmed by its brightness and disappeared. And so the two moons drifted, star by star, toward one another across the vault of the heavens until they finally melted together into a single disk of light . . . while he sat without moving and watched.

He was tired. His eyes burned. When he finally turned away from the window, the oil lamp had already gone out. No more flame, no fire. That was good. He no longer knew exactly why, but it was good.

He could go now with his mind at rest. It was time. Out to the entryway to take his cloak from the hook, not because he would need it, but to tidy up, to leave no unwelcome traces behind. He mustn't trouble anyone with the odds and ends of a failed life. He didn't need that guilt, too.

Then open the door and close it slowly behind you. And just let your legs carry you along . . . along the street to the city gate and beyond, away from the city, farther and farther, and farther still, until your path meets the two moons and you melt away into their light. . . .

V

The Peddler Woman

ON HER TRAVELS between the isolated country houses of the carpet makers, she often saw only women for weeks at a time. The carpet makers' headwives, subwives, and daughters could hardly wait to invite her into their kitchens. However, it wasn't for her textiles and household implements that they waited so impatiently, but for the news she could tell about other families and about goings-on in the city. Then she sat there for hours with the women, and it was often difficult and required skillful manipulation of the conversation to bring up the subject of her wares. New recipes. That was her favorite trick. Ubhika knew an extensive number of unusual recipes—both for food and also for beauty aids of all kinds—that all had one thing in common: for each of them, either a special utensil was needed or a special spice, or some other special thing, which had to be purchased from her.

If she was lucky, she also got a bed for the night, since, with all the chatter and gossip, it often grew late. Today she had not been lucky. And what irked her most especially was that she should have seen it from the beginning. Hospitality had never counted for much in the house of Ostvan—not even in the days of the old Ostvan, and especially not in the house of his son. Shortly before dusk, the young carpet maker had walked sourly into the kitchen and said it was high time for the peddler woman to move on. And he spoke in a tone of voice that made everyone start with fear and wonder what sin they had committed. For a moment, Ubhika had felt like an adulteress instead of an itinerant peddler.

One of the women, at least, had helped her to pack up the yuk mules with her baskets and leather bags and bundles. Without that, she would not have made it down the steep descent from Ostvan's house in daylight. Dirilja was the woman's name. She was a small, quiet woman, considerably past her marriageable years, who never said much during the discussions; she always just stared sadly into the distance. Ubhika would have liked to know why. But that's the way it was with the womenfolk of the carpet makers: they appeared at some point and were simply there, and most of them told little about their past. Dirilja was the last wife old Ostvan took, shortly before his death. Which was odd, because his carpet must already have been finished by then, and Dirilja's hair was dry and brittle and thus not of the appropriate quality for a hair carpet. Ubhika trusted her judgment about that, because her own hair had been like that, even in the days when the silver-gray of age had not begun to show. This Dirilja, what could she have been up to with old Ostvan? A puzzling story.

The sun sank quickly toward the horizon, casting long, bothersome shadows between the hills and bare rocks, and it became noticeably cool. When Ubhika felt the wind nipping up under her skirt, she was peeved for allowing herself to be delayed so long. If she had set off earlier, she could have reached Borlon's house, where she was always allowed to stay the night.

But now, once again, there was no choice but her tent. Ubhika kept an eye out for a protected spot, a small cave or an overhang, and finally she found a hollow in the lee of a rock toward which she led her animals. She tethered them to stakes, which she painstakingly hammered into the ground. She removed the loads from the two pack yuks and blindfolded all three animals—the surest way to avoid having to search far and wide in case some noise spooked them in the night. Then she set up her small tent, padded it with a couple of layers of her cheaper fabric, and crawled in.

And once again, she lay there in the night, listened to the cracking of stones and the rustling of insect feet, and sensed that she was all alone in the middle of the wilderness, protected by nothing but a tiny tent and two packs on either side of her filled with foodstuffs, fabric, and utensils. And she thought, as always, that she would never get used to it. That it really should have been different. And, as always before going to sleep, she rubbed her hands over her body, as though to reassure herself that it was still there. She stroked her breasts, which were still firm despite her age and felt good to the touch; she ran her hands over her hips and regretted that no man's hands had ever touched them.

When she was of marriageable age, she didn't get a husband, and with her brittle hair she couldn't hope to become a carpet maker's subwife. So she was left only with the lonely business of an itinerant peddler woman. Occasionally, she had considered responding to the coarse suggestions of a craftsman or a herdsman, but in the meantime, even those advances had stopped.

As always, she eventually fell asleep and woke up in the early chill of the morning. When she crawled shivering out of her tent with a length of fabric wrapped around her body, the sun was just rising from the silvery morning twilight. And the vast view into the solitude all around made her feel like an insect, tiny and unimportant.

She could never bring herself to eat where she had spent the night. She untied her yuks, loaded them, removed their blindfolds, and was in a hurry to move on. Along the way, she chewed on dried baraq meat from her supplies or ate fruit if she had any.

Borlon's house. It was a good place to arrive in the morning, as well. Narana, Borlon's young subwife, would make tea for her; she always did. And then she would buy some new fabric from her, because she enjoyed needlework and did a lot of sewing.

But when Ubhika caught sight of Borlon's house, still a long way off, she immediately thought something was odd—much darker than she remembered it, almost black, as though charred. And when she got closer, she saw that, in fact, all that remained of Borlon's house were those bits even a mighty fire could not destroy.

Driven by morbid curiosity, she rode on toward it until she finally stood before charred wall fragments, smelling of fire and destruction, with the ashes of the wooden beams and shingles piled between them. She felt like a scavenger arriving late at the scene of a dramatic event, when the only thing to do is to make use of whatever is left. Maybe a few coins still lay somewhere in the ashes.

Ubhika recognized the foundation walls of the kitchen where she had sat many a time with the women, and next to it, the small chamber where she had often slept. She had never been farther into the house than that. Only now, as she shuffled through the sooty ruins, stirring up ashes and the smell of smoke with her feet, did she see what other rooms there were in a carpet maker's house. Which one might have been the carpet-knotting room? She would really have liked to know.

She found sooty footprints that led away from the rubble and disappeared somewhere on the rocky ground—the carpet maker's family appeared to have survived the fire.

But she found no money and nothing else worth taking. Finally she decided to move on. Still, she now had some interesting news to report. With a little elaboration, it could help her make some good sales and maybe even get her a meal here and there.

And then a man was suddenly standing there at the side of the trail. Just like that, in the middle of the wilderness.

Suspicious, Ubhika maneuvered her riding yuk closer, keeping one hand on the grip of the cudgel she carried on her saddle. But he gave her a friendly wave and smiled. And he was young. . . .

She caught herself involuntarily straightening her hair as she slowly rode closer. After all, I'm still young, too—the thought startled her— it's just my body that's betrayed me and gotten older. Nevertheless, for fear of appearing ridiculous, she lowered her hand.

"My greetings to you," said the man. It sounded odd. The way he spoke had something harsh about it, something foreign.

And he was oddly dressed, as well. He wore an outfit made of a fabric Ubhika had never seen before and which covered him completely from his neck to his feet. He wore a glittering piece of jewelry on his chest, and a belt around his waist to which all sorts of pouches and small, dark containers were attached.

"My greetings to you, stranger," Ubhika responded hesitantly.

The man smiled even more broadly. "My name is Nillian," he said, and he seemed to be making an effort to match the rhythm of his speech to that of Ubhika. "I come from very far away."

"From where?" Ubhika asked almost automatically.

"From Lukdaria," the man said. He said it with a slight hesitation, like someone who is taking refuge in a lie and fears being found out.

Ubhika had never heard of a city or a region with that name, but that might mean nothing. After all, it was obvious that the stranger had come from very far away. "My name is Ubhika, she said, and wondered why she was nervous. "I am a traveling peddler, as you can see."

He nodded. "That means you sell the things you have with you?"

"Yes." What else would that mean? she thought, and she studied his face. He looked strong and full of life—a man who could dance wildly and laugh out loud and drink along with everyone. He reminded her a bit of a boy she had loved when she was a very young girl. But nothing had happened there; he had married someone else, had learned the craft of a potter, and had died several years ago.

She admonished herself to get her mind on business again. Whoever the man was, he had asked what she had to sell. "Yes," she repeated. "What do you want to buy, Nillian?"

The man looked the yuk mules over, with their tall packs. "Do you have clothing?"

"Sure." Actually, she had mostly fabric, but there were also a few ready-made garments for men.

"I would like to dress the way that is customary in this region."

Ubhika looked around. She saw no mount anywhere. If the man came from so far away, how had he gotten here? Surely not on foot. And why was he standing here as though he knew he would come across a peddler? Something was going on that she didn't understand.

But business first. "Can you pay?" Ubhika asked. "Because that's customary in this region, too—paying."

The man laughed and said with a broad sweep of his hand, "That's not such an unusual custom; you find that one everywhere in the universe."

"I don't know anything about that. But I do have clothes for you if you have money."

"I have money."

"Good."

Ubhika dismounted, and she noticed that the man's eyes were following her. Instinctively, she moved more energetically than usual, as though she needed to prove that she was still strong and agile and not as old as her skinny body and her wrinkled, weathered skin suggested. Then she was immediately cross with herself, and she roughly yanked the bundle containing men's clothing out of her pack.

She rolled it out on the ground, and when she looked up, he was holding a few coins in his outstretched hand. "This is the money we get where I live," he explained. "Look first to see if you want to take it."

Ubhika took one of the coins from his hand. It was different from the coins she knew—more finely minted, shiny, made of some metal she had never seen. A beautiful coin. But not real money.

"No," she said with regret and gave him back the coin. "I can't sell you anything for that." And a little unexpected sale like this would really have been just what she needed.

The foreigner looked at the coin as though he were seeing it for the first time. "What's wrong with it?" he asked. "Don't you like it?"

"I like it fine," Ubhika responded. "But that's not the question. With money, it depends on whether other people like it."

She began to roll her bundle together again.

"Stop, wait!" the man called out. "Wait just a moment. Let's trade. Maybe I can give you something in exchange."

Ubhika paused and looked him over from head to toe. "What, for example?"

"I don't know.... Maybe the clothes I'm wearing?"

Ubhika tried to imagine who would wear such a peculiar garment. Nobody with half his senses. And whether she could make something else out of it was very questionable.... She shook her head. "No."

"Wait. Then something else. Here, my bracelet. My mother gave it to me; it really is very valuable."

He's not a very good trader, Ubhika thought with amusement. He wanted her miserable items of clothing at any price, and he wasn't even trying to hide it. He was like an open book. Every one of his gestures said, Please give them to me; I'll pay whatever you want. She almost felt sorry for him.

"You don't have our money, Nillian, and I can tell by your speech that you come from far away," she said, "so it won't do you much good to dress like the people here."

"The bracelet," he repeated, and held out the jewelry, which Ubhika seemed to remember he had worn on his right wrist. "How do you like it?"

She took the bracelet from his hand and felt a shiver at how heavy and cool it was to the touch. It was of a smooth metal that shone yellow and bore delicate, glittering designs on the outside. When she looked closely at the patterns, she noticed that the bracelet exuded a strong odor, a heavy, musky aroma that reminded her of the smell of oil from the musk glands of young baraq buffalo in heat. He must have worn this wristband a very long time. Maybe day and night since his mother gave it to him.

But was that story true? And why would someone give away a gift from his mother, and such a valuable one, for a few poor rags?

It didn't really matter. "Take whatever you want," Ubhika heard herself say; she was completely lost in examining the bracelet.

"You have to tell me what I need!" the man protested.

Sighing, Ubhika bent down to her bundle and fished out a pair of pants and a long shirt of crudely woven material and a jacket of the kind the herdsmen wore. Of course, she didn't have any herdsmen's boots; instead she gave him a pair of simple sandals.

"That won't fit me."

"Of course, it will fit you perfectly."

"I won't believe that until I've tried it on," the man replied, and to her boundless amazement, began to take off his clothes.

He did turn away from her, at least. He opened the jacket portion of his outfit at a seam that separated with a smacking sound, and he slipped out of the arms. A strong, naked torso appeared which shimmered velvety in the sunlight while the man began to fumble around with his belt.

Ubhika, who had forgotten to breathe, gasped in surprise and involuntarily looked all around as though she feared someone might be watching them. That had never happened before, that a man had undressed in front of her!

But the foreigner didn't seem to think anything about it. He stepped out of his pants and pulled on his newly bought trousers.

Ubhika stood there and stared at the naked, muscular back, so close she could have reached out her hand to touch it. And her hand actually twitched. Why not? she asked herself and was almost unable to master the desire to grasp the smooth, radiant skin of the man—just to experience for once how it would feel. And she saw his backside, small and powerful, covered only with a tight bit of clothing that looked like short trousers but lay incredibly tight against his skin. And she felt a peculiar wave of warmth spread throughout her abdomen.

And crazy thoughts entered her head. . . .

She rotated the wristband indecisively between her fingers. The patterns on the outside glittered wonderfully. Maybe she could give him back the bracelet and ask him instead to do the things with her that a man does with a woman—just once. . . .

What a crazy idea. She shoved the bracelet firmly over her left wrist. Impossible. She didn't want the humiliation of having him reject her and tell her she was too old.

"You're right," she heard him say innocently. He stretched out his arms in all directions and looked down at himself. "It really does fit."

Ubhika said nothing. She was afraid he could read her thoughts in her face.

But the stranger who called himself Nillian smiled distractedly at her and gathered up his things. He rolled the glittering outfit up into a bundle, which he held under his arm, and he draped the belt over his shoulder. He thanked her kindly and said this and that, which the peddler woman hardly heard, although she did remember later that she had answered him. And then he said good-bye.

She watched him go and he walked away, straight across the countryside. Not in the direction of the city. Shortly before reaching a depression in the ground, he turned again and waved to her. Then he disappeared.

Ubhika stood there for quite a while and stared blindly into the distance. Sometime later she came to her senses again, raised her left arm, and looked at the bracelet: it really was there. It wasn't all a dream.

She suddenly felt as though there were people all around her, behind every rock and hill, whispering secrets she wasn't supposed to hear. She made haste to roll up the remaining clothes and to pack them away. Then she took the reins of the two pack yuks, climbed on her mount, and kicked him in the ribs to get him to move. She felt a pressure on her chest that she couldn't quite explain.

And she tried not to think about the evening ahead. Tonight would be difficult.

VI

The Man from Someplace Else

"A HARSH PLANET, MOSTLY DESERT and steppes. Population estimated at three to four hundred million. Many medium-size cities, all in a state of deterioration. Few mineral resources, agriculture only under the most difficult conditions. Shortage of water."

It was Nillian's incredible dynamism he admired, the almost animal energy he radiated; it gave him a wild, untamable quality. Maybe it was because he seemed not to think too much: his words, his actions, and his decisions came more from his gut—immediate, unaffected, unpretentious, and barely thought out. Since he had been flying with Nillian, Nargant often noticed how his own thought processes made endless twists and turns, even to reach totally insignificant decisions, and how much energy he wasted, almost without thinking about it, trying to protect himself on all sides against all eventualities.

He watched Nillian from the side. The young copilot sat back relaxed in his seat with the microphone of the recorder at his lips and attentively studied the video monitors and the readouts of the tele-analysis instruments. His concentration was almost tangible. Various pictures of the planetary surface glowed on the video screens, gray brown without dramatic contours. The computer had superimposed several white lines, together with data about the dependability of the analysis.

"The instruments show something," Nillian continued, "that may, with a fair degree of probability, represent the rudimentary remains of a highly advanced, vanished culture. From space, straight lines are visible to the naked eye; the coloring suggests that they are foundation walls of earlier large structures. Very large structures. In the atmosphere, I register decomposition products of radioactive elements, small amounts of residual radiation. Possibly an atomic war several tens of thousands of years ago. There is some limited electromagnetic activity, presumably a simple form of radio communication, but we can locate no large energy sources. In other words," he concluded, and his voice took on a note of impatient irony, "the picture is very similar to all the previous surveys. I don't believe we will learn more as long as we continue the policy of prohibiting landings on the planets we visit. Naturally, that's my personal opinion, but I would not object, if the expedition leadership were to interpret this as a recommendation. Report from Nillian Jegetar Cuain on board the *Kalyt 9*. Standard time: 15-3-178002. Last instrument calibration: 4-2. Position: map quadrant 2014-BQA-57, orbiting the second planet of sun G-101. Out."

"Do you really want to send something like that?"

"Why not?"

"Those last comments are a bit . . . impertinent, aren't they?"

Nillian grinned and shook his head; he leaned toward the armatures of the communication unit and with the familiarity of routine, initiated the multiformat broadcast of his report. "Your problem, Nargant," he declared, "is that your education was unconnected with the practical reality of life. You grew up believing that rules are more important than all the facts you could ever uncover, and that the slightest disobedience is deadly. Aside from that, you didn't learn much, but this duty to obey has become your flesh and bone, and on some distant day after your death, when they cut you apart, they'll probably find crystallized obedience in the place of your bone marrow."

Nargant stared at his hands, as though he were trying to see through his skin to find out if Nillian might be right. "You won't be able to change me into a rebel, Nillian," he mumbled uncomfortably.

The stupid thing was that he felt it himself. Since he had been traveling with this former rebel and had observed himself in contrast, he always felt like a fossil.

"No, Imperial Soldier, and you won't turn into a rebel either," Nillian responded. Now he was serious. "And thank God that's no longer necessary. But I would appreciate it very much if you could forget your old drills just a little. How long have we been under way now? Nearly forty days. Forty days, just you and me in this little expedition ship, and to tell the truth, I still don't have any idea if you even like me. Or if you are just sticking it out with me because you were commanded to do it."

"I do," Nargant said. "I like you." It sounded terribly wooden. Have I ever actually said that to anyone else? he wondered in amazement.

"Thanks. I rather like you, too, and that's why it bothers me when you tiptoe around me as though I had to report after the flight on your orthodoxy to a commission of priests or even just to the Rebel Council."

"Tiptoe? . . ."

"Yes! So careful, so cautious . . . at all costs, don't let an improper word slip out, and always behave correctly. . . . I think you should stand in front of the mirror every morning and evening and shout out loud to yourself, 'There is no Emperor anymore!' You should do that for at least a couple of years."

Nargant wondered whether he was really serious.

"Well, I can try it."

"I only mean that, once in a while, you should turn off that damn censor they planted in your brain and say flat out what comes into your mind, regardless of what I think. Do you suppose you can do that—at least once in a while?"

"I'll try." Sometimes he found the rebel quite irritating. For example, why was he laughing at this answer?

"And do you think you could disobey a couple of rules sometime? Interpret a few directives a little more loosely?"

"Hmmm . . . I don't know. What, for example?"

A conspiratorial look entered Nillian's eyes. "For example, the directive that we shouldn't land on any of the planets?"

Nargant caught his breath. "Surely you're not planning . . . ?"

Nillian nodded wildly, and his eyes sparkled with eagerness for adventure.

"But you can't!" Even the thought of it made him tremble. And after the previous conversation, he felt himself really in a bind. He felt his heart beat faster. "We have orders—strict orders!—not to land on the planets we visit."

"But we're not really landing." Nillian grinned broadly. It was hard to decide if it was a malicious or a satisfied grin, or both. We just dip down into the atmosphere a bit—"

"And then? . . ."

"You drop me off in an airboat."

Nargant took a deep breath and clenched his fists. Blood was pounding in his temples. He looked away and anchored his gaze on one of the unfamiliar stars that could be seen silent and mysterious through the hatch windows. But there was no help there.

"We can't do that."

"But why not?"

"Because it's disobeying a direct order!"

"Tut tut," Nillian clucked. "Terrible." And he said nothing.

Nargant avoided Nillian's eyes; he was acquainted well enough with the former rebel to know Nillian was watching him in anticipation.

Planet G-101/2 hung above them like a great dirty-brown ball. There were no cities visible with the naked eye.

"I don't know what you think you'll gain," Nargant finally sighed.

"Knowledge," Nillian said simply. "We don't know much yet, but we do know one thing for sure: we won't find out what's going on around here by approaching one planet after another and taking standard measurements from orbit."

"We've found out a whole lot of things," Nargant contradicted him. "All the planets we have observed up until now are populated. Everywhere we find planetary civilization at a rather primitive level. And everywhere we've found traces of a very ancient war that was fought with atomic weapons."

"Boring," the young copilot countered. "Basically, that's only confirming what we already knew."

"But those were only wild legends, barely believable stories from a handful of smugglers. Now we finally know it from our own experience."

Nillian jumped up so suddenly that Nargant recoiled. "Does all this just leave you completely cold?" he shouted in agitation. "We're cruising here in a galaxy that appears to have been part of the Empire for unimaginable ages—but that isn't recorded on a single star map! We've discovered a vanished part of the Empire, about which there are no documents in the Imperial Archive. And nobody knows why. Nobody knows what's waiting for us here. After all, that's an incredible mystery!"

He sank back again as though this outburst had exhausted him. "And when you imagine that the trail leading to this mystery came to light only through a chain of coincidences..." With fingers spread wide, his hands began to trace wondrous circles in the air. "All these coincidences had to fit together just to bring us here to this point. There was the magistrate of Eswerlund, who had a smuggler's hideout tracked down, as though he didn't have more pressing matters to attend to... there was the technician who looked through the memory units on board the confiscated spaceships instead of just erasing them and happened to find the star maps of the Gheera Galaxy... there was the vote in the Council that only decided on this mission by a one-vote majority.... And here we are. And damn it, it's our duty to find out as much as possible about what's going on here and how it was possible that an enormous chunk of the Empire could have disappeared and been forgotten for tens of thousands of years."

Nargant was silent. With his index finger he traced slowly over the torn upholstery of the main steering knob; it felt scratchy in some spots where the stuffing was spilling out through the cracks and tears.

"What's your plan?" No matter what, he wanted to be able to say later that he had not agreed to this.

Nillian sighed. "You drop me off in the atmosphere in the airboat. I'll land near a settlement and try to make contact with the inhabitants."

"And how do you plan to communicate with them?"

"To judge by the radio transmissions we've picked up, they speak a very old form of Paisi. It may require a little getting used to, but I think I can manage."

"And if not?"

Nillian shrugged his shoulders. "Maybe I'll pretend to be deaf and dumb. Or I'll try to learn the language." He hoisted himself up out of his seat. "I'll think of something." Then he climbed down the narrow ladder leading into the lower part of the spaceship.

Nargant recognized that the rebel wouldn't be deterred from his plan, and he gave up his resistance. Bowing to fate, he followed him below and watched with uneasiness as Nillian loaded equipment into the airboat—the tent that was actually intended for emergency landings, some food, and a few of the instruments for planetary exploration that were supposed to stay in their storage cabinets during this flight.

"Take a weapon," he advised.

"Nonsense."

"What do you intend to do if you get into a dangerous situation? There are humans down there, after all!"

Nillian paused and turned around. Their eyes met. "I'll rely on you, partner," the young rebel said finally with a strange smile that Nargant didn't know how to interpret.

A brief whine of the engines was sufficient to slow the expedition ship down in order to leave its low-level orbit and descend. The planet loomed larger and larger, and soon the nerve-racking whistling sounds of the first atmospheric particles sailing past the shell at tremendous speeds came from everywhere. The whistling turned to howling and finally to a deafening roar as the spacecraft fell deeper into the layers of atmosphere.

Nargant continued to brake and went into a parabolic trajectory, which, at its lowest point, would come quite close to the surface and would then catapult the ship back out into space.

"Ready?"

"Ready!"

Just before reaching the lowest point of the arc, he disengaged the airboat. As elegantly as if their pilots had practiced nothing else for years, the two craft separated. Nargant shot up into the black sky and went into a very high stationary orbit in which he followed the rotation of the planet and would remain approximately above Nillian's location. As the thundering of the engines died down and the spaceship recovered with crackling sounds from its exertion, he made radio contact.

Nillian was already recording a running report.

"I'm flying over a settlement. You could almost call it a city . . . very spread out, many small huts and narrow streets, but also some broad roads. I see some greenspace and gardens. A kind of wall encloses the entire settlement, including the gardens. Outside the city wall, there seems to be nothing but desert and steppes, but with hardy vegetation in some places. I see some grazing animals; so there may be some breeding of domestic stock."

Nargant checked the recorder. The sturdy unit was running constantly, recording every word.

"On my right side is a dark, towering rock formation, easily recognizable from the air. The sensors suggest possible caves there. That's where I'll land; maybe it will be a good base location."

Nargant pulled a face. Caves! On such a desolate planet, wouldn't there be other—and, above all, safer—places to set up an inflatable tent?

"Whoops! There are also a few buildings in the area outside the city. Some of them are quite far from the settlement, several hours by foot, I would guess. The infrared sensors show that the structures are inhabited. I also see something that could be smoke from a chimney."

It was insanity. The whole undertaking was insanity. Nargant massaged his neck and wished he were far away.

"Now I'll fly in a wide loop toward the south until I see the rock I'm heading for. It really is useful as an excellent optical marker from the air. I'm coming in there for a landing."

Nargant pulled out a rag and began to polish the covers of the gauges. I advised him against it, he thought. Maybe I should have insisted on recording my opposition in the logbook.

The harsh sound of the landing gear touching down was followed by the whining slowdown of the gravity motor.

"I've landed. I just opened the hatch and am now breathing the planetary atmosphere. The air is breathable, quite hot and full of smells—it smells of dust and excrement, and there's another sweetish smell, like something rotting. . . . Naturally, I'm especially sensitive now after breathing only sterile air for months in the ship, but I think I can get by without breathing through a filter. I am going to get out now and scout around the rocks for a good location for the tent."

Nargant sighed and looked up. Through the viewing hatch at his right he saw the larger of this planet's two moons. The planet had a second, significantly smaller satellite circling in the opposite direction and requiring less than two planetary days for a complete orbit. But at the moment the smaller moon was not in view.

"It's quite rocky and steep here. I think I'll break the connection for a while and hang the unit on my belt so I'll have both hands free. Do you still read me, Nargant?"

Nargant bent toward the microphone and pressed the ON switch. "Of course."

"It's a relief to know that." He heard Nillian laugh out loud. "I just realized that I am several million light-years from home, and that it's a long way on foot if you leave me in the lurch. Okay, until later."

Some brief static; then the loudspeaker was quiet. The recorder stopped automatically. The familiar sounds of the spaceship closed in around Nargant: the almost inaudible hissing of the air supply system, occasionally an oddly resounding clank from the engine, and the diverse whispering and clattering noises of the instruments in the control panel.

After a few minutes, Nargant realized that he was staring as though hypnotized at the numbers on the ship's clock and waiting for the next radio contact. Irritated, he stood up and climbed down into the lounge to have something to drink.

I'm angry at myself, he realized. Now Nillian has his adventure, and I'm hanging here in orbit, dying of boredom.

It took a distressingly long time for Nillian to make contact again.

"I just had my first contact with a local inhabitant. An older man. The communication went quite well, better than I expected. But I probably confused him a bit with my talk. I had thought there were no people hereabouts, but from what he said, there must be some sort of gemstones in these caves, and sometimes people come here looking for them. He was quite chatty; we had a good conversation. Interestingly, here, they still consider the Emperor to be the immortal, godlike lord, even if they don't know very much else about the Empire. When I told him about the Rebellion, he wouldn't believe a word of it."

Nargant could still remember well the time in his life when the Emperor had also been the center of the universe for him. Even now, after twenty years of difficult, bloody secularization, he still felt pain in that place where this faith used to be, a pain that was tied to shame, to a sense of having failed—and also to a feeling of loss.

The young rebel had it good. Back then, he was still just a child, and in his education he was never subjected to the all-stifling religious machinery of the priestly caste. He surely couldn't even imagine the burden of anguish someone like Nargant would carry around with him for the rest of his life.

"It's fortunate I landed the airboat in a spot where it can't easily be seen. I don't think he saw it. But still, I'll look for a different place to bed down for the night."

The rest of the day passed quietly. Nillian flew to various places and took pictures, which he transferred up to the ship. Nargant was able to look at the photographs on the monitor: shots of broad, desolate landscapes, of crooked, old huts in need of repair, and of hardly recognizable footpaths winding endlessly through rocky ravines.

The next morning, Nillian gave up on his original idea of simply walking into the city and looking around. Instead, he spent the entire day locating individual wanderers who were either under way on foot or were mounted on riding animals. He landed at a safe distance, walked up to them, and asked them questions. In one of these contacts he bought himself a complete outfit of local clothing in exchange for his immensely valuable wristband. This willingness on Nillian's part to make sacrifices instinctively impressed Nargant, and he had to admit to himself that his fears were eased by the caution with which the rebel was proceeding.

Around noon on the following day, Nillian discovered a man who had apparently lost his way in the desert. "I've been observing him for a while. It puzzles me why a man would be under way here on foot. He can only have come from the city, so he must have been walking for at least an entire day. Down here, the heat is merciless and there's no water anywhere. He seems to keep falling down." He was silent for a while. "Now, he's not getting up any more. He's probably lost consciousness. Well, now I can at least spare him the sight of the airboat. I'm going to land."

"Give him a tranquilizer shot," Nargant advised. "Otherwise he'll wake up on board your airboat, and you have no idea how he'll react."

"Good idea. Which vial is that? The yellow one?"

"Yes. Just administer half the dosage; his circulation system is probably significantly weakened."

"Okay."

By listening to the sounds from the loudspeaker, Nargant followed as Nillian picked up the unconscious man and transported him to a cool, shady place. There he hydrated him with one and a half bottles of water. Then he could only wait until the rescued man awoke.

"Nargant, this is Nillian."

Nargant started. He had dozed off in the pilot's chair.

"Yes?"

There was a little crackling and popping in the loudspeaker, and then Nillian asked, "Does the concept 'hair carpet' mean anything to you?"

Nargant scratched at his head and thought about it. "No," he said. "I could only guess that it refers to a carpet made of hair or, at least, having that appearance. Why do you ask?"

"I talked with the man a bit. He told me that he was by profession a knotter of hair carpets. *Profession* is maybe the wrong word; the way he described it sounded more like a social caste. Anyway, I asked to be sure, and he really did mean that he ties carpets out of hair—human hair."

"Out of human hair?" Nargant was still trying to wake up fully. Why was Nillian telling him all of this?

"It must also be an enormously time-consuming business. Unless I completely misunderstood, he needs his entire lifetime to tie just one of these carpets."

"Sounds rather odd."

"I told him that, too, and he was absolutely astonished at my attitude. Making these carpets must be something like a sacred rite here. By the way, because I didn't know what a hair carpet is, his conclusion was razor-sharp: that I must come from another planet."

Nargant gasped for air. "And what did you say?"

"I admitted it. Why shouldn't I? I find it interesting that the people here know there are other inhabited worlds. Since everything seems to be so primitive, I wouldn't have expected that."

To his own amazement, Nargant noticed that his hands were shaking. Only now did he sense that he was sick—sick with fear. He was filled with anxiety that would not ease until this adventure was over and Nillian was on board again, an anxiety that was trying—against all reason—to protect the two of them from the consequences of their obvious insubordination.

"What are you planning to do now?" he asked, and hoped his voice was not betraying any of that.

"The hair carpets interest me," came his untroubled reply. "I asked him to show me the carpet he is working on, but he says he can't. No idea why—he muttered something I couldn't understand. But we'll visit one of his colleagues, another carpet maker, and I can see his carpet."

It was a physical matter. His mind knew that the rebels had a different concept of discipline, but his body didn't understand it. His body was more prepared to die than to disobey a command.

"When are you going there?"

"I've given him an energy compound; I'll wait until it takes effect. Maybe an hour. The man was in bad shape. But I can't get out of him what he was doing there in the desert. A rather mysterious story, the whole thing."

"Are you wearing the local clothing?"

"Of course. Incredibly uncomfortable, by the way. It makes places itch you didn't even know you had."

"When will you report in again?"

"Right after the visit to the other carpet maker. We have a two- to three-hour walk ahead of us; fortunately the sun is already rather low, and it isn't quite so hot now. It could be that he will invite us to stay the night, which I won't refuse, of course."

"You'll have the radio with you in case of an emergency?"

"Of course." Nillian laughed out loud. "Hey, are you worrying about me?"

Nargant felt a twinge at these words. He realized that, in all honesty, he wasn't, and it made him feel shabby and vile. Actually, he was worrying about himself, about what would happen to him if something unfortunate occurred to Nillian. He didn't deserve the friendship the young rebel was extending to him, because he was incapable of returning it. All he could do was envy Nillian's easy attitude and inner freedom and feel like a cripple in comparison.

"I'm dead tired," he said, avoiding the question. "I'll try to sleep a little. Good luck. Out."

"Thanks. Out," Nillian responded. There was an audible pop, and the recorder turned itself off again.

Nargant remained in his chair, laid his head back, and closed his eyes. He felt as though his eyeballs were vibrating. I'm sure I won't be able to sleep, he thought. But he was asleep before he could manage to lift his eyelids one more time, and he slipped into a restless dream.

When he awoke, it took a while before it came to him where he was and what had happened. As he stared at the ship's clock, his dull brain tried without success to figure out how long he had slept. At any rate, the counter on the recorder hadn't moved, which meant that Nillian hadn't yet reported in again.

He walked to the viewing window and looked out, down at the enormous sphere of the planet. An endless twilight stretched across the dirty-brown surface from pole to pole. It was like a shock when he suddenly realized that it was already early morning in Nillian's location. He had slept the entire night.

And Nillian hadn't reported in.

He reached for the microphone and hit the activation switch much too hard.

"Nillian?"

He waited, but everything remained silent. He became more formal, "*Kalyt 9* calling Nillian Jegetar Cuain, please respond!" That also brought nothing.

Time passed, and Nillian still didn't check in. Nargant sat in his pilot's chair and spoke Nillian's name into the radio again and again for hours. He rewound the recorder and listened to the reports, but there really was nothing, no radio message from Nillian. He was unaware that he was constantly chewing his lower lip and that it was already starting to bleed.

He felt virtually torn in two by opposing powers pulling at him like two forces of nature. On the one hand, there was the command, the clear, unambiguous and unrescinded order, not to land on the planets under observation and also his sense of obedience, of which he had once been so proud. He had known from the beginning that this adventure had to go wrong—from the beginning. One single man, alone on an unknown planet in an unknown culture, which had had no contact with the Empire for tens of thousands of years—what could such a man expect to accomplish except to hasten his own death?

On the other hand, there was this new feeling of friendship, the knowledge that now, somewhere down below was a man who might be trapped in a dangerous situation and who was hanging all his hopes on him. There was a man who believed in him and had worked to gain his friendship, even though he knew that those things were difficult for this former imperial soldier. Maybe Nillian was looking up into a dark night sky at this very moment, where he knew there was a small, fragile spaceship, and was waiting to be rescued.

Nargant drew in a deep breath and steeled himself. He had made a decision, and that gave him new strength. With practiced hands, he prepared to send out a multi-format broadcast message.

"Nargant, pilot of Expedition Boat *Kalyt 9*. Calling Heavy Cruiser *Trikood* under Capt. Jerom Karswant. Attention. This is an emergency."

Pause. Without noticing it, Nargant wiped beads of sweat from his brow. He felt as though this were more than a radio message, as though he had to engage his entire body and all its strength to say and do what was necessary. He knew that he couldn't think about it too much; otherwise, he wouldn't be able to send the message. Just talk and send it immediately, and then let the consequences come. He released the PAUSE button.

"Disregarding our orders, my partner Nillian Jegetar Cuain landed on the surface of Planet G-101/2 three days ago standard time, in order to do additional research among the inhabitants. His last planned radio contact is now eight hours overdue. The following events should be noted. . . ." He reported the facts briefly, completely, and without regard for the trembling in his legs. "Please advise. Nargant, on board *Kalyt 9*. Current standard time 18-3-178002. Last instrument calibration: 4-2. Position: map quadrant 2014-BQA-57, orbiting the second planet of sun G-101. Out."

By the time he sent the message, he was wet with perspiration. Now everything would take its course. Reduced to information particles in an incomprehensible dimension, the message raced toward its goal, and no one could hold it back. Nargant lowered the microphone and settled in for a long wait. He was tired, but he knew he wouldn't be able to sleep.

In the hours that followed, he called Nillian's name into the electromagnetic radio again and again. His nerves seemed to glow, and he was plagued with a premonition of approaching disaster.

Suddenly, the orange-red signal for incoming messages lit up on the transmission unit, and the recorder switched on automatically. Nargant started from his fitful half-sleep. The flagship of the Gheera Fleet was calling!

"This is Heavy Cruiser *Trikood*. *Kalyt 9*, we confirm your message, sent standard time 15-3-178002. The expedition headquarters is issuing you a directive to interrupt your research and to return as quickly as possible. Out."

Time seemed to stand still. Suddenly, Nargant heard nothing but the wild pounding of his heart and the rushing of hot blood in his ears. He thought he could hear "Error! Error! Error!" in the rhythmic meter of the beating of his pulse. He had made an error. He had allowed an error to be made. He had been disobedient, and he would be punished without leniency. The only thing he could do, for the sake of his honor, was to return as quickly and as humbly as possible to accept his punishment.

Nargant's hands flew over the armatures. The whispering and murmuring of the instruments in the control panel died out as the colossal engines in the depths of the spaceship came to life and made the outer shell vibrate. Fear had swept away every thought, even the thoughts of Nillian. A needle crept up from the red into the green zone while massive power units boomed as they pumped energy into the ship's drive. Then Nargant accelerated and sent the ship tearing toward the dark fabric of stars. Each of his movements bespoke a lifelong routine; even half-dead, he could still have flown the ship. Without a single wasted movement, he made preparations for trans-light-speed flight, and soon after that *Kalyt 9* slipped into that dimension that is governed by other laws ... where there is no limitation on movement through space, but where everyone is alone. No message can reach a spacecraft under way within this incomprehensible superspatial dimension.

That was the reason that Nargant missed the arrival of the real answer to his emergency message by several minutes.

"*Kalyt 9*, this is Capt. Jerom Karswant on board the *Trikood*. Attention. This countermands the previous order you received. That order was a standard directive to all expedition boats. Nargant, stay in orbit around G-101/2 and continue your attempts to make radio contact with Nillian. I am sending the Light Cruiser *Salkantar*. Calculate the closest entry point for a ship of that size, and send the exact coordinates, so that the *Salkantar* can reach you as quickly as possible. Repeat: Do not return to base. Maintain your position, and facilitate the arrival of the *Salkantar*. Help is on the way."

Much later, after the arrival of the expedition ship *Kalyt 9* at the Gheera Expedition Base, and after repeated conversations with the *Salkantar*, which tried without success to locate the star G-101 using imprecise and error-filled star maps, it became clear to Nargant: in his panic, he had not noticed that the message he assumed to be an answer to his emergency call had arrived much sooner than the laws of physics would have allowed; it was a routine message to all expedition boats. It also became clear, that with his rash return, he had abandoned his comrade Nillian and had probably condemned him to death.

He had an unpleasant interview with the bullish captain of the expedition fleet, but the rebel general didn't punish him. And that was perhaps the severest punishment.

From then on, Nargant said every morning aloud to himself in the mirror: "There is no Emperor anymore." And every time he spoke these words, he felt within himself the profound fear that was still crippling him, and he recalled the man who had given him trust and friendship. He had wanted so much to return both those gifts, but it had been beyond his ability.

VII

The Tax Collector

HE HAD BEEN FOLLOWING the trade route markers for days, and he really had no cause for worry. The rough-hewn waystones were set at regular intervals and were easy to recognize, and only in a few places had dunes drifted over the firmly trampled road. Still, he breathed a sigh of relief when Yahannochia finally appeared on the horizon.

His jibarat was indifferent. The mount didn't change its steady, rolling gait, not even when he tried, against his better judgment, to urge it ahead by striking it with the flat of his hand. In regard to the proper tempo for long, overland trips, jibarats had more sense than people.

Now he could see the estates of the hair-carpet makers scattered among the hills. Depending on the age and style of the houses, some were showy and colorful, others gray brown and inconspicuously hugging the cliffs. There were houses with pitched roofs and walls of red-fired clay. Others were flat and constructed of cut stone. He even saw a house that was completely black and, from a distance, appeared to have been gutted by fire.

No one paid him any attention as he rode through the city gate.

Children ran about quarrelling loudly, and a few women stood chatting at the corner of a house. Only once or twice did he see unmistakable fright in the eyes of those whose glance fell on the insignia on his saddlebags: the insignia of the Imperial Tax Collector.

He still knew his way around. Not much had changed since his last visit, which was now a good three years ago. He still found his way through the narrow alleys past wretched, dusty workshops and dark pubs, past stained walls and moldy piles of wood to the City Elders Hall.

A tight smile played about his lips. They would not fool him. He would assess and tax them without mercy. Of course, they knew that he would come; they always knew. And he had been in the Imperial service for decades; he knew all the tricks. No need for them to imagine that they could deceive him with their wretched housefronts. A closer look would find fat hams hanging in the cellars and fine linens in the cupboards.

Godless thieves! They were asked to sacrifice nothing from their pitiful lives but a little tax, and they even tried to evade that.

He stopped his jibarat in front of the City Elders Hall and, without dismounting, rapped on one of the windows. A young man stuck his head out and asked what he desired.

"I am Kremman, Imperial Tax Collector and Judge. Announce my arrival to the city elders."

The boy's eyes widened when he saw the Imperial seal. He nodded hastily and disappeared.

They tried all the tricks. At Brepenniki, his last stop, they had burned the General Tax Ledger. Of course, they hadn't admitted it; they never admitted something like that. They claimed that a blaze broke out in the City Elders Hall, which destroyed the book. As though they could get around paying taxes with a story like that! The only thing they accomplished was a delay in his schedule. A new ledger had to be created, and every city resident had to be assessed anew. There had been weeping and gnashing of teeth, but he had not been swayed and had done his duty. He knew they would be more cautious in the future. They wouldn't try that again with him.

The door to the City Elders Hall flew open, and a fat old man came rushing out, still slipping into the sleeves of his well-worn ceremonial robe. Wheezing, he came to a halt before Kremman, finally finished donning his robe, and looked up at the tax collector with tiny beads of sweat on his forehead.

"Greetings in the name of the Emperor, Kremman!" he called out nervously. "It is good that you have arrived, very good, as a matter of fact, because we've had a heretic in the dungeon since yesterday, and we don't know what to do with him. But now Your Honor can pronounce judgment."

Kremman looked disdainfully down on the man. "Don't waste my time. If he's a heretic, then hang him as the law requires."

Snorting loudly, the city elder nodded so eagerly that it seemed that he might fall over at any moment. "I would never pester Your Honor with the matter if he were a common heretic, never. But he is not a common heretic; as a matter of fact, he's an extremely uncommon heretic, and I am absolutely convinced . . ."

The things they could dream up! If only they would direct this resourcefulness to their work instead of using it to try to fool him!

He stemmed the man's torrent of speech with a motion of his hand. "First I want to deal with the books, which is the reason I have come."

"Certainly, of course. Pardon my thoughtlessness. Your Honor must be exhausted from the trip. Do you want to see the books immediately, or may I first show you to your quarters and have some refreshment provided?"

"First the books," Kremman insisted, and heaved himself from the saddle.

"First the books, very good. Follow me."

Kremman took the bag with the implements of his profession and followed the old man into the cellar vaults of the City Elders Hall. While he spread out his utensils on a large table with motions practiced hundreds of times, he silently watched the old man fumble with a rusty key and open the large, iron-fitted cabinet in which the General Tax Ledgers were kept.

"Now bring me the Book of Changes," Kremman ordered when the city elder had placed the sealed ledger on the table.

"I will have it brought immediately," the man mumbled.

Kremman smiled maliciously as the city elder shambled through the door. He had surely planned to distract Kremman from his work with these tales. And now he was disappointed, because it had not worked.

He would get them. Sooner or later he got them all.

Then he set to work. First he had to determine whether the seal of Yahannochia's tax book was really intact. He carefully felt the bands of the seal that encircled the book; they were undamaged. On to the seal itself. He hefted it thoughtfully and looked it over with a critical eye. In his lifetime, he had broken and attached thousands of seals, but at this point he always paused and did not allow himself to fall into a routine. The seal of the tax ledger was the most sensitive point in the system. If they should ever succeed in faking a seal without his noticing it, then they would have him. If that were to become public, it would cost him his head. And if it did not become known, then they would be able to blackmail him to the end of his days.

The youth who had opened the window—probably the town page—entered and brought the city's Book of Changes. Kremman indicated with an ungracious nod of the head that he should lay it on the table, and when he noticed the boy's curiosity, he stared at him so venomously that the boy decided to disappear as quickly as possible. He needed no spectators for this work.

Kremman cautiously pressed his signet over the wax seal. To his relief, it fit. Even a careful examination with a strong magnifying glass revealed no irregularities.

They would not dare. They hadn't forgotten that it was he, as a young tax collector, who had discovered the counterfeit tax seal in Three River City. They had not forgotten the harshness with which he had reassessed the entire city and had imposed a supplementary tax penalty so severe that the eyes of the townspeople had filled with tears.

Now the last test. After a short glance at the door to ensure that there was really no one watching, he took a small knife and began to scratch the image on the seal carefully. That was the secret, which no one had discovered by breaking or melting down the seal: under the first image there was a second one, which could be revealed only by dexterous and experienced fingers. Kremman scraped away with infinite care until an unremarkable shift in color in the sealing wax indicated the line of separation. And now with just a small twist of the knife, which had taken him years to learn, the upper layer of the wax split away cleanly. There lay the secret seal, a tiny signet imprint known only to the Imperial tax collectors. Kremman smiled in satisfaction, reached for a candle, and melted the seal completely away. He let the wax drip into a small iron bowl; when his work was finished, he would fashion a new seal from it.

Then he opened the book. This moment had electrified him as long as he could remember, this moment of power. In this book were recorded the belongings of all the townspeople, the riches of the rich and the scanty property of the poor; in this book, he determined with the stroke of a pen the hardship or the well-being of an entire city. Almost tenderly, he turned the pages, which crackled with age, and with his eyes, he caressed the faded sheets filled with ancient entries, numbers, signatures, and stamps. The city elders might wear their beautiful robes for show and fluff up their feathers before the people—but, with this book and his legal authority to write in it, he was the one who held true power in his hands.

He could hardly tear himself away. With an almost inaudible sigh, he picked up the second book, the city's Book of Changes. Immediately, this felt much more common, almost ordinary. He could literally feel that everyone was allowed to write here; it was a whore of a book. With some disgust he opened it and looked for his last entry. Then he skimmed the subsequent pages with all the changes, the births and deaths, the marriages, the moves into and out of the city, and the changes in vocation. After such a long time, there were not as many as he had feared. He would soon be finished with the assessments and then enough time would remain for some spot checks. He wanted to find out whether everything in this peaceful city was really on the up and up.

With a slight wrinkling of his nose, he read the last entry. Recently they had stoned to death their only teacher, apparently on the command of an itinerant preacher. The charge formulated against him after the fact was for doubting God. Kremman did not approve of unknown preachers from who-knew-where taking on the role of judges. And in a city without teachers, sooner or later, the tax revenues decreased; experience had shown that over and over again.

It was pleasantly quiet in the cellar vault. Kremman heard only his own breathing and the quill scratching across the paper as he drew up his lists. He would give the first list to the city page; it contained the names of all the people who would be summoned to the City Elders Hall for interrogation, people whose property ownership or marital status had changed since the last time. On the second list, he noted the names of those he would visit himself for an on-site assessment. A few of the names came from the Book of Changes—when the situation made a personal assessment imperative. The rest of the names were prompted by his intuition, his feel for corrupt intrigues, and his instinctive understanding of the human desire to keep as much as possible while giving out as little as possible and to cheat one's way around one's lawful responsibilities. He trusted this instinct absolutely, and it had so far served him well. He read the registry of the city residents, read their profession, age and position, and their last assessment, and with some names he felt something like an inner alarm. Those were the names he wrote down.

He could well imagine what was going on the city right now. Already the word of his arrival had surely spread to every last hut, and they were all discussing anxiously whether it was their turn this time. And of course, they were busy hiding all their valuables: jewelry, new clothes, good tools, smoked meat, and crockery filled with salted meat.

While he sat here and wrote his lists, they were putting on their oldest clothes—gray, worn-out rags; they were rubbing their hair with fat, their faces with grime, and the walls of their houses and huts with ashes; and they were bringing manure into the houses to attract vermin.

And he would see through their masquerade. They thought they could trick him with unkempt hair and dirty faces, but he would examine their fingernails and check their hands for calluses and would know the truth. He would find things under the straw of their bedsteads, behind cabinets, under rafters, and in cellars. There were not really so many hiding places, and he knew them all. On days when he was in a good mood, he could enjoy the sport, the challenge of it. However, such days were rare for him.

When he had finished the two lists, Kremman closed the General Tax Ledger and rang for the town page.

"Are you familiar with the procedures of a tax levy?" he asked him. "You're very young, and I don't know you. That's why I ask."

"Yes. That is, no. It's been explained to me, but I've never personally—"

"Then do what I tell you. Here's a list of names of the city residents I will assess here tomorrow. I have divided them into four groups for morning, late morning, afternoon, and early evening. You have to see to it, that they're all here on time. Do you understand?"

The young man nodded tentatively. He's a real greenhorn, Kremman thought disdainfully. "Can you manage that?"

"Yes, of course!" the page hastened to assure him.

"How will you proceed?"

He had him. Kremman saw him swallow and look back and forth

around the floor with wide eyes, as though the answer might be found someplace there. He mumbled something incomprehensible.

"What did you say?" Kremman persisted with cruel satisfaction. "I didn't understand you."

"I said I don't know yet."

Kremman looked him over as he would examine a repulsive insect. "Do you know the people on this list?"

"Yes."

"What about dropping in on each one of them today to inform him?"

The boy gave a tense nod, but still didn't dare look him in the eyes. "Yes, yes. I'll do that."

"What's your name?"

"Bumug."

Kremman handed him the list. "It's your turn in the afternoon."

"Afternoon?" Now he looked at the tax collector again, confused. "My turn? What do you mean?"

Kremman smiled sardonically. "Naturally, you're on the list, too, Bumug."

. . . .

As always, the Imperial Tax Collector moved into the guest quarters of the City Elders Hall. Every city he visited found itself in a quandary in respect to furnishing this apartment and feeding the guest. On the one hand, everyone was anxious that he not lack any amenity, so as not to rouse his displeasure; on the other hand, nobody wanted to give him the idea that he was dealing with a wealthy city.

To his good fortune, the need to bribe him usually won out, including here in Yahannochia. He found a clean room, a bed worthy of a king, and a richly supplied table. He placed the General Tax Ledger under his pillow before sitting down to eat. As long as the book remained unsealed, he wouldn't let it out of his presence for a moment.

When he walked over to the City Elders Hall the next morning, clasping the book under his arm, there was already a long line of people waiting respectfully. Kremman took a breath and strode out with an especially severe, determined gait, in order to drive every weakness out of himself—every trace of sympathy, good humor, or other emotions that did not suit a tax collector. An exhausting day awaited him, a day during which he would have to listen to piteous tales from morning until evening. And he could not allow himself a moment of inattention, a moment of weakening, without betraying his duty: his sacred mission to collect taxes for the Emperor.

So he strode past the rows of local citizens. With no look of acknowledgment in their direction, he sat down at the table prepared for him with writing material and a jug of water. He opened the General Tax Ledger and called out the first name on his list. "Garubad!"

A sturdy man with a weathered face and gray hair, the personification of sheer physical strength, dressed entirely in well-worn leather, stepped forward and said, "I am Garubad."

"You are a stockbreeder?"

"Yes."

"What sort of animals do you raise?"

"Mostly keppo sheep. Besides that, I have a few baraq buffalo."

Kremman nodded. All of that was recorded in the General Tax

Ledger. The man made an honest, God-fearing impression. Not a difficult case. "How many keppos? How many baraqs?"

"Twelve hundred keppos and seven baraqs."

Kremman consulted his book. "That means the number of sheep
has increased by one fourth; the number of baraqs has stayed the same.
So I will raise your taxes by the same percentage. Do you have any
objections?"

The breeder shook his head. "No. I give it for the Emperor."

"I accept it for the Emperor," Kremman responded with the ritual
phrase and made a corresponding notation. "Thank you—you can go."

That had been a good start. The tax collector loved it, when an assessment day started out this way. Here, too, he relied on instinct to
tell him when he had to place someone on his list for random property checks and when he could accept what they said at face value.

It turned out to be a busy but, all in all, agreeable day. Naturally
there were the usual heartrending laments about ruined harvests, per-
ishing cattle, dying children, and runaway husbands, but not as many as
he often heard, and Kremman even believed some of the stories. With a
trace of kindness that even surprised him, he granted in one case a re-
fund to a woman whose husband had died. Let it not be said that tax
collectors are monsters. He was just doing his duty, nothing more—his
sacred duty in the service of the Emperor.

It was late evening when he wrote the last entry by the glow of a tal-
low lamp and excused the last man. He looked with satisfaction at his
second list, which contained five names. He would need no longer than
one day for the random property checks, and then it was just a matter
of adding up all the figures.

Just as he slammed the book closed, the city elder arrived again in his untidy ceremonial robe. "May I remind you, that we still have this evildoer in our dungeon and—"

"First the taxes," Kremman advised him wearily, and stood up. "First the taxes and then everything else."

"Of course," the old man nodded submissively. "As you wish."

. . . .

He entered the first house without advance notice. For the random checks, it was important to show up without warning, even though he had no illusions in this regard: his progress through Yahannochia's side streets was watched furtively by many eyes, and everything he did was immediately passed along in whispers.

But this couple was genuinely surprised. They jumped up in shock when he came through the door. The woman hid her face and disappeared into another room, and the man positioned himself, as though by chance, in front of the tax collector so that his view of the woman was blocked. Kremman knew why: a beautiful, young woman in a house was a reason for many a tax collector to impose a painfully high assessment—only to offer a reduction in exchange for the woman's favors. But Kremman had never done that. And besides, the city elders of Yahannochia had, with wise forethought, brought him a young woman last night, a very young woman—they knew his predilections—and he had been satisfied in this regard.

"I am Kremman, tax collector of the Emperor," he announced to the young man who looked just as angry as he was fearful. "According to my records, you married last year. I have to make a valuation. Show me everything you own."

The woman had already disappeared when they entered the next room. The sharp eye of the tax collector noticed that the window was slightly ajar. Kremman gave a grim smile. She must have fled through the window.

He opened cupboards, looked in jugs, tested the straw of the bed with his hands, and knocked on wooden beams and on walls. As he had expected, he didn't find anything in particular. Finally he entered a figure in his list that seemed appropriate.

The young man's relief was unmistakable. "I give it for the Emperor!" he shouted out.

"I accept it for the Emperor," Kremman responded, and departed.

The General Tax Ledger had been sealed again and locked in its cabinet, a copy of the current tax list had been produced and attached to the Book of Changes, and the only thing left to do was to issue the Tax Levy Declaration.

Collection of the taxes was actually carried out by the city; he had nothing to do with it. His responsibility was simply to determine the amount due. He also had nothing to do with the transport of the money; the next hair-carpet trader who came to Yahannochia would take care of that. The Tax Levy Declaration was for the trader, because he would have to account in the Port City for the amount of money that had been entrusted to him and his steel cart.

Most people believed that the taxes were sent to the Emperor, but that was incorrect. The money never left the planet. This world discharged only one sort of payment to the court of the Emperor—the hair carpets. The tax monies were simply used to pay for the carpets.

That's why the hair-carpet traders were given the responsibility for the transport of tax money. When they reached the Port City, they delivered the hair carpets, the remaining money, and the declarations of the tax collectors. These figures were then balanced against the records sent to the Port City by the guildmasters of the carpet makers, and it could thereby be determined whether a trader had done his duty or had unjustifiably enriched himself.

"The taxes have been levied," Kremman said casually when the city elder entered the room. "If you have any other disputes to be resolved by an imperial judge, now is the proper time."

"We have none," the old man responded, "except, as I said, the heretic."

"Ah yes, your heretic." Kremman interrupted his writing of the Declaration and leaned back. "What sort of mischief was he involved in?"

"He said all sorts of blasphemous things; for example, that the Emperor doesn't rule anymore, that he had been overthrown, and other such nonsense. And that was in the presence of two highly respected carpet makers, who are prepared to testify about the incident."

Kremman gave a bored sigh. "Oh, these old rumors. These stories have been making the rounds now for a good twenty years, and there are always more crazies who think they have to heat them up again. Why don't you just hang him? A misguided fellow, nothing more than that. That's what the law is for."

"Well," the city elder drawled out his response, "we weren't sure whether the law was applicable in this case. The heretic is a foreigner, and a very strange foreigner, at that. We don't know where he comes from. He claims to come from another world, so far away that it can't be seen in the sky."

"That's not so peculiar; the Emperor's realm is immense," Kremman interjected.

"And he says he belongs to the rebels who claim to have overthrown the Emperor—pardon my words, but I am just repeating what the foreigner said. He said that he came down from a rebel spaceship that's circling our world."

The tax collector laughed out loud. "Absurd! If such a spaceship existed, it surely wouldn't have hesitated to undertake some effort to free him. A crazy man, as I already said."

"Yes, we thought that, too," said the old man, nodding thoughtfully, and he paused a moment before adding, "but the thing that convinced us to wait for your judgment was that we found a radio device on the foreigner."

"A radio device?" Kremman pricked up his ears.

"Yes. I brought it along with me." From the depths of his cloak, the elder drew a small black metal box into view, on which nothing but a microphone membrane and several buttons could be seen.

Kremman took the device in his hand and hefted it with curiosity. It was astonishingly light and in strikingly good condition, free of the scratches and scrapes common to nearly every technical device the tax collector had ever encountered during his lifetime.

"And you're sure it's a radio?"

"The foreigner claimed it was. And I can't imagine what else it could be."

"It's so . . . small!" Kremman had once owned a radio many years ago, a great, bulky crate. Back then, he had reported his tax valuations directly to the Port City. But one day he happened into a sandstorm; his mount fell, and his valuable possession was smashed against a rock.

Kremman examined the little device more closely. The switches weren't labeled; only on the back side was something stamped—like a number, but in written characters that only vaguely reminded him of the ciphers with which he was familiar.

A strange fear crept into the tax collector the longer he held the apparatus in his hand—the sort of fear that befalls you when you are standing on the edge of a cliff and are forced to look down into a dark, immeasurably deep abyss. This device, he realized, was an irrefutable argument. It was a foreign body. Whatever it meant, its mere existence proved that things were afoot here, which went beyond the realm of his judicial competence.

This sudden insight allowed him to take a relieved breath. There was a path he could take, which freed him from all responsibility and was also in complete accord with regulations.

"The heretic should be sent to the Port City," he pronounced finally. "He . . . and the device with him."

"Should I bring him before you?" asked the elder.

"No, that's not necessary. I'll record my decision in the Declaration. The next carpet trader who visits Yahannochia will transport him and bring him before the Council."

Rapidly, as though he wanted to preclude any possible objections, he entered a suitable notation in the lower margin of the Tax Levy Declaration, dribbled sealing wax beside it, and marked the wax with his signet.

VIII

The Hair-Carpet Robbers

THE GIGANTIC CARAVAN of the trader Tertujak, with its wagons and tent-carts and mounted soldiers, surged slowly across the broad lowland plain toward the Zarrak Massif, which stretched endlessly from horizon to horizon like a dark, impenetrable wall.

Tertujak sat in his wagon poring over his account books. He felt the distinct shift when cart wheels began to grind their way through yielding sand and no longer rumbled over hard rock and gravel—where every pothole and every rock in the road had given him a hard, almost painful jolt through the wagon frame. He had traveled this route often enough in his life to know, even without glancing through his window, that the climb had begun to the only point where the Zarrak Massif could be crossed, the pass at the foot of Fist Rock.

After brief consideration, he decided it was time to see that everything was still in order. He heaved his massive body out of the pillows and opened the narrow door that led to a platform by the coach-box. It was almost too narrow to accomodate the trader's substantial corpulence, but Tertujak squeezed himself through, grasped the handgrip intended for just this purpose, and nodded curtly to his driver before looking around.

Once again, he was sure he would find all sorts of things that displeased him. His people were sometimes like children; he had to be constantly on his guard, couldn't let them get away with any of their many sloppy practices that could otherwise become habits. For example, the train was already too spread out again; the provision carts, instead of being grouped all around the hair-carpet wagon, were following behind it in a long crooked chain. The fault lay, as always, with the sutlers hawking their wares, who preferred to hang back at the end of the trek to carry out their questionable little deals with the soldiers undisturbed, and also to demonstrate that they were not under the command authority of the trader.

Tertujak gave a disapproving snort through his nose, while he considered whether it was imperative to intervene. He let his eyes wander down the long, straight line of the Zarrak mountain chain that rose up before them. Directly ahead of them stood Fist Rock; the black karst stone towered high and seemed almost threatening. It was named for its shape: five deep clefts leading down from an inaccessible high plateau toward the plain and a ledge on the side gave the impression of a giant's fist, which seemed to guard the only pass through the massif. They would cross over the mountain saddle near the bent thumb of the fist, and from there, for the first time in years, they would be able to see the Port City, the destination of their journey.

The prisoner came to mind again. Not a day passed without his wondering about this peculiar man who had been turned over to him in Yahannochia. Naturally, he hadn't been eager to take on the extra burden, but he had not been able to refuse. Now the prisoner was sitting up front in one of the trade wagons between two large bolts of cloth, chained and guarded by soldiers with strict orders not to speak with him and to silence him if he should talk. The prisoner was considered a heretic, and whatever he said might be intended to pervert the heart of a pious man.

What was it about this man that made it necessary to bring him before the Council at the Port City? They would probably never find out.

Tertujak sought the attention of his cavalry commander and waved him over with a curt gesture.

"What do the scouts report?"

"I would have spoken with you soon about that, anyway, sir," said the commander, a lanky, gray-haired man named Grom who was keeping his mount trotting with almost dancelike steps alongside the trader's cart. "The ascent is very sandy this time; I don't think we will even reach the pass before nightfall, let alone get beyond it."

That agreed with Tertujak's assessment. He shoved out his lower jaw a bit, as he always did when he had made a decision. "Let's make camp," he ordered. "We'll start off tomorrow morning at first light; be sure everyone is ready then."

"As you wish, sir," Grom responded with a nod, and rode away. As Tertujak withdrew into his spacious cart, he heard Grom blowing commands on his signal horn.

Setting up camp occurred as it did every evening, and everyone who belonged to the trader's caravan knew exactly what he had to do. They circled the wagons around the trader's cart and the armored hair-carpet wagon: the wagons filled with trade goods formed an inner ring, and the provision wagons made an outer ring beyond them. In the area between the inner and outer rings, tents were set up where the mounted soldiers would bed down. The draft animals, mostly baraq buffalo, were unyoked and tied to long ropes so that they could lie down. The mounts were herded together; they slept standing up. The foot soldiers, who had been lying the whole day on various wagons and had dozed the time away under awnings, were the only ones who had to wake up now; their duty was to stand guard around the camp the entire night.

The trader's personal cook pulled his little camp kitchen up to the huge, richly decorated wagon of the trader. Tertujak had opened his cart and stood waiting in the doorway.

"Sir, we still have some salted baraq meat," the cook began eagerly. "I could roast you some karaqui and prepare a salad of new-moon herbs, with a light wine to go with it—"

"Yes, fine," Tertujak growled.

While the cook was busy with his pots, Tertujak looked around as though searching out the source of the inner unease that filled him this evening. It was already twilight; Fist Rock high above them was nothing more than a silhouette against the dark silver of the sky, which still shone bright just above the horizon but was already black at its zenith. Tertujak heard the voices of the men setting up the last tents. Elsewhere, fires were already being lit. They had to be sparing with fuel, so there were only a few fires, just enough to cook food for the members of the caravan. A jolly, easygoing atmosphere prevailed. The strenuous work of the day was past, tomorrow they would cross over Fist Rock Pass, and then it was only a few days' trip to the Port City.

Three foot soldiers appeared out of the twilight. One of them approached the trader with deference and reported that the night watch had been posted.

"Who is the officer of the watch?" Tertujak asked. It was the duty of that officer to walk the chain of posts throughout the night to be certain that none of the soldiers fell asleep.

"Donto, sir."

"Tell him to be especially alert tonight," Tertujak said, and added a little more quietly: "I have an uneasy feeling."

"As you command, sir." The soldier disappeared again, and the other two took up positions next to the trader's wagon.

Tertujak scrutinized the wagon standing behind his, the hair-carpet wagon; it was twice as big, with eight wheels and equipped with harnesses for seventy-four baraqs. It contained the most precious treasures transported by the entire caravan—the hair carpets and also immense sums of money. Even in the fading twilight, he could see places where the metal armor was beginning to rust. He would have to have the wagon refurbished after the carpets had been shipped off and the accounting had been completed in the Port City.

He returned to his cart, had his meal served, and ate silently, lost in thought.

They had managed to buy enough hair carpets, but it had taken longer than he had planned. That meant they would arrive in the Port City after the other traders, and he would once again get one of the less attractive routes for the next trip. Then it would be even more difficult to reach the prescribed number of carpets, and some-time . . .

He didn't want to think about this "sometime."

He shoved his plate away abruptly. He ordered the cook to clean up and had another bottle of light wine brought to him.

In the light of an oil lamp, he brought out one of his most precious possessions, an ancient trader's logbook his forefathers had begun several hundred years ago. The pages of the book crackled with dryness, and in many places the columns of figures were now difficult to decipher. In spite of that, this book had given him much valuable information about the various hair-carpet routes and about the cities along them.

It was only a few years ago when he realized that this book could enlighten him about something else, namely the changes that had occurred over long periods of time. They were creeping, unnoticeable changes that nobody perceived; it was only when he compared and added up the figures of several centuries and nearly ten generations that the evolution became clear. There were fewer and fewer hair carpets. The number of carpet makers was slowly declining, and also the number of carpet traders. The route a hair-carpet caravan had to cover in order to collect the number of carpets prescribed by tradition was becoming longer on average, and the competition among the traders for the good, productive routes in the Polar Regions was becoming stiffer.

Tertujak was very good at calculations, like all traders, but he had also inherited the extensive mathematical gifts of his ancestors. It wasn't difficult for him to chart these comparative numbers in expressive curves: the curves pointed downward. In fact, they were almost crashing downward; the trend had drastically increased in recent years. They were the curves of a dying organism.

The logical conclusion would have been to get out of the business with hair carpets. But he would never be able to do that. He was bound to the Guild by his oath to the end of his life. Producing hair carpets was the sacred duty given to this world by the Emperor—but, for some reason, the vitality behind this duty seemed to have waned.

And in this context, Tertujak had to think about the prisoner again and about what was said of him. They accused him of the most incredible things in Yahannochia. They said he claimed to have come from another world. And still something else, something that profoundly shocked everyone, but was nevertheless always passed along: that the Emperor, the Lord of the Heavens, the Father of the Stars, the Keeper of all their Destinies, the Middlepoint of the Universe—that the Emperor no longer reigned!

Tertujak looked at his depressing charts, and something inside him wondered whether that could be the explanation.

He raised himself to his feet and opened the wagon door. Night had fallen in the meantime. There was laughter from the soldiers who were chasing after the few women in the caravan. Because these women were, without exception, camp followers, it was not a matter with which the trader had to concern himself. He waved to one of the two watchmen.

"Get Commander Grom for me."

"Yes, sir."

Grom soon entered. Permission to enter the trader's residence cart when he was summoned was the privilege of his rank. "Sir?"

"Grom, I have two requests for you. First, see to it that not all the mounted soldiers drink themselves senseless. I want to know that at least some of the men are battle-ready. Second," Tertujak hesitated a moment and then continued decisively, "I would like to have the prisoner brought to me discreetly."

Grom's eyes opened wide. "The prisoner? *In here?* In the wagon with you?"

"Yes."

"But why?"

Tertujak gave an irritated snort. "Do I owe you an explanation, Rider Commander?"

The officer winced. His rank was totally dependent on the pleasure of the trader, and he wasn't about to lose it. "Forgive me, sir. As you wish."

"Wait awhile until most of them are asleep. I don't want any gossip about it. Take two or three discreet men to escort the prisoner, and bring along a chain to tie him up here."

"Yes, sir."

"And remember: utmost discretion!"

Tertujak awaited the prisoner's arrival with nervous impatience. Several times he came close to sending one of the soldiers on watch to hurry things along, and it required almost physical effort to restrain himself.

Finally, there was a knock at the door. Tertujak opened quickly, and two soldiers brought the prisoner inside. They chained him to a support post, after which the trader dismissed them with a quick nod.

Then he scrutinized the man who was now sitting on one of his most valuable pelts. So that was the heretic. His clothes had been torn into dirty rags; his tousled beard and his matted hair were also covered with filth. He reacted to the scrutiny of the trader with a dull, uninterested stare, as though he no longer cared what happened to him.

"Maybe you're wondering why I had you brought here," Tertujak began finally.

He thought he could see a spark of interest ignite in the apathetic eyes of the prisoner.

"The truth is that I don't know precisely myself." Tertujak thought about the silhouette of Fist Rock against the dark blue evening sky. "Maybe it's because tomorrow we will see our destination, the Port City, for the first time. And I don't simply want to hand you over to the Port Council without finding out just who it is that I have been transporting."

The man gave him a dumb stare, as expressionless as before.

"What's your name?" asked Tertujak.

Endless time seemed to pass before the prisoner answered. His voice was a dusty croak. "Nillian . . . Nillian Jegetar Cuain."

"Those are three names," the trader said, surprised.

"We all have three names where I am from." The man coughed. "We bear our birth name, our mother's name and our father's name."

In the heretic's manner of speech, there really was a foreign sound that the trader had never heard in his travels.

"Then it's true, that you come from another world?"

"Yes."

"And why are you here?"

"I was stranded here."

"Where is your home world?"

"Far away."

"Can you show it to me in the sky?"

The prisoner stared so long at Tertujak that the trader thought he hadn't understood the question. But then he suddenly asked, "What do you know of other worlds? What do you know of travel between the stars?"

The trader shrugged his shoulders. "Not much."

"What do you know?"

"I know about the starships of the Imperial fleet that take the hair carpets on board. I've been told that they can travel between the stars."

The unkempt fellow, who claimed to come from the stars, seemed to revive.

"The hair carpets," he repeated, and bent forward, supporting his elbow on his knee. "Where are they taken?"

"To the Palace of the Emperor."

"How do you know that?"

"I don't know," Tertujak admitted. "That's what I was told."

The man who called himself Nillian nodded, and Tertujak saw a bit of sand trickling from his hair onto the floor. He would have to have the room cleaned tomorrow. "They lied to you. There are no hair carpets in the Palace of the Emperor. Not a single one."

Tertujak squinted his eyes with suspicion. That sort of statement was to be expected from someone who was considered a heretic. But what if he wasn't a heretic? "How do you know that?" he asked.

"I've been there."

"In the Imperial Palace?"

"Yes."

"Maybe you didn't notice the hair carpets."

For the first time the foreigner laughed. "That's impossible. I've seen a hair carpet; it was the most finely worked and most extravagant work of art I've ever seen in my life. Such a work of art wouldn't remain undiscovered. And we aren't talking about just *one* carpet here; we're talking about thousands and countless thousands. But not a single one of them is to be found in the palace. Our language doesn't even have a *word* for them!"

Could that be true? And if it were a lie—what purpose could the man have for telling it?

"They say," Tertujak began, "that the Palace of the Emperor is the largest building in the universe."

The man thought for a moment. "Yes, that's probably true. But that doesn't mean nothing can be found there. It would be easier for a man to hide in any of your cities than in the entire Star Palace."

"But surely there must be private chambers for the Emperor where no one else is allowed?"

"Once there were such rooms." The foreigner stiffened his posture. "I'm in prison here because I said this once, so I can certainly repeat it: The Emperor's reign ended approximately twenty years ago, according to your time."

Tertujak stared at the man sitting there, bound hand and foot with chains, ragged and filthy, and knew that he wasn't lying. Of course, this claim was sheer heresy. But he felt deep inside himself a certainty that what the stranger had said was nothing but the truth.

"Then the rumors that have been circulating here for two decades are true," he muttered thoughtfully. "That the Emperor abdicated?"

"Well, I would say that these rumors have been prettied up."

"What do you mean by that?"

The expression in the prisoner's eyes was suddenly steely. "Sir, I am a rebel, and my entire life I was a member of the Silent Wind movement. Twenty years ago we attacked the Central World, conquered the

Palace, and overthrew the Emperor. Since that time, there has been no Empire. You may like it or not, but it is a fact."

Unsure of himself, the hair-carpet trader looked the stranger over. What he was saying seemed to pull the ground from beneath his feet.

He pointed toward the window with a vague gesture. "Out there I see the stars in the sky, and they are still shining. I was always told that they couldn't shine without the Emperor."

"The Emperor has nothing to do with that," responded the rebel. "That's a legend."

"But didn't the Emperor call them into existence?"

"He wasn't capable of that any more than I would be. He was a human being, like any other. They told you all that just to maintain power over you."

Tertujak shook his head. "But isn't it true that he has ruled for countless millennia? How could he do that unless he's immortal?"

The stranger raised his eyebrows. "Well, however he managed that, now, at any rate, he's dead."

"Dead?"

"Dead. A rebel cornered him in a remote room during the occupation of the Palace and shot him."

Tertujak remembered what he had been told about the circumstances of the foreigner's arrest. He had been a guest of two carpet makers and had suddenly begun to make blasphemous statements. They had arrested him and charged him with heresy.

"You said those things to the carpet makers?" he said in astonishment. "It's a miracle that they didn't kill you outright."

"They gave me a blow to the skull—it's a miracle I survived it," growled the prisoner. "One of the two kept eagerly asking me questions, while the other one slipped around behind me and—whack! When I woke up, I lay in a dungeon and was in chains."

Tertujak began pacing back and forth nervously. "You say there aren't any hair carpets in the Imperial Palace. On the other hand, I see tens of thousands of hair carpets leaving this planet year after year. Where are the Imperial Shipsmen taking them, if not to the Palace?"

The stranger nodded. "I've already realized that this is the most interesting question of all. And I don't have a ghost of an answer."

"Maybe we aren't talking about the same Emperor?"

"We're talking about this man," said the prisoner, and pointed to the photograph of the Emperor hanging on the wall. Tertujak had inherited the picture from his father, who had in turn inherited it from his father, and so on. "Emperor Aleksandr the Eleventh."

"Emperor Aleksandr?" For the first time this evening, Tertujak was totally astounded. "I didn't even know he had a name."

"That also slipped into obscurity. He was the eleventh in a series of Emperors, all named Aleksandr. The first ten also lived to be quite old, but he ruled longer than all the others combined. And his rise to power happened so unimaginably long ago that it seemed as though he had ruled since the beginning of time."

"Well." Tertujak shook his head and then began his nervous pacing again. The stranger watched him silently.

Was that it? Was that the explanation? The explanation for the diminishing number of hair carpets?

He sat down again on his divan.

"What you say," he admitted, "awakens a resonance inside me. But at the same time, I can't comprehend it. Do you understand? I can't imagine that the Emperor could be dead. He seems to be somehow inside me, a part of me."

"That concept of the Emperor as a superhuman being is a product of your education, since you, after all, never saw the Emperor." The foreigner struggled with something on his belt, as best his chains allowed. "I have a picture that I actually wanted to keep hidden until I finally have some sort of a trial."

He brought out a photograph, which he handed to the trader. Tertujak examined the image. With sickening clarity, it showed the dead body of a man who had been hung by his legs from a flagpole and who dangled there headdown. Through his chest was a hole bigger than a fist, the edges of which were seared as though by fire.

When he turned the picture upside down to take a better look at the face of the dead man, it hit him like a bolt of lightning, and he thought his heart would stop that very instant. He knew this face, knew it better than his own! The dead man really was the Emperor!

With a wordless moan, he tossed the photo aside and sank back into the pillows on his seat. That was impossible. That was . . . He reached for the picture again to be sure. The Emperor. Dead. Dead in his parade uniform, the imperial cloak around his shoulders, hung without honor on a flagpole.

"Now you feel like someone has struck you on the forehead with a hammer," the voice of the rebel seemed to reach him from a great distance. "If it's any comfort, you aren't the first one to feel like that. This photograph is today perhaps one of the most widely circulated pictures of all time, and it's our most important aid in freeing people from the stranglehold of their fixation on the Emperor as a god."

Tertujak barely heard him. Behind his forehead was a sensation like boiling water. His mind was working at a crazy pace; it raced through all the images in his memory, tried to see and organize them anew: everything, everything had to be rethought. None of the things that had always been true were true anymore.

What was this foreigner babbling on about? He didn't understand him. He saw only this image and tried to comprehend the truth in its full measure: The Emperor was dead.

". . . the noise outside?"

"What?" Tertujak emerged from the whirlwind of his thoughts and feelings as though from a nightmare. Now he heard it, too. Loud noises penetrated in from outside, shouts and screams and the clang of metal against metal. It sounded dangerous.

With one leap, the hair-carpet trader was on his feet at the entrance. He tore the door open and stuck out his head. He saw torches, running people, shadows, and the dark contours of mounted animals hurtling straight through the camp. Battle sounds. He slammed the door again and fumbled with his fleshy hand at the thin chain he wore around his neck.

Everything is falling apart, he thought.

"What's happening?" the stranger asked.

"Robbers," the trader heard himself say with unnatural calm. "They're attacking the camp."

"Robbers?"

"Hair-carpet robbers." So his uneasy premonitions had been right. Of course, here just before the only pass over the nearly endless Zarrak Mountains, here was the ideal place for an ambush.

"You mean they want to steal the hair carpets?"

"They sell them to other traders," Tertujak explained hastily while he was searching feverishly for a way out of this catastrophe. "For as long as anyone can remember, there has been a set number of carpets that a trader must present when he returns to the Port City from his route. If he can't fulfill that quota, the honor code of the traders requires that he take his own life."

"And the robbers sell the stolen hair carpets to traders who are having difficulty with their numbers, but are fond of staying alive?" the rebel guessed, and his eyes now glistened with complete attention.

"Exactly."

A thought was suddenly clawing at the back of the trader's mind, an ancient voice from the dust, saying, You lent the heretic your ear, and he has seduced you. You believed him, you really believed him—now take the punishment you deserve!

Tertujak picked up the photo of the dead Emperor and handed it to the prisoner.

"Don't you have a weapon?" the stranger asked, and pulled uneasily at his chains.

"I have soldiers."

"They don't seem to be of much use."

Yes, thought Tertujak. This must be the end.

The battle sounds came closer and closer, wild bellowing and the blows of steel on steel. A bone-chilling scream rang out, and something that sounded like a human body struck the wagon. The broken fragments of his thin necklace slipped from the trader's fingers, fell to the floor, and disappeared among the pelts.

For a terrible moment, everything was quiet. Then the wagon door was ripped open, and in the light of a sooty torch, they stared into blackened, bloodstained faces.

"Greetings to you, Trader Tertujak," the first man boomed out derisively, a bearded giant with a knotty scar across his forehead. "And please forgive us for disturbing you so late in the evening."

He vaulted into the interior of the wagon, followed by three accomplices. The scornful grin disappeared from his face as though it had been too much trouble. He directed no more than a passing glance at the prisoner, then pointed at the hair-carpet trader.

"Search him!" he commanded.

The men fell over the trader, tore open his clothes, and fumbled through them until nearly everything hung from him in tatters, but they didn't find what they were looking for.

"Nothing."

The ringleader stepped up to the merchant and gave him a vicious look. "Where's the key to the hair-carpet wagon?"

Tertujak swallowed. "I don't have it."

"Don't tell me any fairy tales, you sack of fat."

"One of my men has it."

The bearded man laughed out loud in disbelief. "One of your men?"

"Yes. A soldier I trust completely. I ordered him to flee if we should be attacked."

"Damn!" Enraged, the leader punched him in the face so hard, his head flew sideways. The blow split Tertujak's lower lip, but the trader made no sound.

The other men became nervous. "What'll we do now?"

"We'll take the entire wagon with us," suggested one of them, a stocky man whose right arm was crusted with blood that didn't seem to be his own. "Somehow we'll get it open—"

"Crap!" the bearded one shouted at him. "Why do you think the wagon is armored? That won't work. We need the key."

The robbers looked at one another. From outside, the sound of occasional fighting could still be heard.

"At daybreak we could search the whole area," suggested another. "A man without a mount can't get far."

"How do you know he doesn't have a mount?" the stocky one asked.

"We would have noticed—"

"Shut up!" the leader ordered with a surly wave of his hand and turned again to the hair-carpet trader, whose lip was dripping blood. "I don't believe you," he said in a dangerously quiet tone. "I don't believe that a trader would let the key to his hair-carpet wagon leave his body." He looked at Tertujak with suspicion. "Open your mouth."

The trader didn't react.

"I ordered you to open your mouth!" the bearded one shouted at him.

"Why?" Tertujak asked.

"Because I think you're trying to trick us." With sudden, brutal force, he grabbed the trader's chin and forced his mouth open.

"I see a couple of fresh cuts in your throat," he announced, and gave the trader a sympathetic look. "I don't believe in your soldier. Do you know what I believe? I believe you swallowed the key!"

The trader's eyes grew unnaturally large. He was incapable of speech, and his eyes were his only confession.

"Well?" the robber rasped. "Am I right?"

Tertujak gave a strangled gasp. "Yes," he managed to say.

Every glimmer of human mercy suddenly disappeared from the eyes of the bearded one as he reached behind him and pulled a knife with a long, sharp blade from his belt.

"You shouldn't have done that," he said quietly. "You really shouldn't have done that."

IX

Flute Fingers

THE NARROW STREET was still sleeping. A light early-morning fog hung suspended between the squat gables and was mixed with cold smoke from hearths in which the fires had gone out in the night. When the first sunrays flicked across the roof ridges of the crooked little houses, everything seemed bathed in an inappropriately dreamy and delicately misty light. Like little piles of dirt, beggars lay in some dark corners, sleeping on the bare ground, ragged blankets twisted up over their heads. A few small rodents crawled dully through the garbage, feeling sated enough to circle mercifully around the sleepers, and a few of them were brave enough to sniff their way to the narrow gutter, where the water moved sluggishly along the middle of the alleyway.

They leapt aside in fright and shot back into their holes as though drawn by strings when a cloaked figure approached with rapid steps; wheezing, stumbling, and flitting from shadow to shadow, the figure finally hurried toward the house of Flutemaster Opur. Then came the sound of two dull blows with the doorknocker.

Upstairs in the house, the old man awoke instantly from a restless sleep, stared up at the ceiling, and wondered if the sound he had just heard had been dream or reality. There was another knock. Well, then—reality. He threw back the blanket and slid into his slippers, reached for his worn housecoat and put it on before he shuffled to the window to open it. He looked down onto the street, which lay there empty and forlorn, stinking of rancid fat, just like every other morning.

From the shadow below the house, a boy stepped out timidly, looked up at Opur, and pulled back the wrap with which he had covered even his head. Master Opur saw blond locks framing a face he had never expected to see again in his life.

"You?!"

"Help me, Master," the skinny boy whispered. "I ran away."

The sudden joy that had filled the old man's heart gave way to painful disappointment. For a fraction of a second he had thought everything would be as it had been in the past.

"Wait," he said. "I'll come down."

The boy, what had he done? Opur shook his head sadly as he hurried down the steps. He had plunged himself into misfortune—that's what he had done. Nothing good would come of this. Opur knew that, but something inside him wanted to believe the opposite.

He slid back the heavy bolt on the door. There stood the boy, trembling and looking at him with terror in his eyes—the big, blue eyes that had once looked so trusting and enraptured. His face was marked by fear and privation.

"Come in," the old flutemaster said, and still didn't know whether he should be happy or afraid. But then, when the boy stepped into the narrow, dark entryway and stooped under the low ceiling, he took his arm without another thought.

"Master Opur, you must hide me," the boy whispered, shaking with fear. "They're after me. They're hunting me."

"I'll help you, Piwano," Opur muttered, and listened to the echo of this name in his mind, a name he had not spoken since the Guild had drafted the boy for service with the Imperial Shipsmen: of all people, they had drafted this boy—his best student and the most gifted triflutist in living memory.

"I want to play the triflute again, Master. Will you teach me?" The boy's lower jaw quivered. He was at the end of his strength.

Opur patted him gently and, he hoped, reassuringly on the back. "Of course, my boy. But first you have to sleep. Come."

He removed the large picture that hid the door to the cellar steps and set it aside. Piwano followed him down into the cellar, where the floor was packed clay and the walls were only roughly bricked. One of the old, dusty racks of shelves could be rotated on unseen hinges and gave access to a second, hidden, cellar room with a bedstead, an oil lamp, and a few supplies. This was not the first time in his life that the venerable flutemaster had hidden a fugitive.

It took only a few minutes for the boy to fall asleep. He slept with his mouth open, and sometimes his breathing faltered, only to restart with gasps. With jerky motions, one of his hands clenched at some unseen resistance, finally relaxing again only after a long spasm.

Opur finally nodded his head with a sigh. He carefully lifted the oil lamp and placed it in a safer location. Then he left the sleeper alone, closed the secret door, and went upstairs. For a moment, he considered getting a little more sleep himself but then decided against it.

Instead, he made himself breakfast in the first light of day and ate it silently; he completed a few household chores and went up to his lesson room, to pore over the old music notations.

On this day, his first student arrived shortly before midday.

"I'm sorry about the tuition money," she immediately began to babble on, almost before he could open the door. "I know it's due today, and I remembered it already last week and I've thought about it the whole time. Well, what I'm trying to say is that I didn't forget it."

"Yes, okay." Opur nodded with displeasure.

"It's just that I have to wait for my brother; he should arrive in the city any day now—actually, he should have already been here long ago. You see, he travels with the trader Tertujak, you may know, and he always gives me the money I need when he comes back from a trip. And Tertujak's arrival was expected by now; you can ask anybody—"

"Okay, fine," the flutemaster interrupted her impatiently, and waved her ahead to climb up the stairs to the lesson room. "Then you can pay next time. Let's get started."

Opur sensed his own inner agitation. He had to find his equilibrium, as best he could. They sat down on two pillows facing one another, and after the woman had unpacked her triflute and her music sheets, Opur had her close her eyes and listen to her own breathing.

The flutemaster did the same. He felt his agitation fall away. Inner composure was important. Without inner composure, playing an instrument as difficult as the triflute was hopeless.

As was his habit, Opur first reached for his own flute and played a short piece. After that, he allowed his student to open her eyes again.

"When will I be able to play something like that, Master?" she asked quietly.

"That was the *Pau-Lo-No*," Opur explained calmly, "the simplest of the classic pieces. It will be the first classic piece that you will someday play. But, like all the traditional flute pieces, it is polyphonic—in other words, you must first master monophonic technique. Let me hear how your drills are coming along."

She held the triflute to her lips and blew. After Opur's playing, it sounded like dreadful discord. And, as he had done so often, the venerable master had to muster all his self-control to keep a pained grimace from his face.

"No, no, the first drill again. Above all, you have to play the note *cleanly. . . .*"

The triflute was composed of three individual flutes, each with eight holes that could be covered with the fingertips. For this reason, the flutes were bent into a peculiar S-shape, so that they would fit the hands of the player and the varying lengths of the fingers. Each flute was made of a different material: one of wood, one of bone, and one of metal. Each of the three flutes gave a different timbre to the notes, and all of them together produced the inimitable sound for which the triflute had always been famous.

"You have to remember to keep your small finger relaxed . . . relaxed and limber. It has to be stretched out, because the construction of the flute and the placement of the holes require that, but that can't restrict its movement."

Long, agile fingers with prominent finger joints were an important prerequisite for a triflute player. A long little finger was a particular advantage. The technique was not like that for a normal flute, where each hole is simply covered or uncovered. That was only for beginners, in order to become familiar with the basics of flute technique and the musical theory. An advanced flutist, however, played harmony. By skillful bending and angling of the individual fingers, he produced a different note on each flute; for example, he could raise the middle knuckle of several fingers in such a way as to keep the holes on the outer two flutes covered, while the finger holes of the middle flute were open.

"Good. Now try the ninth drill. It contains a short two-part passage. Here. At this point, you raise your two lowest fingers, so that holes of the two outside flutes are free while you cover the holes of the middle flute with the corresponding knuckles. Try it."

He was impatient today, in spite of all his composure. She really was trying hard, and when she controlled her excitement, she achieved some very acceptable passages.

"Stop, stop. This symbol means that you should block two of the flutes with your tongue, blowing only into one of them—until right here. Again now, and pay attention to the difference."

By the end of the lesson, she was very happy to have mastered the drill to some extent, and Opur was relieved to have survived it. He managed to say good-bye without additional long-winded conversation.

Then he hurried immediately down to the cellar to check on Piwano.

The boy sat with his back against the wall and was hungrily devouring everything edible he had found in his hiding place. It seemed that he had not been awake for long, but he looked much better than he had early this morning. When Opur opened the secret door, he smiled happily.

"Tell me everything," the old man suggested. "Start from the beginning."

Piwano put down his bread and told him. About the harsh training he had to endure; about the rough, boorish environment in which he had to live on board the Imperial spaceships. About inhospitable, foreign worlds, about bone-numbing work, about illnesses, and about hateful attacks by the other shipsmen.

"They chased me away when I played, so I hid in the engine rooms just to play," he recounted with a quivering voice. "Then they smashed my flute, and when I tried to make another one, they smashed it, too."

A band of steel seemed to draw around Opur's chest as he listened to the boy's story.

"You've put yourself in great danger, Piwano," he said earnestly. "You've run away from the Emperor's service. That carries a death penalty."

"Master, I can't be a shipsman!" Piwano shouted. "I can't live that way. If that's the only way I can live, I would rather die. It's not because I don't want to serve the Emperor; of course, I love the Emperor, but . . ." He paused.

"But you love the flute even more, don't you?"

Piwano nodded. "Yes."

Opur sat in silent thought. He wasn't sure what he should do. He was old; he wasn't afraid for himself, no matter what happened. He was only afraid for the boy.

Desertion was a serious matter: that much he knew about the laws of the Imperial Shipsmen. Even if Piwano turned himself in voluntarily, he would have to expect serious punishment, probably a long sentence at hard labor on an undeveloped planet. And for a fragile, sensitive boy like Piwano, that would be the same as a death sentence.

"Master, may I have a flute again?" Piwano asked.

Opur looked at him. That glow of absolute, unmitigated devotion to something bigger than himself still shimmered in the boy's eyes—that glow the old flutemaster had discovered in the eyes of an eight-year-old.

"Come," he said.

They went upstairs to the lesson room. Piwano looked around, eyes sparkling at finding himself again in the room where he had spent so many years of his childhood; it seemed that an invisible force was filling him with new life.

Opur went to the windows that opened onto the street to be certain that no guild soldiers were in sight. Then he motioned the boy over to him.

"Piwano, I am willing to hide you, even for years, if necessary," he declared earnestly. "But you must never leave the house, even if nothing outside seems suspicious—never. The Guild has disguised spies, and you never can tell who is in their pay. And as much as possible, you should stay away from the windows. You can play the flute in your hideaway, at least during the day when it can't be heard on the street. Agreed?"

Piwano nodded.

"But in case you should ever need to get away, I'll tell you about an escape route known only to a few." Opur pointed to a building diagonally across from the flutemaster's house; it was set somewhat back from the street and wedged between the displays of a basketmaker and the bar of a dark, greasy soup-kitchen. "That's a laundry. That's where you run in. From the front, it's obvious that there's a large drying yard behind the building where linens are nearly always hanging out to dry. You can't be seen between the sheets. A pursuer will immediately think of the numerous exits from the drying yard that lead to other alleys. But you must turn immediately left and you'll come into the soup-kitchen from the rear. A trapdoor in the floor leads to the cellar, and down there is a set of shelves—similar to the one here—that you can swing aside. Behind it, a hallway runs for a long distance and finally opens into the underground water system of the Upper Town. So, even if they discovered your entry point, there are literally thousands of possible exits for you."

Piwano nodded again. Opur had seen the boy memorize whole pieces of music with just one look; so he felt sure that he had understood everything and would never forget it.

He walked over to the cabinet where he kept his written music, books, and instruments. After brief consideration, he removed a small case, opened it, and took out a triflute, which he presented to Piwano.

"This is a very, very old flute, which I have saved for a long time . . . for a special moment," he explained. "And I think this is that moment."

Piwano held it reverently in his hands, turned it over, and looked at it carefully. "There's something different about it," he said.

"Instead of the flute of bone, it has one of glass." Opur closed the empty case and put it aside. "The glass has become milky with age. You will have to get used to it a bit, because a glass flute has a sharper tone than a bone flute."

Carefully, Piwano raised the triflute to his lips and wrapped his fingers around the three interwoven flutes. He played a few chords. They sounded harsh and dissonant. The old man smiled.

"You'll master it."

. . . .

Ten days later the Imperial spaceship took off. The whole time, the silver colossus had been visible in the distance on the shabby, old spaceport grounds. But this morning, the air over the city vibrated with the whine of the rocket engines. Opur and Piwano watched together from the window, as the spacecraft's shiny metal hull rose above the houses, awkwardly at first, then climbing—faster and faster, higher and higher—until it had shrunk to a tiny point that disappeared far above them in the sky. The silence that then descended was like a feeling of salvation.

"You must not become careless now, Piwano," the old man warned. "They have flown off and won't be back for two years. But the Guild is still looking for you."

Months passed. Piwano soon rediscovered his old virtuosity. He sat for hours in his hideaway and played the classical pieces, honed his technique, and attempted variations; he was tireless and eager. Opur sometimes sat with him and just listened; sometimes they played together. Besides, there was hardly anything more he could teach him.

Piwano beamed with excitement. Soon he was ready to try the most difficult pieces—pieces that had always been problematic even for Opur. And to the utter amazement of the old flutemaster, the boy even succeeded in mastering the *Ha-Kao-Ta*, one of the classical pieces generally regarded as unplayable.

"What are those words below the notes?" Piwano asked when Opur placed an old manuscript in front of him.

"Transcriptions of a lost language," the master said. "The classical triflute pieces are all very old, some of them hundreds of thousands of years and more. Some flutemasters say that the triflute is older than the stars and that the world was created out of its music. But, of course, that's nonsense."

"Does anyone know what the words mean?"

Opur nodded. "Come with me."

They climbed up from the cellar to the lesson room. Opur went to a small table beneath the street-side window and, from the top of it, he picked up a case decorated with worn wood carvings.

"The old flute pieces are actually stories, written in an ancient, forgotten language. The words of that language are not words like the ones we speak, but rather motifs of notes on the triflute. In this chest, I have the key to this language in safekeeping. It is the secret of the flutemasters."

He opened the lid of the case. His own flute lay inside, along with a stack of old papers, note transcriptions, and handwritten notations ... some of them yellowed and brittle.

Piwano took the manuscripts Opur handed to him and examined them. He nodded slightly when he had understood the principle: the length of the notes, the rhythm and the accent were determined by the requirements of the music, but the sequences of note motifs and chord rows represented words and concepts.

"I have deciphered some of the stories. The oldest of the classical pieces are about a lost Golden Age of wealth and happiness in which wise, generous kings ruled. Other pieces tell of a terrible war, which ushered in the dark epoch, and they tell of the last king, who lives imprisoned in his palace for a thousand years, doing nothing but shedding tears for his people."

He replaced the papers and closed the lid again.

"Before my death, I will pass this chest along to you, because you will be my heir," he declared.

. . . .

The end of the year arrived, bringing with it the preparations for the annual student concert. Opur wondered if the circle of triflute players and the handful of listeners—most of them relatives or friends—would ever be large enough that he'd lack for space to accommodate them in his lesson room. In recent years, this performance had seemed to attract a smaller and smaller audience. But the concert was important, because it gave his students a goal, and the competition with others provided them with perspective.

Shortly before the concert, Piwano confessed his desire to perform, as well.

"No," said Opur firmly. "It's much too risky."

"Why?" Piwano persisted stubbornly. "Do you think the Guild will plant a spy in the audience? You have known all the people who will be here for years."

"Don't you realize how quickly the word will get around that someone can play the *Ha-Kao-Ta*? Don't be foolhardy, Piwano."

Piwano clenched his fists. "Master, I *must* play. I can't sit in the cellar forever and make music for myself. It's not . . . not *complete*. Do you understand? It only becomes art if it touches other people. If I play with nobody listening, then it makes no difference whether I play at all."

The flutemaster felt irritation rising inside him, and also fear for the boy. But he knew him well enough to realize that Piwano would always do in the end what he believed was right, even if it might cost him his life.

"Okay, I'll allow it," he relented. "But only on one condition: You won't play any difficult pieces, nothing that might draw attention. You will play easy polyphonic pieces that others have mastered, as well. Nothing above the level of the *Shen-Ta-No*." He was absolutely serious. He was prepared to threaten Piwano with being thrown out on the street if he didn't agree.

But Piwano nodded thankfully. "Agreed, Master."

In spite of that, Opur had an uneasy feeling as the concert approached. His anxiety spread to his other students and made them nervous. Never before had he found the necessary preparations so difficult. He rearranged the performance order endlessly and, just as often, the seating. He became dissatisfied with the pillow covers and almost got into an argument with the cook from the soup-kitchen, who was supposed to provide the refreshments.

Then the evening of the concert arrived. Opur greeted all the visitors personally at the door; upstairs one of the students showed them to their seats. All of them arrived in their best clothes, which, of course, didn't mean much for people living in this part of town. As a small boy, Opur had once experienced a concert his own master had given in the Upper Town: sometimes he suspected that he was always trying to copy the wasteful splendor of that day with the concerts he presented—but without ever managing more than a parody of a great festival.

As was customary, the flutemaster said a few words at the beginning. He reviewed the past year and commented on a few of the pieces on the program. Then the youngest beginners started first—a practice that had proved practical since they suffered the most from stage fright, and he didn't want to make them wait too long.

The beginning was tough. The first student forgot a repetition and got off beat when he realized it. Then he played faster and faster in an attempt to get it over with more quickly. There were some indulgent smiles and he still got applause when he bowed his scarlet face. The second student, an older woman, surprised even Opur with the unusual fluency of her playing; it seemed that this time she really had practiced. Gradually, the concert smoothed out, even became quite good, and

Opur felt the worry that had gripped him in recent days slowly subside.

Then Piwano began to play.

As soon as he put the triflute to his lips and blew the first note, a jolt passed through the audience. Suddenly, there was electricity in the room. Heads raised and backs straightened, as though pulled up by invisible cords. The instant the first note rang out from the flute, it was clear that a star was rising. Everything else was in shades of gray; here was color. Everything else was successful effort; here was effortless perfection. It was as though the cloud cover had suddenly opened to allow a ray of pure light to break through.

Piwano played the *Pau-No-Kao*, an easy polyphonic piece that one of the other students had already played. He played nothing but what those before him had played—but the way he played it!

Even Opur, who had heard him play immeasurably more difficult things and had the highest possible regard for his talent, was awestruck. It was a revelation. With this simple piece, the willowy blond boy had completely outdone himself; he had attained a new level of triflute virtuosity as though in a quantum leap. With this simple piece, he outclassed everyone around him, showed them their place, and made it clear once and for all who in this room was a beginner and who was a master. No one would later remember any of the other pieces, and everyone would remember this one.

His fingers danced over the flutes as lightly and with as little effort as others need to breathe or speak, to laugh or love. Simply playing the polyphony of the piece was not enough for him. He exploited the fact that precisely the same note on the metal flute had a different timbre when played on the wooden flute, and he interchanged notes between the flutes to create contraposed, subliminal movement in the music. He used the glass flute's tendency to slip into a sharp treble when blown too hard in order to imbue some passages with a sense of drama that no one had ever made audible in that way before.

The others *played* their triflutes—this boy become one with his and forgot himself completely in absolute devotion.

Most of the listeners didn't understand what he was actually doing, but everyone sensed that something unheard of was happening, that here in this humble little room they were seeing into a wondrous, forgotten world. God was here. God was revealed. He danced within music that had been unheard by humans for thousands of years, and everyone held his breath.

And after it was over and Piwano had accepted the applause with a transfigured smile, Opur was gripped by fear.

. . . .

They came two days later, shortly before sunrise. Without warning, they kicked in the entry door, and before Opur had jumped from his bed, the whole house was already filled with soldiers, with barked commands and the stomping of boots.

A black-bearded giant in the leather uniform of the Guild Patrol stepped toward the flutemaster.

"Are you Opur?" he asked imperiously.

"Yes."

"You are under suspicion of hiding a shipsman who has deserted the Emperor's service."

Although everything inside him was trembling, he met the eyes of the soldier with courageous calm. "I know nothing about a shipsman," he declared.

"So?" The bearded soldier closed one eye and gave him an evil look with the other. "Well, we'll see about that. My men are searching the house."

He couldn't voice an objection. Opur focused all his energy on maintaining his composure and appearing unconcerned. Maybe they would be lucky.

But they weren't lucky. Two soldiers brought a terrified Piwano up the steps and presented him to the commandant, who laughed triumphantly.

"Well, then," he shouted. "This must be Cargo Loader Piwano from the Third Loading Brigade of the *Kara*. Sooner or later, we get them all. And all of them regret it—every one."

The flutemaster stepped up to the patrol commandant and fell to his knees.

"I beg you, be merciful," he implored. "He is a poor shipsman, but a good flutist. His gifts in this life are not an Imperial Shipsman's strong shoulders, but his flute fingers. . . ."

The commandant looked down at the old man scornfully. "If his flute fingers hinder him in his service for our Lord, the Emperor, then it is our duty to help him out," he mocked, and grabbed Piwano's right hand to force it roughly against the balustrade of the steps. Then he reached for his heavy wooden cudgel.

Sudden horror shot through Opur when he realized that the man intended to break Piwano's fingers. Without thinking, he sprang to his feet and rammed the soldier's stomach with all his strength, which was multiplied by his fear for Piwano. The commandant, who had never imagined he would be physically attacked by the aged flutemaster, doubled over with a wheezing sound, stumbled, and fell. Piwano pulled free.

"Run!"

Suddenly Piwano moved with the agile speed of a rabbit, a quality Opur had never seen in his starry-eyed pupil, except when he was playing his flute. The boy sprang in one courageous leap over the edge of the balustrade and disappeared below, before even one of the soldiers could react.

Opur pulled himself together and flew to the window; he tore it open and grabbed the chest containing his own flute. Below, Piwano was just rushing out of the house.

"Master Piwano!" Opur yelled, and threw the chest down to him.

Piwano paused, caught it, and gave his master a last, irrationally roguish smile. Then he sprinted off and disappeared into the broad doorway of the laundry.

The soldiers were already on his heels. They paused in front of the laundry building, one of them issued commands, and they split up and ran to seal off the nearby alleys, hoping in this way to entrap the escapee.

Opur felt the heavy hand of a soldier on his shoulder and closed his eyes in resignation. The light had been preserved and passed on to the next generation. There was no more he could have done.

X

The Emperor's Archivist

ONCE, THIS HAD BEEN his realm. Once, when the Emperor was still alive. Back then, silence had reigned in the great marble halls containing the documents of the glorious history of the Empire, and he had not had to hear any sounds but the shuffling of his own steps and the rush of his own breathing. Here he had spent his days, his years, and had grown old in the service of the Emperor.

The most exalted hours were when the Emperor himself came—came to him here in the Archive he guarded for the Divine One. He always had the giant steel entry doors thrown wide open and all the lamps brightly illuminated, and then he waited on the lowest step of the semicircular staircase until the Emperor's sedan drove up. And after that, he stood modestly in the entry hall, somewhat to the side, near one of the columns; he kept his eyes directed humbly toward the floor, and his greatest reward was when the Emperor walked past and nodded regally at him, just slightly, but in view of everyone else. Nodded to him, the hunchback. To him, Emparak, his most faithful servant. To him, who knew the Empire better than any other mortal.

But then the new lords had arrived and degraded him to a messenger boy, to an unprivileged administrator of an unappreciated heritage. Just good enough to polish the costly marble, to clean the glass cases, and to change the burned-out lighting elements. How he hated them! *Deputies of the Provisional Council for the Investigation of the Imperial Archives.* They could come and go as they pleased, could rummage through all the documents and archive cabinets, and defile the silence of millennia with their bickering chatter. Nothing was sacred to them. And when they spoke to him, it was always in a manner that made it clear that they were young and beautiful and powerful, and he was old and ugly and powerless.

Of course, it was intentional that they stationed two women right here in front of him. They wanted to humiliate him. The women dressed in the new fashion, the fashion of the Rebellion, which revealed much and suggested even more. And they always pressed so close to him that even with his shortsighted old eyes, he couldn't miss seeing the curves of their seductive bodies, close enough to touch, but still unattainable for a limping old cripple like himself.

Just now they had arrived, unannounced as usual, and had spread out their papers in the Great Reading Room, the center point of the Archive. Emparak stood in the shadow of the columns in the entryway and observed them. The red-haired woman sat in the middle. *Rhuna Orlona Pernautan.* How they put on airs, these rebels, with their triple names! Beside her stood the woman with blond hair that never seemed to end; as far as he understood it, the assistant to the redhead. *Lamita Terget Utmanasalen.* And they had brought a man along whom Emparak had never seen before. But he knew him from government documents. *Borlid Ewo Kenneken, Member of the Committee for the Administration of the Imperial Estate.*

"We're way behind on this!" the redhead shouted. "He's arriving in two hours, and we haven't even developed a theory yet. How do you intend to pull this off?"

The man opened a large satchel and pulled out a stack of files. "There has to be a way. And it doesn't have to be perfect. He just needs a clear, concise report, so that he has some basis for a decision."

"How much time will he have for us?" the blond woman asked.

"At most, an hour," the man replied. "We'll have to limit ourselves to the essentials."

Emparak knew they considered him simpleminded and senile. Each gesture, each word directed at him told him that. So, fine. Let them think it. His time would come.

Oh, he knew exactly how things looked in the Empire today. Nothing was a secret from the Emperor's archivist. He had sources and channels, through which everything he needed to know came to him. He still had *that*, at least.

"What does he know about the background of the Gheera Expedition?"

"He knows about the discovery of the star maps on Eswerlund. He was one of the councilors who voted to send out the expedition."

"Good. That means we can forget about that much of it. What does he know about the reports up until now?"

"Almost nothing." The blond woman looked to her colleague for help. "As far as I know."

"As far as I know, too," she responded. "It's best if we present a chronology of the events, a summary of about, say, a quarter of an hour. Then he will have time for questions—"

"For which we should be prepared, of course!" the man interjected.

"Yes."

"Let's start," the redhead suggested. "Lamita, you could make a list of possible questions, things that occur to us about each of the individual points."

Emparak observed the blond woman, the way she reached for a writing pad and pen and the way her hair fell forward when she bent over to make notes. He found her attractive, of course, and, in the past, he would . . . But she was so young. So ignorant. Sat here in the middle of tens of thousands of years of momentous history and didn't feel it at all. And he couldn't forgive that in anyone.

Didn't she know that once *he* used to sit there? Emparak saw everything before his eyes again, as though no time had passed. There at the oval table sat the Emperor and studied documents the archivist had brought him. Nobody else was present. Emparak stood submissively in the shadow of the columns that stretched high up above the hall to support the glass cupola, from which pale light streamed down, bathing the scene in a shimmering glow that elicited thoughts of eternity. The Emperor turned the pages in his inimitable, graceful manner, which arose from his quiet confidence in his own power, and he read calmly and attentively. Surrounding him, ten tall dark doors led to ten radial hallways, along which ranged bookshelves, data storage units, and archive capsules. On the ten wall surfaces between the doors hung the portraits of the Emperor's ten predecessors. No place had been reserved for his own portrait, because he had said he would rule until the end of time. . . .

And now it had apparently come, the end of time. These young people symbolized it with their noisy, superficial bustling about. They understood nothing, nothing at all. And they took themselves so terribly seriously. In their boundless arrogance, they had dared to dethrone the God-Emperor—and even to kill him. Emparak felt his heart begin to rage with wrath at the thought.

He knew what the Empire was once like, and he knew what it looked like now. They weren't up to the task—of course they weren't. People were hungry again, and plagues were raging whose names had been forgotten for millennia. Everywhere was turmoil; in many places, bloody wars were being fought, and everything was going to the dogs. They were slitting open the belly of the Empire, gutting it with its heart still beating, and shredding it into raw tatters of flesh. And all the while they thought they were so important, and they invoked the word *freedom*.

The man leaned back in his chair and put his head in his hands, his fingers spread like a fan and locked together. "Good, where should we begin? I suggest the expedition boat that found the first clues about hair carpets. The ship was the *Kalyt-9* and the man we can thank for the information was Nillian Jegetar Cuain."

"Is his name important?"

"Not really. But I have heard that he is a distant relative of the councilor; so maybe it would be good to mention him by name."

"Okay. What about him?"

"He vanished. According to his companion, he disobeyed a direct order and landed on Planet G-101/2 in Sector HA/31. We have radio messages from him and a few photos, but no pictures of a hair carpet. Nillian discovered the hair carpets, but then he disappeared."

"Didn't they search for him?"

"There was some miscommunication about orders . . . crossed messages. His fellow pilot left him in the lurch and returned to base; a rescue ship only made it back weeks later and found no trace of Nillian."

The red-haired woman drummed nervously on the tabletop with the tip of her pen. Emparak cringed at the noise, which sounded almost obscene to his ears. This table was already old before her home world was even colonized.

"I'm not sure we should go into all that," she suggested. "There will surely be an inquiry—the whole thing is an unfortunate affair, the sort of thing that happens, but it isn't really what matters. The only important thing is that this Nillian discovered the hair carpets, and that's what sparked interest in the whole matter."

"Exactly. It will be more important to explain what these hair carpets are and what they mean. They're large, densely knotted rugs, made of human hair. The people who make them are called hair-carpet makers. They use exclusively the hair of their wives and daughters, and the whole process is so incredibly time consuming that a carpetmaker must spend his entire life tying just one single carpet."

The blonde raised her hand for a moment. "Can we show a sample of such a carpet?" she suggested.

"Unfortunately not," the man admitted. "Naturally, we've requested one, and that's been approved, but as of this morning . . . nothing. I had hoped that the Archive—"

"No," the blond woman said immediately. "We've looked. There's nothing like that in the Archive."

In his quiet corner by the columns, Emparak smiled. Level 2, hallway L, sector 967. Of course the Archive had a hair carpet. The Archive had everything. It just had to be found.

The man looked at his watch. "Okay, let's continue. We have to make clear what these hair carpets are and what an immense expenditure of effort they represent. As the sociological report points out, the entire planetary population is engaged in almost nothing else."

The red-haired woman nodded. "Yes. That's important."

"And what becomes of all the hair carpets?" the blonde asked.

"That's another crucial point we have to emphasize. The entire hair-carpet production has a religious motivation. And that means the old state religion—the Emperor as god, as creator and protector of the universe, and so on."

"*The* Emperor?"

"Yes. Without question. They even have photographs of him. So this also proves that the inhabited portion of the Gheera Galaxy really was once a part of the Empire. The whole superstructure of religion and power politics is the same as in the known parts of the Empire, and the language common on the Gheera worlds corresponds to a dialect of our Paisi, as it was spoken, so the linguists tell us, approximately eighty thousand years ago."

"That would give us a point of reference as to when contact between Gheera and the rest of the Empire was severed."

"Precisely. By the way, on many of these worlds there are indications of atomic explosions very long ago—long-term atomic decomposition products and such—all of which suggests there were military conflicts. And these trace elements have also been dated back to at least eighty thousand years."

"That strengthens the theory."

"But what does that have to do with the hair carpets?" the blonde persisted.

"The carpet makers produce these carpets as service to the Emperor. They believe the carpets are destined for the Emperor's Palace."

Perplexed silence. "For the Emperor's Palace?"

"Yes."

"But there is nothing in the Palace that is anything like a hair carpet."

"Exactly. That's what is so puzzling."

"But . . ." The blond woman began to calculate. "That must be a heck of a lot of carpets, added all together. A whole world with an estimated population . . ."

"The quantities are phenomenal," the man completed her thought. "Save yourself the trouble; it gets better. The people on G-101/2 believe they are the only producers of hair carpets. They know that the Emperor's realm contains many worlds, but they believe that the other worlds deliver other things to the Emperor's Palace. A kind of interplanetary division of labor." He examined his fingernails intently. "Then, soon after that, the Gheera expedition discovered a second world, where the people also produce hair carpets in the belief that they are the only ones."

"*Two* worlds?" The women were astonished.

The man looked from one to the other, obviously enjoying the expectant curiosity in their faces. "The latest report of the expedition shows," he continued, "that, to this point, they have found eight thousand three hundred forty-seven planets on which hair carpets are knotted."

"Eight thousand . . ."

"And there is no end in sight." The man smacked the table loudly with the flat of his hand. "That's the point we have to make. Something is going on there, and we don't know what it is."

I know, Emparak thought with satisfaction. *And the Archive knows. And if you understood how to search it, you could know it, too. . . .*

The blond woman jumped up and walked over to Emparak, pressing her enormous breasts almost into the hunchbacked archivist's face. "Emparak, we have two points of reference," she said, and looked at him. Eighty thousand years. The Gheera Galaxy. Can we find something related to those in the Archive?"

"Gheera Galaxy?" Emparak croaked. She had startled him with her sudden approach, and the proximity of her alluring body wakened forgotten appetites in him that momentarily overwhelmed him and rendered him speechless.

"Let him be, Lamita!" the red-haired witch called in the background. "I've tried that often enough. He has no idea, and the Archive is nothing but chaos, without any sort of organizational system."

The young woman shrugged her shoulders and returned to her seat. Emparak stared at the redhead, seething with rage. How dare she? They were failing by the hundreds and thousands in their attempt to fill the shoes of a man like the Emperor, but she dared to call the Archive chaos. What did she call the mess the self-appointed Provisional Council was creating out there? What word did she have for the infinite loss of direction in the souls of the people whose lives they had destroyed? What word for the deterioration of morality, for the spreading degeneracy? How would she describe the results of their limitless failure?

"So what is actually happening in Gheera with the hair carpets?" the redhead asked. "They must be stacked up somewhere, after all."

"Transporting the hair carpets is undertaken by a large fleet of ships that are aging, to be sure, but are quite adequate for space flight," the man reported. "A separate caste, the Imperial Shipsmen, is responsible for that. They seem to be the keepers of the technological heritage, since there is nothing to be found on the planets themselves beyond the level of primitive, postatomic cultures."

"And where do they transport the carpets?"

"The expedition was able to track them to a gigantic space station orbiting a binary star that has no planets. One of the two stars is a black hole. I don't know if that means anything."

"What's known about this space station?"

"Nothing, except that it's extremely heavily guarded and armed. One of our ships, the light cruiser *Evluut*, was attacked and heavily damaged when it approached."

Naturally. To this day, Emparak couldn't understand how the rebels—these conceited, know-it-all weaklings—had managed to wrest power from the immortal, omnipotent Emperor and seize the Empire. The rebels couldn't fight! Lie, deceive, hide, and spin treacherous intrigues—they could do all those things—but fight? Until his dying day, he would never understand how they had succeeded in overcoming the mighty, invincible military machine of the Emperor. It would have taken ten or more of these rebels to match a single Imperial Soldier.

"Okay." The redhead closed her folder in order to end the discussion for the time being. "Let's get prepared. I think we should set up a projector and keep the chronological charts ready, in case someone is looking for historical connections." She glanced in the old archivist's direction. "Emparak, we need your help!"

He knew what sort of help they wanted. He was supposed to get the projector and set it up. Nothing else. All the while, he could have answered all questions and solved all riddles in the blink of an eye. If they had only been a little friendlier to him, a little more obliging, a little more respectful . . .

But he would not buy their respect. Let them slave away by themselves. The Emperor always had reasons for his actions; he surely had his reasons in this case, too, and it wasn't the archivist's job to question him.

Emparak shuffled from the reading room back into the entry hall and turned to the right. He was in no hurry. In contrast to the three young people, he knew exactly what had to be done.

He descended the broad staircase leading to the underground regions of the Archive. Here the light was dim and he couldn't see very far. They liked to be upstairs—the young women—between the endless shelves of the domed building. He had seldom seen them down here. It was probably a bit eerie for them, and he could understand that. Down here you couldn't escape the smell of history. Down here lay incredible artifacts, testaments to unimaginable events, documents of inestimable value. Down here you could touch time with your hands.

He unlocked the door to the small equipment room at the foot of the staircase. Eighty thousand years. They said that so casually—these clueless fools—as though it were nothing. They said it without being overcome with awe, without feeling a shudder at the edge of this chasm of time. Eighty thousand years. In that amount of time, mighty empires could rise, then crumble again and be forgotten. How many generations came and went in that length of time, lived their lives, hoped and grieved, achieved things and then sank down again into the merciless maelstrom of time! Eighty thousand years. They said that in a tone of voice as though they were speaking about eighty minutes.

And still, it was only a part of the immeasurable history of the Empire. Emparak nodded in thought while dragging the projection equipment up the stairs. Maybe he should give them a little hint. Not much, just a little scrap. A clue. Just to show that he knew more than they thought. Just so they might then have some idea of the greatness of the man they had shot down like vermin. The Empire could never have existed for so long without that man, without the eleventh Emperor who had achieved immortality. Yes, thought Emparak. Just a clue, so they could uncover the rest themselves. In their foolish pride, they would never accept more than that.

"He should be here any minute," said the redhead, who was now continually looking at her watch, while the others were organizing their papers. "How are we supposed to address him?"

"His title is Councilor," the blond woman said.

Emparak placed the projector on the table and removed the cover.

"He doesn't like titles," the man interjected. "He prefers to be called by his name, Jubad."

At the sound of this name, an icy chill seemed to spread through Emparak all the way to his fingertips. *Berenko Kebar Jubad! The man who murdered the Emperor!*

How dare he? The Emperor's murderer dared enter this place where the glory of the Empire was preserved. An affront. No, it was worse than that: insensitivity. This common, narrow-minded man was not even capable of comprehending the meaning of his action, the symbolism of his visit. He was just going to show up here to listen to a stupid little report from the mouths of stupid little people.

Well, let him come. He, Emparak, would stand there and be silent. He had been the Emperor's Archivist and would still remain that until his final breath. He was ashamed for coming so close to deciding to cooperate with these loudmouthed upstarts. Never. Never again. He would be silent; he would be silent and would polish the millennia-old marble until one day the polishing rag would fall from his hands.

The redhead walked to the control panel in the entry hall and opened one wing of the entrance door. Just one. Emparak nodded in satisfaction. They had no sense of style, of appearance. They had no greatness.

The whole reception of the rebel leader seemed like a ridiculous imitation to Emparak. A small vehicle drove up, and Jubad stepped out—a short, gray-haired man whose movements seemed fidgety and nervous and who walked slightly bent as though weighed down by the burden of his responsibility. He hurried up the steps like a jittery marionette, and without even noticing the magnificent atmosphere of the entry hall, he headed directly toward the redhead so that she could show him into the reading room.

Emparak took his usual place near the columns and observed Jubad while he was listening to the report of the other three. The rumor was that he suffered from a chronic, perhaps incurable disease. Emparak was inclined to believe it when he looked at the rebel leader's face, which was marked with suppressed pain. Maybe it was coincidence. But maybe it was also the punishment of fate.

"So nothing is known about the final disposition of the hair carpets?" Jubad drew his conclusion at the end of the presentation.

"No."

"Inside the space station?"

"It's not large enough," the man replied. "It's only necessary to estimate the total volume of the hair carpets produced up until now and to compare that with the volume of the space station—the carpet volume would be many times larger."

"Perhaps the hair carpets aren't kept at all," the blond woman suggested. "Perhaps they're destroyed."

"That could be," said Jubad in passing. It was clear to look at him that he was occupied with completely different thoughts. "The frightening possibility for me is that an undiscovered Imperial Palace might exist somewhere in the universe, where, in the meantime, mountains of hair carpets are stacking up. And if there is an undiscovered palace, who knows what else is there—perhaps undiscovered armies that have been lying in hibernation for millennia?"

The redhead nodded. "Maybe a clone of the Emperor who is also immortal?"

"Exactly," Jubad agreed earnestly with her. "We don't know how the Emperor managed to stop aging and to live on and on for this immeasurable time span. There is so much we don't know, and we must have more than an academic interest in some of these unsolved mysteries, because they may hold hidden dangers."

Emparak had to admit grudgingly that this Jubad had a surprisingly keen mind. A little of the Emperor's greatness seemed to have rubbed off onto his vanquisher. And he was right: even the Archive knew nothing about the immortality of the Emperor.

Jubad leafed quickly through the papers while the others watched him silently and patiently. He couldn't get past one sheet; he read it through and passed it to the man. "What's this about?"

"The star Gheerh hasn't been found," he explained. "The first order for the expedition fleet was to verify the accuracy of the star maps that were discovered. Several of the catalogued stars bore no numbers, only names, and one of these—the star Gheerh—couldn't be found."

"What does that mean, it couldn't be found?"

The man shrugged his shoulders. "Simply not there. The sun, together with its planets, simply swept away out of the universe."

"Could that have anything to do with this presumed war eighty thousand years ago?"

"The names are immediately striking. Gheerh. Gheera. Maybe Gheerh was the main world of the realm named Gheera and was therefore destroyed in that war."

Jubad looked across to the red-haired woman. Silent horror showed in his eyes. "Did the fleet of the Empire have that ability—to destroy an entire solar system?"

Yes, Emparak thought. They did it often enough.

"Yes," the redhead said.

Jubad became lost again in contemplation. He stared at the papers as though this might force them to reveal their secret.

"One of the two parts of the binary star, around which the space station is orbiting, is a black hole?" he asked suddenly.

"Yes."

"How long has it been a black hole?"

The women and the man were surprised and didn't know what to say. "No idea."

"That's a rather dangerous combination, isn't it? The riskiest possible place to build a space station—constant, heavy radiation and always the looming danger of being devoured by one's own environment . . ." Jubad eyed the others one after another. "What do the old star maps show?"

"Huh." The blond woman bent over her portable data unit and pressed a few keys. "They show no black hole. Only the red giant. No double star at all."

"That means something!" Jubad stood up. "I'll use my position in the Council to see that a battle fleet is sent to Gheera with orders to attack and take the space station. We have to solve the mystery of the hair carpets, and I am of the opinion that the space station is the decisive key to it." He gave an expressive nod. "Thank you."

With that he rushed out to his car, which carried him away.

The man leaned back with a relieved sigh and sprawled out his limbs.

"Well?" he blurted out. "It went well, don't you think?"

The redhead stared at the tabletop in front of her with dissatisfaction. "Those things about the binary star were embarrassing. We should have noticed that ourselves."

"Oh, Rhuna, you eternal perfectionist!" the blond woman responded. "Aren't you ever satisfied? There's been a decision—that's all we wanted to achieve."

"If he had said, It's all a waste of time, let's recall the Gheera expedition—that would have been the worst outcome," the man suggested.

"And maybe it wasn't so bad that he figured it out for himself," the blond woman speculated. "That was probably more convincing for him than if we had presented it predigested to him."

"Well, that's true, too." The redhead smiled and started gathering up her files. "So, guys, let's be happy about it. Let's pack up and consider where we want to go to celebrate."

The blonde signaled to Emparak. "You can take down the projector now. Thank you very much."

Why was she thanking him? And why was she watching him so strangely?

Emparak said nothing. He picked up the projector cover and shuffled to the table to attach it. The three young people left, loaded down with their bags and folders and without another word of acknowledgment to him.

"You'll see, we'll still figure out what's going on with the hair carpets. . . ."

Those were the last words Emparak heard, and they hung for a while in the air as though they were hoping for an echo from the unfathomable depths of the Archive.

Emparak watched them go; his face was expressionless. In his mind's eye, he could see the archive cabinet that hid all the answers and could have resolved all their questions.

Just keep looking, he thought as he closed the steel door. Keep butting your heads against it. You think you've uncovered a great mystery. You have no idea. You haven't even scratched the surface of the history of the Empire.

····· XI ·····

Jubad

HIS LEFT HAND PRESSED his right hand to his chest, a gesture that had become his trademark and was often imitated—both by admirers and by detractors—and his eyes swept over gardens flooded with sunlight and flower beds bursting with blossoms, over glittering ponds and idyllic walking paths. But he saw only the murky, gray gloom of a past age. His car was following a route which snaked playfully between impressive architectural monuments from every epoch and which would lead them to the center of the former Imperial Palace. But Jubad's eyes saw nothing but the massive, dark, columned edifice they had just left.

The Emperor's Archive . . . He had always avoided entering the ancient building that housed documents and artifacts from the entire Imperial Age. Perhaps he should have also avoided it today. But for some reason, taking part in the meeting there today had seemed inescapable to him, although he could not now recall the reason why.

When the discussion was finished, he had practically fled the building. He had said yes and of course and then he had fled, as though compelled to escape the spirit of the dead monarch. Jubad suddenly had to draw a deep, tortured breath, and out of the corner of his eye, he noticed his driver's concerned look. He wanted to say something to reassure him, but didn't know what to say. He could hardly remember the subject of the meeting, because he had had to fight off waves of memories that threatened to engulf him. Memories of a past that had shaped his life.

Berenko Kebar Jubad. He had so often heard his own name in speeches and read it in history books that it had begun to seem like someone else's name of long ago. Jubad the Liberator. Jubad, Conqueror of the Tyrant. Jubad, the man who had slain the Emperor.

Since the end of the Empire, he himself led the life of a ruler. He sat on the Council of Rebels, spoke before parliament, and wherever he went and whatever he said, he sensed reverent glances and devout affection. Because his word was respected, he had been able to influence significantly the decision to grant the Tempesh-Kutaraan region its autonomy, and the liberation of Baquion Province was, at least in part, also his work. But these were not the accomplishments later generations would remember. He would be remembered for all time as the man who had dealt the fatal blow to the despot.

Responding to a sudden whim, he had the driver stop the car. "I'm going to walk part of the way," he said, and when he noticed the driver's worried glance, he added, "I'm not as old as I look. You should surely know that."

He was only fifty-four, but was often taken for seventy. And when he climbed out of the car, he almost felt it was true. He stood and waited until the vehicle was out of sight.

Then he breathed deeply and looked around. He was alone. Alone in a small garden, encircled by delicately foliaged, blue-green bushes with dark red buds. Somewhere a bird was singing a lonesome song, the same sequence of tones over and over again. It sounded like a diligent rehearsal.

Jubad closed his eyes, listened to the birdsong that reminded him more of flute tones than of the birds of his homeland, and enjoyed the warmth of the sun on his face. Delightful, he thought, just to stand here . . . anywhere . . . and to be totally unimportant. To be observed by no one. Simply to be alive.

To his surprise, when he opened his eyes again, a small boy stood before him and stared. He had not heard the boy's approach.

"You're Jubad, aren't you?" said the boy.

Jubad nodded. "Yes."

"Were you just thinking about a difficult problem?" the child asked. "That's why I didn't bother you."

"That was very thoughtful of you," said Jubad, and smiled. "But I wasn't thinking about anything in particular. I was just listening to the bird."

The boy opened his eyes wide. "Honest?"

"Honest," Jubad assured him.

He watched the little boy, who shifted his hips nervously and clearly had something on his mind. Suddenly it burst out: "I want to ask you something important!"

"Really?" Jubad responded instinctively. "So ask!"

"Is it true you killed the Emperor?"

"Yes, it's true. But that was a long time ago."

"And was he really dead? Did you see for sure?"

"I saw for sure," Jubad assured him as earnestly as he could. With effort he suppressed a smile. "The Emperor was really dead."

Suddenly the boy seemed distressed. "My father always says none of that's true. He says the Emperor is still alive and that he just gave up his body so he could live among the stars and planets. He has lots of pictures of the Emperor in his room, and he says you are a liar. Is that right? Are you a liar?"

A familiar pain shot through Jubad. The past. It would never let him go.

"Look," he explained cautiously, "when your father was a child like you are now, the Emperor was still ruling and your father had to attend a priest's school like all the children. There the priests hurt him and put really, really terrible fear into him . . . fear that he might sometime do something that would displease the Emperor. And this fear has not left him his whole life. He's still afraid now—that's why he says such things. Can you understand that?"

It was almost too much to expect of a child who may have been four or five years old and who, nevertheless, had to fret about such things because he loved his father.

For a while the struggle was evident in his little face as the boy tried to come to some resolution. But suddenly it seemed that all the fretting was swept away, and he beamed: "I don't think you're a liar!"

"Thank you," Jubad said dryly.

"Besides," the boy continued cheerily, "the Emperor would have punished you bad if he was still alive!" With that he hopped away, relieved and full of energy.

Jubad watched him leave, somewhat overwhelmed by this childish insight.

"Yes," he finally mumbled. "That's a logical conclusion."

. . . .

When Jubad entered his apartment, a man was sitting calmly at the table as though he had been waiting for some time. Beside his hand on the tabletop lay a small, dark case.

Jubad paused for a moment, then closed the door deliberately.

"Already that time again?"

"Yes," the man said.

Jubad nodded and then began to close the shutters on all the windows. Outside it was already dusk, and several of the seven moons had appeared in the sky as though embedded in black velvet.

From one of his windows Jubad had a good view of the great dome at the center of the palace. It contained the magnificent former private rooms of the Emperor, now locked and accessible only to researchers with special permission. But unbelievably, some people had suggested that Jubad himself should move in there—an idea he immediately rejected, of course.

"Did anyone see you?"

"I don't think so."

"Aren't you sure?"

The man at the table laughed softly. "Of course. But it will never be possible to completely get rid of the rumor that you have some serious illness."

Jubad closed the last shutter, turned on the light, and also sat down at the table.

"We're talking about one of the most vital state secrets," he said seriously. "Not even the Council may hear of it."

"Yes." The man opened the small case, took out a syringe, and began to fill it with a light blue fluid. "But how long will you be able to stand this?"

"As long as I can."

He refused to become superstitious about it. It was just coincidence, nothing more. He must have picked up the virus somewhere when he was young, probably even during his first trip on behalf of the Revolutionary Council, which had taken him to Jehemba. And then the sickness had lain dormant inside him—many long years—without the slightest symptoms.

Gradually the fluid in the syringe became darker. It had to be injected as soon as it reached a specific dark tint, nearly black. It would burn like hell for hours, but it would retard the progress of the disease. Jubad began to remove his shirt.

Fleshblight. That's what they called the disease on Jehemba. Carefully, Jubad undid his shirt cuff, which simulated healthy skin. Beneath it appeared the skin of an ancient man; wrinkled, cracked, and withered, it covered hard, shriveled cords of muscle hardly thicker than a small finger.

Suddenly he thought about the Archive again—and about the little boy. And about the past, about a time long ago, when the Emperor was still alive and had him, Jubad the rebel, in his power.

It had to remain a secret. No one must find out that the right arm of Berenko Kebar Jubad was shriveling away—the arm with which he had killed the Emperor.

The Emperor and the Rebel

HE EXPECTED NOTHING NOW but death. And it would be terrible, terrible for him and still more terrible for those who depended on his silence. The lives of thousands, possibly even the future of the entire movement depended on his ability to keep the secrets entrusted to him. And he knew he would not be able to keep them.

The Emperor's henchmen would use every method at their command to break his silence. And those were horrible methods, cruel procedures, against which he had no defenses. Pain awaited him, pain more intense than anything he had ever experienced. And pain would not be all. There were other means—wily, cunningly designed methods—against which strength of will was useless. They would work on him with drugs. They would insert probes into his nerves. They would utilize devices he had never heard of, and in the end they would get him to talk. At some point, they would find out everything they wanted to know.

There was only one possibility of deliverance, only one hope: he had to die before they got him to that point.

But that was not so easy. If he had seen a chance to end his own life, he would not have hesitated for an instant. But they had taken everything from him—first the poison capsule every rebel carried with him and then every other weapon, everything. They had searched every body cavity for hidden objects and had scanned him from head to toe. The only thing he now had on his body was a thin, lightweight suit made of cottony fabric.

The cell into which they had put him was small and totally empty, almost antiseptically clean. The walls were of steel, as smooth as a mirror, also the ceiling and floor. There was a small tap that dripped lukewarm water when he turned it on and a container fixed firmly to the floor for his bodily waste. That was all. No mattress, no blanket. He had to sleep on the bare floor.

He had thought of smashing his skull against the walls in an act of sudden despair—so quickly they would not be able to stop him. But a power field extended a hand's width from the wall; it made rapid movement impossible and prevented such an attempt much like a rubber pad, only better.

It was warm. Walls and floor seemed to be heated. He guessed that some large machine was installed near his cell, perhaps a generator, because he felt tiny vibrations when he lay on the floor. The light from the three elements in the ceiling never went out, and he was sure he was being observed, even though he had no idea how.

There was a semicircular flap in the door that sometimes closed. When it opened again, it contained his daily meal. It was always the same, a thin mush in a transparent bowl. That was the only threat he had received: if he refused food, he would be tied down and fed artificially. So he ate. There was no spoon; he had to drink the mush. The bowl itself was soft and delicate and not suitable for cutting open arteries and such.

That was the only diversion and his only measurement of time. Other than that, he usually sat in a corner with his back against the wall and let his thoughts wander. The faces of his friends appeared as though to say good-bye, and episodes from his life returned as though to demand an accounting. No, he regretted nothing. He would do everything exactly the same way again. Even this reconnaissance flight, which had turned out to be an elaborate trap. He could not have known that. He had done nothing wrong.

Sometimes even his thoughts were silent. Then he just sat there watching his indistinct reflection in the opposite wall and did nothing but sense that he was still alive. He would not be for long. Now every moment was precious.

In these moments he was at peace with himself.

Then there were moments of fear. The certainty that death is near and inescapable awakens an animal fear millions of years old, a fear that denies all attempts to understand it, that sweeps aside every rational consideration and crushes every higher need beneath it. It wells up from the darkest depths of the soul to become a terrible flood. Like a drowning man, he sought hope and some relief in those hours, and found only uncertainty.

Gradually he lost his sense of time. It was soon impossible for him to say how long he had been imprisoned—days or months. Maybe he had been forgotten. Maybe he would simply stay locked up here for years on end . . . would get old and die.

They came while he was sleeping. But at the sound of keys in the lock of his cell door, he was awake and on his feet in an instant.

The time had come. The torture was beginning. He counted sixteen soldiers of the Imperial Guard pressed close together in the hallway, all of them armed with narcotic guns. They always thought of everything. He didn't have a chance.

One of them, a stocky man with thinning hair and a severe face, stepped into the doorway.

"Rebel Jubad? Come with us!" he commanded brusquely.

Two soldiers approached cautiously and shackled him, so that he could only take small, toddling steps. Then they bound his wrists together and fastened a chain around his waist. Jubad did not resist. When they signaled him to move, he obeyed.

They passed along a brightly lit hallway to a broad tunnel where a heavily armored transporter awaited them with open doors. There was no possibility of escape and no way to throw himself into an abyss or into a barrage of gunfire. They ordered him in, seated themselves around him, and the journey began.

They seemed to go straight ahead for hours. Sometimes they rode through complete darkness, and in the dim light from the instrument panel, the faces of the soldiers, who never took their eyes from him, looked like grotesque demonic masks. Several times they had to stop at energy shields that shimmered threateningly—to await a thorough inspection by guards who sat in armored cubicles and made lengthy telephone calls before shutting down the shields and allowing them to proceed. The whole time, not a word was spoken inside the transporter.

At some point, as they were again riding through the darkness toward a distant speck of light, the transporter suddenly shot out of an opening in a sheer cliff face and floated straight ahead through the air on its antigravity field. Jubad looked around in amazement and took in the overwhelming sight. They continued their course high above a calm, ink-blue sea that stretched from horizon to horizon and bore the great, flawless azure dome of the sky above them. They left behind them a rugged rock face falling steeply to the ocean, and before them . . . there before them lay the Emperor's Palace, glistening in the sunlight and almost beyond comprehension in its unimaginable size.

The Star Palace. Jubad had seen pictures, but no picture could adequately reproduce the proud, extravagant splendor of this gigantic edifice. This was the seat of the Emperor, the immortal ruler of all mankind, and was therefore the heart of the Empire. There was no rebel who had not dreamed of reaching this place—as a victor. Jubad came as a prisoner. His eyes clouded over at the thought of the horrors that might await him there.

The transporter descended until it was shooting so low over the surface of the sea that he could have touched the crests of the almost imperceptible swells. The outer walls of the Palace approached rapidly and rose higher and higher. A gate opened like a great maw and swallowed them, and behind it, the transporter landed in the center of a tall courtyard.

"You are being transferred to the Life Guard of the Emperor," said the commander.

Jubad flinched. That could mean nothing good. The Imperial Life Guard—they were the most devoted of the most select, the elite of the elite, devoted to the Emperor unto death and ruthless with themselves and others. Twelve of them, powerful giants in gold uniforms, all resembling one another like brothers, awaited him on the landing pad.

"Too much honor," he muttered nervously.

He was placed in the center of the Life Guard contingent, and they waited with expressionless faces until the transporter had departed. Then one of them stooped down and removed his shackles. There was condescension in this act: he seemed to be saying, You can't possibly escape from us even if you can run.

They led him through endless hallways. Fear throbbed in Jubad, but still he took in everything, every step and every impression. Soon, maybe in the next hallway or in the one after that, a door would open to a room where his life would end. The sterile glow of the instruments in that room would be the last light to enter his eyes, and his own screams would be the sounds he would carry with him into the darkness of eternity.

They climbed a broad stairway. Jubad noted it with confusion. He had instinctively assumed that the interrogation rooms and torture chambers would be located in the lower levels of the Palace—in the cellars where no one lived and where no one would hear any screams. But to the beat of their marching, the guardsmen led him across polished marble floors, through gold-trimmed portals and magnificent halls filled with art treasures from all the galaxies of the Empire. When they stepped through a small side door, his heart beat like a mallet in his chest, but behind the door was nothing but an unadorned white room. With the exception of several armchairs and a table, it contained only a small control panel. They signaled him to stop, took up positions around the room and at the doors, and waited. Nothing happened.

"What are we waiting for?" Jubad asked finally.

One of the guardsmen turned to him. "The Emperor wants to see you," he said. "Be quiet."

Jubad's thoughts leapt back and forth and tied themselves in knots; his lower jaw suddenly dropped open without control. The Emperor?

He felt searing terror ignite within him. No one had ever heard of the Emperor participating in person in an interrogation.

The Emperor wanted to see him. What could that mean?

It took quite a while before it dawned on the rebel what that meant. It meant that soon the Emperor would come here himself. Here into this room. Probably through the door that was guarded by two soldiers on either side. The Emperor would come here to confront the rebel.

Jubad's thoughts stampeded about like a spooked herd of animals. Was this an opportunity? If he tried to attack the Emperor himself, they would certainly kill him, they would *have to* kill him, quickly and painlessly. Here was the chance he had been waiting for. He would show the tyrant that a rebel knows how to die.

In the midst of Jubad's thoughts, the door opened. The Life Guardsmen came to attention. With measured steps an older, somewhat stocky man entered; in comparison to the guardsmen, he looked like a dwarf. He had graying temples and wore a monstrously tacky uniform, hung everywhere with spangles and tinsel. He gave a stately look around and then said:

"The Emperor."

With these words, he fell to his knees, spread his arms, and bowed humbly until his forehead nearly touched the floor. The Life Guardsmen did the same, and finally Jubad was the only one still standing.

And then the Emperor entered the room.

There are things one forgets and things one remembers, but among the latter, there are just a very few moments in life that remain burned forever, like oversize, glowing images, into the memory. Whenever Jubad was later asked what the most impressive and most soul-stirring moment of his life was, he had to admit reluctantly: it was that moment.

The presence of the Emperor hit him like the blow of a hammer. Of course he knew the face; every human being knew it. Over the course of centuries, an intimate familiarity with this face seemed to have become part of the heritage of mankind. Jubad had seen films of the Emperor, had heard speeches by him, but none of that had prepared him for—for *this*. . . .

There he was. The Emperor. For tens of thousands of years, ruler over humankind, ruler over the entire inhabited universe, ageless and beyond all ordinary human scale. He was a slender, tall man with a powerful body and a sharply molded, nearly perfect face. Clothed in a simple white robe, he entered the room with infinite composure, without the slightest superfluous movement, and without haste. His eyes fell on Jubad, who had the sensation he was falling into them, as though they were two bottomless wells.

It was overpowering. It was like meeting a mythological figure. *Now I understand why people think he's a god!* was all Jubad's poor brain could think.

"Rise."

Even the sound of his voice was familiar, dark, nuanced, restrained. It was the voice of someone who lived outside time. Around Jubad, the men of the Life Guard rose and stood with humbly lowered heads. Appalled, Jubad realized that he, too, had spontaneously fallen to his knees when the Emperor entered. He leapt up.

The Emperor looked at Jubad again. "Take off his shackles."

Two of the guardsmen freed Jubad from the remaining chains,

which jangled as they rolled them up and slipped them inside the pockets of their uniforms.

"Now leave me alone with the rebel."

Dismay registered on the faces of the soldiers for an instant, but they obeyed without delay.

The Emperor waited motionless until everyone had disappeared and closed the doors behind them. Then he glanced quickly at Jubad with a thin, inscrutable smile and walked past the rebel into the room, carelessly turning his back to him as though he were not even there.

Jubad felt almost dizzy with the heat of something pulsing inside him that said, Kill him! Kill him! This was an opportunity that would not come again in a thousand years. He was alone with the tyrant. He would kill him, with bare hands, with teeth and fingernails, and would free the Empire from the dictator. He would fulfill the mission of the rebels—alone. His hands drew silently into fists, and his heart beat so powerfully that it seemed it must be echoing through the room.

"All your thoughts," the monarch said abruptly, "are focused on the idea of killing me. Am I right?"

Jubad swallowed. The air escaped from his lungs with a gasp. What was happening here? What sort of game was the Emperor playing with him? Why had he sent his Life Guard away?

The Emperor smiled. "Of course I'm right. The rebels have dreamed of a situation like this for centuries—to be alone with the hated despot.... Isn't that so? Come on ... say something. I'd like to know what your voice sounds like."

Jubad swallowed. "Yes."

"You would like to kill me, right?"

"Yes."

The Emperor spread out his arms. "Well, warrior, here I am. Why don't you try it?"

Jubad squinted suspiciously. He scrutinized the God-Emperor waiting there patiently in his unadorned white robe, his hands spread out in a gesture of defenselessness. Yes. Yes, he would do it. At worst, he would die in the attempt. And besides, dying was the only thing he now desired.

He would do it. Now. Immediately . . . as soon as he figured out how to get his body to react. He looked into those eyes, the eyes of the Emperor, the Lord of the Elements and the Stars, the Omnipotent Sovereign, and his inner strength flagged. His arms cramped. He gasped. He would do it. He had to kill him. He had to, but his body did not obey him.

"You can't do it," the monarch observed. "I wanted to show you that. Respect for the Emperor is rooted deeply in all of you, even in you rebels. It makes it impossible for you to attack me."

He turned away and walked to the small control panel, beside which two armchairs faced the wall. With a casual, almost graceful gesture, he extended his hand and activated a switch; a section of the wall slid noiselessly aside, revealing to view a gigantic three-dimensional projection map of a star panorama. Jubad recognized the outlines of the Empire. Each individual star appeared to be represented, and the reflection of the galaxies bathed the room in which they were standing in a spectral light.

"I often sit here for hours and consider the things over which I have power," said the Emperor. "All these stars with their planets are mine. This entire, incomprehensible universe is the realm in which my will is done and my word is law. But power, real power, is never power over things, not even over suns and planets. The only real power is power over people. And my power is not simply the power of weapons and of force; I also have power over the hearts and the thoughts of people. Billions upon billions of people live on these planets, and they all belong to me. None of them passes a day without thinking of me. They honor me; they love me. I am the focal point of all their lives." He looked at Jubad. "Never has there been an Empire greater than mine. Never has a human being had more power than I have."

Jubad stared at the Emperor, this man whose facial features were subject to less change than the constellations in the firmament. Why was he telling him this? What did he intend to do with him?

"You are wondering why I am telling you this and what I intend to do with you," the Emperor continued. Jubad nearly jumped with the shock of realizing of how swiftly and easily the Emperor had seen through him. "And you are also wondering whether I can possibly read thoughts. . . . No, I can't. It's not necessary. What you think and feel is written on your face."

Jubad sensed almost physically how vastly inferior he was to this ageless man.

"By the way, I have no intention of having you interrogated. So you can relax. I am telling you all this because I want you to *understand* something." The monarch gave him an inscrutable look. "I already know everything I want to know. Even about you, Berenko Kebar Jubad."

Jubad could not keep himself from flinching when he heard the Emperor speak his name.

"You were born twenty-nine years ago on Lukdaria, one of the secret base worlds of the rebel organization, the first son of Ikana Wero

Kebar and Uban Jegetar Berenko. At age twelve you undertook your first reconnaissance mission, were then trained in heavy weaponry and ship artillery, named support vessel commandant and then ship's captain and finally appointed to the Consulting Staff of the Rebel Council." An almost mocking smile flickered across the Emperor's face when he saw Jubad's bewilderment. "Should I recount for you some spicy details of your little affair with that young navigator? You had just turned sixteen, and her name was Rheema—"

Jubad was horrified. "How . . . how do you know that?" he stammered.

"I know everything about all of you," said the Emperor. "I know names, positions, and the condition of your armaments on every one of your base planets—Lukdaria, Jehemba, Bakion, and all the others. I know about your shadow government on Purat, your secret alliances on Naquio and Marnak, and I am even familiar with your secret base Niobai. I know every single one of you by name, I know your goals, and I know your plans."

He might as well have run Jubad through with a red-hot sword. The fright was almost fatal. Jubad had forearmed himself against torture designed to tear this information from him, and he had been prepared to die to keep any one of these names secret.

His legs gave way under him. Without noticing what he was doing, he sank into one of the armchairs. After everything he had experienced, he was on the verge of losing consciousness.

"Ah," said the Emperor, and bowed his head respectfully. "I see you are a true rebel."

It took a while for Jubad to understand what he meant: He had taken a seat while the Emperor was still standing. That would normally have been interpreted as an insult worthy of death. Still, Jubad remained seated.

"If you know all that," he said, struggling to bring his voice under his control, "then I wonder what you want from me."

The Emperor looked at him with eyes as unfathomable as the abyss between the stars. "I want you to return and see to it that the plans are changed."

Indignant, Jubad jumped to his feet. "Never!" he shouted. "I will die first."

For the first time, he heard the Emperor laugh out loud. "You believe that will accomplish something? Don't be stupid. You see that I know everything about all of you. From one hour to the next, I could wipe out the entire rebel movement, every last man without a trace. I am the only one who knows how many revolts and rebellions there have already been, and I was always delighted to defeat and exterminate the rebels. But this time I will not do that, because the rebel movement plays an important role in my plans."

"We won't allow ourselves to be your tool!"

"You may not like it, but you have been my tool from the beginning," the Emperor responded calmly and added, "I founded the rebel movement."

Jubad's thoughts were paralyzed—permanently, it seemed to him.

"What?" he heard himself mutter feebly.

"You know the history of the movement," said the Emperor. "About three hundred years ago in the border worlds, a man appeared who gave inflammatory speeches and knew how to incite the people against the rule of the Emperor. He founded the nucleus of the rebel movement, and he wrote the book that has remained the most important work of the movement and whose title gave the movement its name. The book is called *The Silent Wind*, and the man's name was Denkalsar."

"Yes."

"I was that man."

Jubad stared at him. The earth beneath him seemed to crumble away, piece by piece.

"No..."

"It was an interesting adventure. I disguised myself and agitated against the Empire... then I returned to the Palace and fought the rebels I had goaded into action myself. I have traveled around in disguise innumerable times during my life, but that was the greatest challenge. And I was successful—the rebel movement grew and grew, unstoppable—"

"I don't believe you."

The Emperor smiled sympathetically. "Just examine the name. Denkalsar—an anagram of my name, Aleksandr. Did none of you ever notice?"

The ground beneath Jubad finally seemed to fall away completely. The abyss opened up to swallow him whole.

"But—why?!" he burst out. "Why would you do all that?"

He already knew the answer. It had just been a game the Emperor had played against himself in his boredom, just to pass the time. Everything Jubad had believed in with every fiber of his being had in reality only been for the amusement of the immortal, all-powerful sovereign. He had given birth to the rebel movement; he would wipe it out again, when he had tired of it.

There seemed to be no chance, no hope in the face of his omnipresence. Their struggle had been hopeless from the beginning.

Maybe he really was the god people believed him to be, Jubad thought dully.

The Emperor watched him silently for a long time but didn't appear to be seeing him. His gaze was absent. Memories, millennia old, were reflected in his face.

"It has been a long time, and it may be hard to imagine, but I was once also a young man the same age as you are now," he began to explain slowly. "I understood that I had only one spark of life, and I had to grab on to whatever I wanted before that spark went out. And I wanted a lot. I wanted everything. My dreams knew no bounds, and I was prepared to do anything to make them reality, to demand everything of myself in order to reach the pinnacle. I wanted to accomplish what no one had ever accomplished; I wanted to be the master of all classes, the victor in every discipline, I wanted to hold the universe in my hand, along with its past and its future."

He gestured vaguely. "The contents of the conscious minds of the emperors before me still live inside me, and that is why I know they were motivated by the same drive. In my youth Emperor Aleksandr the Tenth ruled, and I was determined to become his heir. I managed to get accepted to his school, The Sons of the Emperor, and I lied and deceived, bribed and murdered, until I had become his favorite. On his deathbed, he bequeathed sovereignty over the Empire to me, entrusted me with the secret of long life, and received me into the brotherhood of emperors."

Jubad hung on every word the monarch spoke. His head reeled at the thought of the unimaginably distant time when all this had occurred.

"But there was still more to attain, still more to achieve. I had power and a long life, and I fought to get more power and more life. I could not rest until I had turned long life into immortality. I made war after war to expand the borders of the Empire farther and farther into the infinity of the universe. The more power I had, the more I craved. There was no end. It was a fever that drove us onward. Whatever we already had, there was always the promise of still more."

The gaze of the Emperor was directed at the star projection. "We achieved power, held onto it, and enjoyed it ruthlessly to the fullest. We made wars, suppressed or exterminated peoples, and always imposed our will without mercy. There was no one who could stand up to us. We committed atrocities that make all history sound like children's tales, atrocities for which language has no words and which no mind can imagine. And nobody ordered us to stop. We waded through blood up to our hips, and no bolt of lightning struck us down. We stacked up skulls into heaps, and no higher power prevented us. We offered up rivers of human blood, and no god intervened. So we concluded that we ourselves were gods."

Jubad hardly dared to breathe. He felt he would suffocate, crushed by what he was hearing.

"We had power over their bodies, and we set about to win power over their hearts. Every mortal beneath every sun feared us, but that was no longer sufficient: he should also learn to love us. We sent out priests who sanctified our name and preached our omnipotence in all galaxies, and we succeeded in driving the old images of the gods from the hearts of men and taking their place ourselves."

The Emperor was silent. Motionless, Jubad stared at him. The air in the room seemed composed of solid steel.

With infinite slowness, the monarch turned toward him. "I achieved what I wanted. Absolute power. Eternal life. Everything," he said. "And now I know it is meaningless."

Jubad sensed an unspeakable desolation in these words, and he recognized all at once the stench of the Empire—this breathless fossilization, this hopeless darkness. It was the reek of decay that was without vitality, because time was standing still.

"Power's promises only exist as long as there are hindrances keeping one from power. We amassed immeasurable power, but we did not solve the riddle of existence. We are closer to the gods than common humans, but we have never attained fulfillment. The Empire—as vast as it is—is still nothing but a speck of dust in the universe, but it is apparent that more power will not bring us any closer to fulfillment. Should I conquer one more galaxy? What's the use in that? We have never found other beings comparable to us humans, and, without exception, all humans live under my rule. And so there has been stagnation for millennia; there's no movement—everything functions, but nothing new happens. As far as I am concerned, time has ceased to exist. It makes no difference whether I have lived for a hundred thousand years or for only one . . . there is no sense continuing on this path. We have recognized that our search has failed, and we have decided to free humanity from our yoke, to give back to them that which we conquered, and to keep none of it."

The words fell like hammer blows into the silence. Jubad could not shake the feeling that he had vanished into smoke.

"Do you understand what I am trying to say?" the Emperor asked.

Yes. No. No, he understood nothing. He had stopped believing that he understood anything at all.

"We," said the Emperor, who held the memories of his predecessors within himself in some mysterious way, "have decided to die."

"To . . . die?"

No. He really understood nothing.

"Someone who has gained this much power can never get rid of it," the Emperor responded calmly. "So we will die. The problem is that the Empire cannot live on without the Emperor. The people are too dependent on me. If I were just to disappear, they would have no future. I cannot simply give up my power without condemning them all to death. To solve this problem, I founded the rebel movement."

"Ah." Jubad sensed voices inside himself beginning to doubt and seeing this whole thing as an inscrutable subterfuge by the tyrant. But deep at the bottom of his heart, something told him that the Emperor was entirely serious.

"Constructing a mental yoke is easy, but removing it again from people's minds is difficult. Human beings will have no future, if they are unable to shake off my control over their minds. So the purpose of the rebel movement was to draw people together and train them in freedom of the spirit."

The Emperor closed the wall in front of the projection map of the Empire. "That has been achieved. We are nearing the final phase of my plan, and now it depends on you rebels. You must conquer the Central World, kill me, take over the government, and divide up the Empire into many individual, viable parts. And above all, you must eradicate—root and branch—the belief in me as God-Emperor from the minds of men."

Jubad became aware that he had been holding his breath for quite some time, and he inhaled deeply. A superhuman weight seemed to lift from his shoulders, and the atmosphere of tangible darkness around him fled.

"But how can we possibly do that?" he asked.

"I will tell you how," said the Emperor. "I know your plans; they are hopeless. When we finish our discussion, while you are being taken back to your cell, you will discover an opportunity to escape. My Defense Department has arranged a completely believable scenario for you. Don't be mistaken; it is all intentional. They have set it up so that you will come into possession of secret documents that reveal a weakness in the Central World's defenses. But these plans are forged; if you were to attack the supposed area of weakness you would blunder into a trap with no escape. Instead, you will feign an attack there, but direct your real attack against Tauta Base. Tauta—don't forget that name. Tauta is one of the bases from which I operate in disguise. From there, a secret transdimension tunnel leads directly here into the Palace. In this way, you can circumvent all planetary defenses and occupy the Palace from the inside."

Jubad's breathing faltered. No one had ever imagined that such an access could exist.

"And now about my death," the Emperor continued calmly. "You will kill me. When you attack, I will wait for you here in this room. You will kill me with a shot through the chest—and be prepared! You've already found out that attacking me is not so easy. When we meet again, you must be able to do it!"

Jubad nodded in bewilderment. "Yes."

"There are two essential things," the monarch stressed. "First you must show my corpse on all media channels in order to prove that I am dead. Show it in some degrading position, maybe you can hang it by its heels. You cannot show any respect—that would be pernicious. Keep in mind: above all, you must undermine faith in the Emperor. You have to demonstrate that, despite my long life, I was just a mortal. And you must prove that it is really my corpse—so don't disfigure my head. Don't suppose you have an easy task. Nothing is more difficult to exterminate than religion, no matter how false it may be."

Jubad nodded.

"The second matter concerns the two of us, you and me," the ageless man continued as he scrutinized the rebel. "It is important that you take this conversation with you as your secret to your grave."

"Why?"

"The people must believe they have taken back their independence themselves; they must be proud of their victory—this pride will help them over the difficult times ahead. They must not find out that it was not *their* victory at all. Never. They must not find out that they had totally lost their freedom and that it required my intervention to give it back to them. For the sake of the self-esteem of future generations, for the sake of the future of all mankind, you must be silent."

Jubad, the rebel, looked into the eyes of the Emperor and saw in them the unfathomable depth of his weariness. He nodded, and it was like taking a solemn oath.

. . . .

When the rebels took the Palace half a year later, Jubad inconspicuously slipped away from his battle unit. They had taken the Palace Guard by complete surprise. There was gunfire everywhere, but the outcome of the battle was not in doubt. Without being challenged, Jubad reached the outlying sectors of the gigantic palace and finally entered the room where the Emperor awaited him.

He stood on the same spot where Jubad had last seen him. This time he wore his official parade uniform with the imperial mantle over his shoulders.

"Jubad," he said simply when the rebel entered. "Are you prepared this time?"

"Yes," Jubad replied.

"Then let's make an end of it."

Jubad drew his raygun and weighed it reluctantly in his hand. He watched the Emperor, who stood looking calmly at him.

"Are you sorry you did this?" the rebel asked.

The Emperor raised his head. "No," he said. The question appeared to surprise him.

Jubad said nothing.

"No," the Emperor repeated finally. "No. I was born into this world without knowing what life was all about. Only power promised fulfillment in life, and I have pursued it—long enough to recognize that it's a false promise and that this road leads to nothing. But I tried. Even if we get no answers to our questions, it is the inalienable right of every living being to search for them—by all means, on all paths, and with all strength. What I did was only what I had a right to do."

Jubad shuddered at the cruelty of his words. The Emperor was merciless toward everyone, even toward himself. To the very end, he was not relinquishing the iron grip he had maintained for a hundred thousand years. Even in death and beyond, he would determine the fate of mankind.

He's right, Jubad realized with dismay. *He cannot rid himself of the power he struggled to achieve.*

The handle of his weapon seemed heavy in his hand.

"A court would perhaps judge differently."

"You must kill me. If I remain alive, you will fail."

"Maybe."

Jubad had steeled himself for the Emperor's anger, but to his surprise he saw only disgust and weariness in the monarch's eyes.

"You mortals are fortunate," the Emperor said slowly. "You don't live long enough to discover that everything is vain and that life has no purpose. Why do you think I have done all this . . . have gone to all this effort? I could have taken all mankind with me to the grave if I had wanted. But I don't want to. I want to have nothing more to do with this existence."

Shouts and the sound of shots reached the room from outside. The fighting was coming closer.

"Shoot now!" the Emperor commanded fiercely.

And Jubad raised his weapon as though by reflex and, without thinking about it, shot the Emperor in the chest.

Later they celebrated him as the Liberator, the Vanquisher of the Tyrant. He smiled at cameras, struck triumphant poses, and gave wildly acclaimed speeches, but he was always aware that he was only playing at being the victor. He alone knew that he was no victor at all.

To the end of his life he would wonder whether even this final moment had also been part of the Emperor's plan.

Understanding alone cannot withstand time; it changes and fades away. But shame is like a wound that is never exposed and therefore never heals. Yes, he would keep his promise and never break his silence, but not out of a sense of understanding but out of a feeling of shame. He would keep his absolute silence, because of this one moment— when he, the rebel, *obeyed* the Emperor.

····· XIII ·····

I'll See You Again!

THE ATTACK HAD COME without warning. From nowhere alien spaceships had appeared and approached the space station without identifying themselves and without responding to contact attempts. And when the battle robots, the station's first line of defense, opened fire, the strangers responded with massive return-fire.

They had driven them off and had even damaged one of their ships severely. But the aliens could be counted on to return. The damage to the station had to be repaired as soon as possible, so that next time, they could confront them, alert and ready for action.

··········

Ludkamon had been assigned to repair duty in Base Sector 39-201, along with a gang of common cargo loaders, and he hated it immediately.

Base Section 39-201, a flat, hall-like module that served as a fully automated intermediate warehouse for containers, had been struck by a blast and had been out-of-order since then. The damage to the exterior had been repaired, and the sector had been flooded with air again, but was still not in service.

"Attention, everyone," droned the leader of the repair squad in a voice used to giving commands. "We'll divide into groups of two and will mark every part of the facility that's not in working order. Then we'll reduce gravity in the zone and offload the inaccessible containers by hand. And quickly, please. The tunnel ship is waiting!"

The bulkhead flew up, opening the way into the gigantic, dim hall filled with shelves and transport rails, many of which were dented and partially melted. It smelled cold and dusty.

Dividing into pairs didn't work out, and Ludkamon headed off alone. He didn't mind. He couldn't stand the cargo loaders, not since Iva . . .

He didn't want to think about that. Maybe it was good that he had work to do, something to concentrate on. He took out the marking pen and devoted himself to inspecting the conveyor tracks: he spun the rollers by hand, listened to the sound of the rotation, and stopped them again. Wherever the rollers didn't rotate or made a suspicious sound on the track, he put a mark on the side.

And then he discovered the toppled container.

There were a lot of toppled containers in the hall. But this one had fallen from a conveyor during the shelling. It had struck the shredded side-support of a shelf and the container lid had been slit open, as though by a can opener.

Ludkamon held his breath. An open container!

His whole life he had wondered what was in these containers that arrived here daily by the thousands to be transferred to the tunnel ships. Knowing what was in them was forbidden. The containers—about as long and as wide as a man is tall and hip-high—were always locked and sealed. And what they contained was the subject of the most fantastic rumors.

Ludkamon looked in every direction. Nobody was watching. Just one step, and he would know. One step and he would bring the wrath of the Emperor down on him.

So what. One step, and Ludkamon bent over the gaping hole in the lid of the container.

A rancid, unpleasant odor struck him. His hand brushed across something soft, like fur. What he grabbed in his hand and drew out through the hole looked like a thick blanket or a thin carpet. It seemed to have precisely the dimensions of the container. And the container was filled with them.

Carpets? Odd. Ludkamon stuffed the soft thing back as best he could.

"You weren't trying to peek into the container just now, were you?" A booming voice gave him a jolt.

Ludkamon sprang to his feet. "Uh, no," he stammered.

The squad leader stood before him and scrutinized him suspiciously from head to toe. "I bet you were. Ludkamon, your curiosity will cost you your head someday!"

. . . .

The doctor bent over the gaping wound with an unemotional but still slightly nauseated expression on his face and a gesture betraying clearly that he considered his presence here an annoying, routine matter. The skull had burst, over an area two hands wide, and the brain mass was oozing out from beneath it—gray and lifeless. He drew the lamp that was suspended above his head down closer, so that its light illuminated the fracture without shadows.

"Well?" the other man asked. His voice echoed in the large, clinically sterile room. "He's no longer functional."

With a sigh, the doctor removed his measuring probe from its bracket and touched the brain, making no particular attempt to be careful. He watched the instruments for a while. Nothing moved.

"He's dead. No doubt," he said finally.

The other man snorted in annoyance. "Dreadful! And now, of all times!"

"You guys think the attackers will come back?"

"Forewarned and better armed. Yes. There's no way around it; we need replacements in the Upper Sector as soon as possible, before the Portal Station is attacked again."

The doctor nodded without emotion. "I'm finished."

He began removing the life-support cables and turning off the machines. The soft, subliminal humming that had been audible in the cool room the whole time fell silent.

. . . .

Ping!

With a signal that sounded metallic, Space Traffic Control sent the alert that a new blip had appeared on the screen. The man at the console looked up. He immediately found the dot flashing alone on the monitor, and his hand moved nervously toward the alarm switch.

Endless seconds passed before the proper identification appeared beside the dot and it stopped blinking. I-70113. One of the Imperial Ships. The man let go of the alarm button and switched on the radio.

"I-70113, Gateway Station here. Boarding time is 108. We're on heightened alert. Prepare to be escorted by battle robots. You're assigned to the southwest approach quadrant. From 115 on, you'll be on an autoguide-ray; your landing assignment is Bay 2."

The voice from the speaker sounded calm and businesslike, as always. "Portal Station, we copy. Approach southwest. Landing Bay 2. Guide-ray beginning at 115. Over and out."

"Over and out," the man confirmed. They had not asked for details. Apparently they knew nothing about the attack by the alien spaceships. Well, now they would find out.

. . . .

From his seat in the glass cabin Ludkamon had a view of the entire landing bay, the enormous airlock gates, the catwalks and stairs, and the mountainous piles of empty containers. *We serve the Emperor.* The individual beads of the Guardschain slid soothingly through his fingers. *Whose word is law.* Who could tell how many times he had recited the Oath of the Portal Guards today to rein in his wildly galloping thoughts? *Whose will is our will. Whose anger is terrible.* Everything was going more slowly since the alien attack. The repairs were mostly completed, and there were long stretches of downtime when he knew no other way to calm himself. *Who forgives not, but punishes. And whose vengeance is eternal.*

Once again the question ran through his mind, why the final bead for the last sentence of the oath was covered with fur, and he thought about the strange fabric he had found in the container. Then he saw Iva, his Iva, flirting with Feuk—with this disgusting, cocky fellow—and the jealousy he had fought so hard to control boiled up inside him.

Ludkamon examined his reflection in one of the inactive monitor screens. He saw a reedy young man who seemed awkward and clumsy, with an otherwise rather inconspicuous appearance. Reluctantly, he had to admit to himself that he could not quite explain why a girl like Iva wasted any time at all on him. He could more easily understand why she liked Feuk, and these thoughts unleashed a fiery pain in his gut, leaving him feeling ugly and small. Feuk was a cargo loader, big, strong and self-confident, a giant with golden locks and muscles of steel. He, Ludkamon, had risen at an amazingly young age to loading supervisor—a position that would always be beyond Feuk because of its mental prerequisites—and he really did feel that he was destined for even higher things. But he had never noticed that women were impressed by mental ability.

A notice appeared on the screen before him. Ludkamon read it reluctantly, and with an angry gesture, switched on the hall loudspeakers for the necessary announcement.

"Space Traffic Control reports the approach of Imperial Ship I-70113. Estimated arrival time: 116."

The loading crew began to move, conveyor belts were shifted into position, counters were reset, and transport trolleys were prepared. A signal light above the airlock gates indicated that the air was being pumped out of the lock chamber. The groans and creaks of the great gates that had to withstand the pressure of the vacuum seemed to announce impending disaster throughout the hall, but the workers were used to it.

Look! Feuk had grabbed her ass, and she was laughing. She just did whatever she wanted. He would never be able to handle her carefree lust for life. Angrily, Ludkamon crumpled up the top sheet of his writing tablet and flung it into the corner.

. . . .

The news was broadcast by all the Portal Station media into the living quarters. "The station administration has announced that the winner of the next championship will be promoted to the Upper Sector."

Hundreds caught the scent of an opportunity. Here was a chance open to everyone to reach the management level. Amazing things were said about the luxury enjoyed by those in the Upper Sector. Nobody had ever seen it: the Upper Sector was strictly sealed off from the Main Sector, and no one who had been promoted to the management level had ever returned. It was rumored that members of the Upper Sector enjoyed treatments to extend their lives. But at any rate, they would never lift a finger again. Never load another container. This was an opportunity.

. . . .

She kissed him long and lovingly, and he felt he would melt completely away. With a sigh, he twined his fingers through her hair, inhaled the heavenly scent of her, and whispered with closed eyes: "Iva, I love you."

"I love you, too, Ludkamon." She gave him another kiss on the tip of his nose and sat up.

He still lay with his eyes closed and savored the tender feelings inside himself. When he realized she was dressing, he suddenly sat bolt upright.

"What are you doing? Where are you going?"

She looked at the clock. "I have a date with Feuk."

"With Feuk . . . !" He almost screamed the words. "But . . . you just said you love *me!*"

"And I meant it." Her smile asked for forgiveness. "But I love Feuk, too."

She kissed him once more and left. Stunned, Ludkamon watched her depart. Then he doubled up his fist and pounded it into his mattress again and again and again.

. . . .

The tunnel transfer ship hung on the side of the Portal Station like a great, blister-shaped growth. In contrast to the Imperial Ships that swarmed around the station like insects around a flower stalk, it was positively monstrous. In an endless stream, the containers vanished into its insatiable cargo holds, guarded by men and women in black uniforms who were referred to with awe as "tunnel riders."

Daily, the Imperial Ships arrived, put in at one of the twenty-four landing bays; they were unloaded and then departed with empty containers. On high-volume days, fifty thousand containers were transferred, sometimes even eighty thousand. Most days, ten thousand containers rumbled along the conveyor tracks and transport belts of the Loading Sector—from the landing bays to the docking station of the transfer ship.

The red light of the nearby sun shimmered dimly on the huge Portal Station's matte exterior skin, which was pocked by particle streams and micrometeorites. Hardly anyone ever looked out into the universe. There were only a very few viewing windows, because there was hardly anything to see. A great red sun, and then the uncanny dark spot in space at whose edges the light of the distant stars was distorted: the Tunnel.

. . . .

Ludkamon confronted her for an explanation in the container warehouse, hoping she would not notice how he was shaking.

"Iva, I can't go along with this any longer. You leave me to go to Feuk and come back to my place from being with Feuk, always back and forth. I can't take it." With these last words, he had to struggle to control himself . . . to keep his voice from dissolving into helpless sobs.

"And what about it?" her tone was snippy. "What do you intend to do? Break up with me?"

Just the thought, just hearing the words made everything cramp inside him. He clenched his fists.

"You have to decide on one of us!" he insisted.

She made an obstinate face. "I don't have to do anything."

"Iva, I love you!"

"The way you say that, it sounds like: I want to own you!"

Ludkamon didn't know how to respond to that. She was right, of course, and it just made him more furious. "You'll see!" he finally blurted out, and turned away. As he walked away, he hoped she would call him back, but she didn't.

. . . .

The next ship that docked in Loading Bay 2 was I-5404. Surprisingly, it brought not only freight, but also relief crewmen, supplies, and replacement parts. The supplies and parts had been impatiently awaited, but the personnel replacements presented a problem. I-22822, which was supposed to take back the departing crew, had not yet arrived. So the narrow, uncomfortable emergency quarters in the Engine Sector had to be flooded with air and heated. The upside was that the battle stations could be temporarily double-staffed.

. . . .

"Feuk!"

Ludkamon shouted across the entire dining hall, and he didn't give a shit that hundreds of people all around could hear him.

"Feuk, I challenge you!"

The broad-shouldered cargo loader turned around slowly. He looked deliberately over the crowd, and muscles like steel ropes were visible beneath his clothing.

"Oh yeah?" he growled with amusement when he saw the willowy loading supervisor rushing toward him.

"Feuk, I want a fight!" Ludkamon stood wheezing in front of his rival.

"Of course," he grinned. "Should we step outside or should I nail you to the floor right here?"

Ludkamon shook his head. "I challenge you to compete with me in the championship. Whoever goes farthest in the competition gets Iva, and the other one shoves off."

Suddenly, there was rapt attention in the dining room.

Feuk thought about it. "I've never taken part in a championship competition," he responded cautiously.

"Neither have I. So it's a fair fight."

Someone mumbled in agreement.

Feuk sized up his challenger. "Oh well," he responded. "I suspect you won't even qualify. So . . . good."

Ludkamon extended his hand. "Agreed? On your honor?"

"Agreed. On my honor," he responded with a grin and shook on it, squeezing Ludkamon's hand so hard, he almost brought him to his knees.

Those around them clapped in approval.

. . . .

The great conference hall directly in the center of the Portal Station was readied for the championship event. The necessary technical installations were easily arranged. More difficult were the organizational problems. They were still on high alert, so the defense systems had to be fully staffed, even during the tournament. However, because the victor's reward was to be promotion to the Upper Sector, no limit was set on the number of participants. Everyone who qualified would be allowed to compete.

. . . .

"Ludkamon! Have you gone crazy?"

"No. I am just keeping myself from *going* crazy."

She was beside herself with rage. Completely against regulations, she had come to his supervisor's cabin during working hours, and now the entire loading crew watched from below while, burning with anger, she confronted him and made a scene. Not being able to hear anything though the glass walls just made it more interesting.

"I thought I must have heard wrong. Fighting for me. You want to beat on one another for me—thanks, very flattering. And nobody bothers to ask me about the matter at all?"

"I *did* ask you, Iva."

"When?"

"I asked you which one of us you wanted to choose."

"But I don't want to choose!"

"And that's why we're resolving the matter between the two of us."

"The matter. Aha. For you two I am 'the matter.' A trophy. First prize to be displayed on a shelf. Or in this case, to be put in bed."

"We just want to finally clear up the situation."

"So why didn't you beat one another up on the spot?"

"Iva, Feuk is a cargo loader, a big hulk of a man. It would have been unfair."

"Ludkamon, how well you do in the championship depends mostly on natural aptitude. The fact that you're a supervisor and Feuk is just a cargo loader doesn't improve your chances."

"Exactly. So it's fair."

She stared at him in bewilderment. "And if you lose, you're just going to drop me?"

"Yes."

"Jerk!"

"But I'm going to win."

An inarticulate scream escaped her throat. "Why didn't you just roll *dice* for me? That would have been fair!" she shouted. Then she tore open the door and screamed into the entire hall: "*Men!*"

. . . .

The qualification officer scrutinized the young man in the chair, who seemed so excessively nervous. "What's your name?" he asked with pen in hand.

"Ludkamon."

"Position?"

"Supervisor of Loading Bay 2."

The man checked his list. Loading supervisor was not an essential position for defense, so it wouldn't be necessary to assign a replacement for him. He lay the form aside and handed the candidate a battle helmet. "Have you ever competed in a championship?"

"No."

Oh, Emperor! Another adventurer dreaming of escape from the daily grind of the Portal Service. Another fellow who thought he was worthy of the Upper Sector, the most exalted caste imaginable.

"Okay, I'll explain it to you," the officer began patiently. "Put on the helmet, and be sure the front sensors are tight against your forehead. Like this. Now lower the visor. What do you see?"

"A yellow ball."

"Good. Move it."

"Move it?" the young man asked, baffled. "How?"

"Simply by *thinking*," the officer explained. "With the power of your thoughts. In the championship, you only fight with your thoughts. The helmet collects these impulses and transforms them into movement. With this model, only you can see the ball; in the championship, the spectators can see it, too. And of course, it isn't just one ball. In the second round there will be three, then five, and so on. You will fight your opponent for control of these balls, and the more balls you can control, the farther you will get."

"Just as long as I get farther than . . . ," the boy began, but then cut himself off.

The officer took notice. "Than who?"

"Nothing. What do I have to do?"

Well, okay. The skinny boy's problems made no difference to him. "Move the ball. In a circle, if you can." The man monitored on a screen what appeared in the helmet visor. The ball moved, tentatively at first, then rapidly becoming steadier, tracing an approximate circle.

"Thank you," the man said, and made a check mark on the form. "You're qualified."

. . . .

The championship usually passed without much notice, but this time it was opened with much pageantry. Nearly everyone not tied to his post by the security alert had collected in the stands. Music was playing, a colorful light show danced across the ceiling, and the mood was casual.

The spokesman for the management level stepped up. The music stopped, the light show went out, silence settled over the crowd.

"It is my honor," he said, "to solemnly declare the opening of the championship with the recitation of our oath, the Oath of the Portal Guards. Please repeat after me."

There were muffled sounds of shuffling and clattering as everyone stood up.

"We serve the Emperor," he began.

We serve the Emperor, repeated the choir of voices, a thousand strong.

"Whose word is law. Whose will is our will."

Whose word is law. Whose will is our will.

"Whose anger is terrible. Who forgives not, but punishes."

Whose anger is terrible. Who forgives not, but punishes.

"And whose vengeance is eternal."

And whose vengeance is eternal.

A fanfare blast. "The championship," shouted the speaker, "is open!"

. . . .

While Ludkamon ran beside the others onto the playing field with his helmet pressing tight against his head, his eyes scanned the stands without finding Iva. There were too many faces. Maybe she had not even come.

He had to concentrate on the game. This was his chance to beat Feuk, the only chance he had.

His first opponent was easy. At the signal, a yellow ball appeared between them, and a pale blue rectangle glowed above the head of each player. Whoever got control of the ball and moved it into the rectangle over his opponent's head was the winner. Ludkamon won in a few seconds.

Then he looked around. Feuk stood some distance away, but seemed to have won as well.

Well, okay then. On to the next round.

This time there were three balls, but Ludkamon held on to all of them and dropped them into the goal. Another win.

He checked out Feuk. He was finished, too, and was also keeping tabs on Ludkamon.

That made him nervous. He wiped the sweat from his eyebrows. He didn't hear the shouts of the crowd; he saw only his rivals. Secretly, he had counted on having a mental advantage over his opponents, but it seemed that Iva was right: in this game the aptitude measures were different. Gradually he began to suspect that this would be no easy fight.

. . . .

"Portal Station, this is I-6937, an Imperial Ship. We request permission to land."

"I-6937, this is Space Traffic Control for the Portal Station. No offloading is possible at this time. Please move to a holding position."

"Space Traffic Control—what's the problem?"

"At the moment, a grand championship match is under way."

On another channel. "Imperial Ship I-12002 calling Portal Station."

"I-12002 this is Space Traffic Control. . . ."

The number of dots of light around the Portal Station kept growing. Work had stopped in the loading bays. Only the loading of the transfer ship continued in spite of the championship.

. . . .

Eleven balls. Ludkamon's eyes burned from the sweat, and the helmet seemed intent on crushing his skull. Eleven balls, and both of them were still in the competition. Feuk shot him a grim glance across the much reduced field of players. He would not give up. He felt passion burning inside him like a consuming flame.

Eleven balls. At this point, they had left many good and popular players behind. Whatever happened, they would end up near the top of the field.

The realization that he, a beginner, had defeated well-known championship players like the technician Pai and the soldier Buk rattled him for a moment, and for an instant, the pattern of the eleven vibrating, dancing balls began to wobble.

He must not lose his concentration now. He clenched his fists and swayed back and forth, legs planted wide, without losing his focus on the balls. His opponent was strong and tricky. From the seven-ball level on, the battles had been hard-fought and long.

. . . .

The final container became wedged against the counting device just before rolling into the interior of the tunnel transfer ship. Because the preset number for the load had not been reached, the entire conveyor system continued to run empty, and the rotating rollers scraped with a nerve-jangling screech against the underside of the container that was stuck in place.

The noise alarmed a transfer ship crewman. The tunnel rider hurried to the spot and tried to free the container from its wedged position, but because of the incessant pressure of the conveyor rollers he could not free it by himself. He got another man to help out.

"Things like that always happen right at the end," he said.

"Yes. How's the match coming?"

"It looks like this time two unknown players will be in the final. Too bad we'll be gone by then."

The tunnel riders were obligated to only one schedule: to the pulsing of the Tunnel, called *tides*.

Together, the two of them managed to shove the container back onto the conveyor track. It rumbled along to its designated place, and then, with a reverberating boom, the entire loading system switched itself off. Instantaneously, it was quiet in the hallways and shafts, with the exception of the continued whirring of a few free-spinning rollers.

. . . .

"Bulkheads locked and sealed."

"Absorbers ready and functioning."

"Umbilical cable disconnected. On-board systems functioning."

The man in his black uniform leaned forward and activated a series of switches. "Transfer ship to Space Traffic Control. We're ready to disengage."

"Space Traffic Control here. You'll miss the championship finals."

"Yes. But our hearts beat to the rhythm of the tunnel tides...." It was a saying among the tunnel riders.

"Of course. Preparing to disengage in ten ... five ... three—two—one—disengage! Have a good flight."

The man in the black uniform smiled. "Thanks, Portal Station!"

Gently, without a trace of vibration, the transfer ship separated from the great space station and slid slowly toward the sinister black spot in the sea of stars.

. . . .

Ludkamon had mocked and provoked Feuk in every conceivable way to stoke up his battle rage. Now that they stood facing one another in the final, he stuck out his tongue one more time. That brought frenetic hooting from the crowd and apparently set off an insane fury in Feuk. Good. Let him be blind with anger—let him fight raging blind and hotheaded. Let him hate, let him forget everything but the desire to defeat Ludkamon.

And he would grant Feuk that desire! Ludkamon grinned with the knowledge of his certain victory.

The gong sounded, and the three-dimensional projection of nineteen game balls appeared above the battlefield.

For a moment, a different thought occurred to Ludkamon, however: if he fought and won, he would discover the secret of the Upper Sector. Maybe it was true what they said—about unimaginable luxury and long life. . . . Maybe he was fighting a silly battle here. The Upper Sector . . . that was an opportunity that would never come again. And to throw that away for the sake of a fickle woman . . .

With sudden horror, Ludkamon saw the nineteen balls abruptly begin to move. They shot toward the goal above Feuk's head and disappeared before Ludkamon could even react.

The tension in the crowd exploded in deafening cheers. Fanfares blared. The referee tried unsuccessfully to make himself heard over the loudspeaker system. Not until the first spectators jumped the barriers and ran toward him did Ludkamon comprehend that—somehow—he had won the championship.

"But . . . I didn't do anything at all!" he stammered.

Feuk! Feuk, the scoundrel! Now everything was clear. Feuk had thought up exactly the same ruse Ludkamon had planned, but he had not hesitated to defeat himself immediately!

Powerless to do anything about it, Ludkamon had to watch Feuk bow before him with a mocking smile. Feuk had outmaneuvered him. Ludkamon closed his eyes tightly. Now there was only one hope left, that the Upper Sector would be adequate compensation. At least in the future, he would never have to lift a finger.

. . . .

Iva had tears in her eyes when she confronted him.

"Are you satisfied now?" she sobbed.

"Iva," he muttered sheepishly. "No one could have imagined. . . ."

She embraced him and pressed him to her with the despair of a final farewell. "Now you've won, but you've still lost, you . . . you idiot!"

"This isn't forever, Iva," he whispered helplessly.

"You'll soon forget me. You'll enter the Upper Sector and never think of me again."

He shook his head and felt a strangling sensation in his throat. "I won't forget you. I'll see you again. I'll see you again, I promise."

. . . .

Overwhelming blackness, vibrating and pulsing, a sinister maelstrom of impenetrable darkness that seemed to devour the stars. The transfer ship was like a fleck of dust as it floated toward the gigantic vortex.

"Now once again into the realm of darkness," said one of the men in the cockpit.

They had risked the descent a thousand times, but the tunnel riders still held their breath.

The blackness seemed to swell. It was a feeling like tipping over the brink of a cataract. The transfer ship disappeared from the universe.

. . . .

The connections lay prepared. The frame that would receive the new member of the Upper Sector had been opened up, the nutritive solutions pulsed evenly through the latticework of transparent tubes.

The doctor checked the instruments. They indicated normal function. A routine case.

Flexible silver hoses disappeared into the half-opened mouth of the patient, light gray cables disappeared into the nostrils and into cuts in the shaved spot on the back of his scalp. Eyes and ears had already been removed and replaced with plug-in modules. The doctor's gaze passed casually over the slender, wiry body of the young man lying naked before him on the table, and he felt a momentary regret. Then he banished these thoughts, applied the saw, and began to separate the head from the torso.

"Iva, you have to finally forget him." Feuk held Iva's delicate hands in his massive ones and looked at her helplessly. She gazed vaguely into the distance. "He's in the Upper Sector now and belongs to the management level. Don't you suppose he could check in any time if he wanted?"

Iva shook her head slowly. "I can't believe he forgot me so soon."

. . . .

He saw out of a thousand eyes and had a thousand arms. In his mind, he heard the commands to be carried out, and using nothing but his thoughts he directed the squadrons of remote-controlled battle robots that cruised through space around the Portal Station. Connected to the Portal Station computer system whose cables and switch units wound through the entire space station, he saw everything, and he would live for centuries.

I see you, Iva. I see you with a thousand eyes. Didn't I promise?

····· XIV ·····

The Palace of Tears

THIS IS A LONELY PLANET, the loneliest planet in the universe and its most cursed. There is no hope here. The sky is always lead gray and covered with heavy, cheerless clouds, and at night there are no stars . . . ever. This planet once had a name, but who can remember it? The rest of the universe has forgotten this world, its inhabitants, and their fate . . . and even its name.

Somewhere on this world is a broad, abandoned plain stretching from horizon to horizon and beyond. Nothing grows here, nothing lives, no shrub, no blade of grass, no plant, and no animal, everything is gray stone and gray dust. If there were someone to undertake a march across this flatland, he would find no hill and no valley for days and weeks, nothing to eat and nothing to drink and no variation but the rising and setting of the dull disk of the sun—until one day he would catch sight of the silhouette of a great edifice on the horizon: this is the Palace of Tears.

The cracked merlons of its parapets tower into the sky like the decaying teeth of an old warrior who will never surrender as long as he lives. From these parapets, magnificently uniformed trumpeters once blared their fanfares into the evening—but that was so long ago. . . .

If time could be turned back—far, far back—this plain would not exist. Where there is now only leveled stone, houses would stand, roads would stretch into the distance, plazas would spread out luxuriously. At that time, a vast city, the capital of a mighty kingdom stood here. Broad roads led in all directions, farther than the eye could see, cutting paths through the sea of opulent buildings. Traffic on the boulevards and squares never ceased, no matter whether it was day or night. Anyway, it was never really night in this city, which was always bathed in a golden glow. Its residents were happy and wealthy, and when they looked into the heavens, they saw the silver bodies of mighty interstellar spaceships leaving their cloudy tracks in the clear sky as they landed at the trade port or as they were leaving the planet's atmosphere to set their courses for faraway destinations with their freight—perhaps to one of the millions of stars that twinkled in the sky and called to them.

But then the stars went out. . . .

Nothing is left of the city that once seemed immortal, invincible. Excavations would never find traces of the people who once lived here. There are no buried remains of foundations, no indications of roads, nothing. There is nothing left but day and night, heat and cold, occasional rain, and always the wind, blowing across the lowlands and driving before it the gray-brown dust that gnaws mercilessly and ceaselessly at the stone ornamentation of the palace, the only structure still standing. Back then, when there were still people here, they considered the palace the most beautiful building in the galaxy. But the destructive forces of time have left no evidence of that. The stone rosettes on the towers, once like delicately unfolding blossoms, have eroded into formless gray clumps. And on the walls, nothing at all is left of the skillfully wrought relief images that people once traveled many light-years to see—not even any traces that might disclose their former location. The palace stands crumbling and abandoned. Cracked walls and collapsed roofs have surrendered to the wind and the rain. Cold and heat gnaw at what remains of the ruined walls; now and again, a stone cracks, sending a fragment tumbling down. Beyond that, nothing happens at all. Nowhere in the courtyards and hallways is there anything left that bears witness to human life.

The only part of the structure that remains completely intact is the throne room itself. With its proud, slender windows, it towers over the rubble and fragmentary ruins. Mysterious powers have protected the finely chiseled decorations on its supporting buttresses, the ornate embellishments on its cornices, and the sharp-edged flutes of its columns from disintegration.

The throne room is a colossal hall whose vault is borne on mighty pillars. Unimaginable ages ago, extravagant festivals were held here, moving speeches were given, and embittered negotiations were concluded. This hall saw numerous victories and just as many defeats. No . . . one defeat too many . . .

Since then, the huge portal has remained locked and sealed. The gold intarsia on the inside of the door wings has survived, but it can't be seen. It is hidden by a gigantic portrait, illuminated by a row of lamps that glow perpetually.

The monarch's gold throne sits against the facing wall on a pedestal. And on this throne, motionless, sits the only living being still accommodated within these walls: the king himself. He sits there, rigid, erect, his arms lying on the armrests. He could be mistaken for his own statue, if his eyes did not blink drowsily and his rib cage did not rise and fall with each breath.

From his vantage, he can look out through the windows at the plain surrounding the palace and see all the way to the horizon. On the table in front of him stand two large monitors that functioned a long, long time ago and showed him pictures of distant cities. But at some point in the past, the pictures began to fade until there was nothing to be seen on the screens but gray flickering—for years and centuries. Finally, first one and then the other screen burned out completely. Since then, the equipment has been sitting black and silent and useless before the king.

The view through the windows is always the same: a monochrome gray plain that somewhere in the distance becomes the monochrome gray sky. And at night the sky is black, infinitely dark with not a single star to be seen. Nothing happens outside, nothing changes.

The king often wishes he would go insane and often wonders if perhaps he already is. But he knows he's not and never will be.

Once in a while a stone falls somewhere, and the king savors the sudden sound for days, recalls it to his ear again and again in order to relish the experience fully, because there is no other diversion.

In the course of eons, the material of the windowpanes followed the pull of gravity; with infinite slowness, it flowed and sank downward. After many centuries, the tall glass panes got thicker at the bottom and thinner at the top until, one day, they cracked along the upper edge and allowed the wind—whistling hesitantly at first and later howling triumphantly—into the throne room that had been silent until then.

Since then, the panes have continued to crumble, and today the wind blows through the hall just the way it blows across the plain. And with it, it brings dust.

Now the precious crystal floor of the throne room lies dust covered and unseen. Dust has settled on the pictures and statues along the walls, on the upholstered seats of the chairs, and on the body of the king himself. Dust lies on his arms and hands, on his lap, his feet and his hair. His face is gray with dust, and only the tears running from his eyes leave tracks down his wrinkled cheeks, along his nose, on his upper lip and down his neck, where they dampen the collar of his coronation robe, which was once rich purple, but is now faded and gray.

So the king watches everything decay around him, and he waits with unspeakable longing for the time when the machine under his throne will stop functioning like everything else and will let him die.

So he sits motionless, but not voluntarily so. He sits motionless because long ago all the muscles and tendons in his body were severed and all nerves were seared off irreversibly. Barely visible steel clamps hold his skull and are screwed firmly into the backrest of the throne. They enter his scalp at the rear of his head, are attached to the temporal bones and extend forward below the cheek bones to fix the position of his skull. Additional clamps hold the lower jaw in place, which would otherwise hang completely slack.

Behind the throne is an immense, silent machine that has forced the body of the king to live for thousands of years. Pipes as big as arms project through the throne's backrest into the king's body, though they would be unseen by any observer who would enter the hall. They force the rib cage to continue to breathe, the heart to continue to beat, and they supply the brain and other organs with nourishment and oxygen.

The eyes of the king are the only body parts he can still move. He can shed as many tears as he wants, and had they not evaporated, the hall would be submerged by the tears he has shed. He can look wherever he wants, but for a very long time he has stared at nothing but the picture across from him. It is a brutish, mocking picture, which has lost none of its cruelty over the endless ages: the portrait of his conqueror. The king stares at it and waits for mercy—he waits, waits, waits and cries.

When We See the Stars Again

THE FIRE IN THEIR MIDST was very small—hardly sufficient in competition with the severe cold to keep the contents of the pot boiling. They sat around it in a wide circle—the women and children and old men of the tribe—and stared silently into the weak flames, their mouths chewing slowly. With hardly a thought, they tried to extend their enjoyment of the simple, tasteless mush they shoveled out of worn wooden bowls with their bare fingers.

The firelight gave only weak illumination to the cliffs surrounding the little group. It flickered bleakly on the haggard faces, graven by the rigors of a lifetime of fleeing. At night, it was the only light. The broad sky above them was black, like a bottomless abyss.

Cheun was the only warrior in the circle. He ate his mush silently, knowing that it would not satisfy him. Full ... it had been years since he last felt full. Back then, they had still lived in the valleys along the river, valleys with lush pastures and fertile soil. Now the enemy occupied these valleys and the pastures had disappeared forever under the gray mass with which he covered everything he conquered.

Cheun ate faster. He had to get back to the other men keeping watch on the mountain above. They were hungry, too, and were waiting for his return.

From the corner of his eye he saw old Soleun set aside his cracked bowl and give a fleeting smile as he drew his hand across his belly—an old habit, just as though he were actually full and satisfied. Cheun gave him only a cursory glance. He knew what was coming next.

"The heavens were not always dark," Soleun began to recite with the thin voice of old age. "Darkness did not always oppress mankind when the night fell. Once, unimaginable ages ago, so long ago that the rain has long since washed all the mountains that were then young to the sea—at that time, there were stars at night in the firmament."

The children loved these old men's tales. Cheun made a dismissive face. It was reason enough to seek a warrior's death, just in order to escape becoming childish in old age.

"Stars . . . Even after all this time, our language has kept a word for them," Soleun continued thoughtfully. "Though no living eye has ever seen a star, we know from the traditions of our ancestors that a star is a small, fine point of light in the night sky. And thousands and thousands of these stars covered the heavens. Back then, the vault of heaven at night was a gloriously glittering fabric of light, like precious jewelry set with diamonds large and small. Then the enemies came. They came from another world to ours and extinguished the stars. Since that time, the night sky has been dark and afflicts our souls."

The words of the old man and the reverent solemnity of his recitation unleashed something in Cheun that caused a shiver at the back of his neck, and he was immediately annoyed with himself.

"Since that day, the enemies have hunted us. Step by step, they drive us before them, kill us, and make our world uninhabitable. No one knows why. They drive us out and extend the Gray Land, farther and farther still. On the outside, they appear to be humans like us, but they are the servants of the Evil One. They are not just *our* enemies, but the enemies of Life itself, for they intend to cover the whole world someday with the Gray Land, so that nothing else remains . . . nothing but the Gray Land and the palace at its center, called the Palace of Tears. But we know that the enemies serve the Evil One, so we know, too, that they are doomed to destruction in the end. Evil does not exist by itself. The enemies may taste victory, but they will be destroyed and will pass into oblivion. We may taste death, but we will live eternally. All these horrors will end one day. Someday the stars will shine again. And when we see the stars again, we will be redeemed."

At these words, the children raised their faces to the dark heavens and shuddered at the oppressive emptiness above them. The eyes of the adults remained gloomily fixed on the ground, and their breath appeared like fog in the light of the little fire.

Someday. Nobody knew when that would be. By then, the rain would probably wash these surrounding mountains to the sea, as well.

Although he had not yet emptied his bowl, Cheun stood up with an angry start. Impolitely, he passed the bowl to the woman beside him and walked from the circle into the darkness.

Here he could see nothing at all. He had to feel his way forward, up the mountain on a path he had memorized during the day. Every sound was important. He noted every small change in the echo made by his footsteps. The path was steep and dangerous.

He was out of breath when he reached the lookout camp, which the men had set up on the opposite face of the mountain ridge. Someone greeted him with a slap on his shoulder. Cheun reached for the hand and recognized Onnen, the tribe's leader.

"Cheun! How do things look below? Are the old men reassuring themselves again with their fairy tales?"

Cheun gave a violent snort. He could sense the presence of the other men, could hear the sound of their breathing and their movements. There was fear in the air, and rage—impotent despair at having no defense against the enemy.

"Soleun is telling the old legends. He says we just have to wait until the enemies are destroyed by their own wickedness."

There were scattered laughs from the darkness, short and hard, like barking. The slight breeze up here blew gently but bitter cold, and it began to sting Cheun's face. His nostrils seemed to freeze from the inside and go numb.

"Has anything happened on the border?" Cheun asked into the impenetrable night.

"No," someone said.

Cheun crept forward until he could see down into the plain. The other light was there, the light of the enemy. An almost imperceptible dark blue rim of light defined the course of the fortified border. The light was so diffuse that no details could be seen, only the angular silhouettes of colossal machines that had drawn up along the boundary.

Cheun remembered the first time he had seen this sight as a child. Before then, the border had been an endless, inconspicuous wire fence that killed everyone who came too close to it with a lightning bolt and whose flickering blue light glimmered at night like an ever-present threat. Then one day the machines arrived—slowly, like great beasts of gray steel. An endless column lined up side by side, one next to the other, until the front of moving machines finally stretched from horizon to horizon.

He had stood there at first and waited to see what would happen next. His tribe had not waited; they had packed up their few possessions and fled. But from a distance, he had continued to watch: men arrived and dismantled the fence. And as young as he was, Cheun still understood that they were clearing the way for the Gray Land, for the enemy who wanted to kill them all, even though they had done nothing to him.

And so it went, on and on. Again and again they had to flee, ever farther north, where it became ever colder and the food ever scarcer. Sometimes they had to fight other tribes whose territories they had entered in their flight from the enemy. And now they had reached the edge of the rocky Northern Massif. Now, the only path led into murderously cold, infertile desolation where they would die between the bare cliffs and steep chasms.

"What do you think, Cheun?" Onnen asked suddenly beside him.

Cheun jumped. He had been absorbed in his thoughts and memories and had not heard the clan chief approaching.

"I don't know where we can run now," he explained. "The only way left to us leads into the stony wasteland and, beyond that, the eternal ice. It makes no difference what we do—we can only choose a quick death or a slow one."

"And what do you choose?"

"I choose to fight."

Onnen was silent for a while. "I had planned to move on toward the sunrise, when it became necessary. If the reports are true, there are warm valleys there with fertile soil and many well-nourished animals. But it would be a long trek, and we would still need the next harvest in order to survive the journey. Their attack is coming too early. The enemies will move in the next few days and destroy our last fields down below, and if we're still there when they come, they will kill us."

"Then there's no other way but to flee and leave the old ones and the weakest behind," Cheun observed. During one escape, he had had to leave his sick mother behind and, from a great distance, had seen her hut disappear in a blast of fire from the enemy.

"I have another plan," said Onnen. "We could try to stop them."

Suddenly, Cheun was not sure whether this was just a bad dream. Stop them? What was the clan chief saying? None of their weapons was capable of inflicting even a scratch on the enemy's steel behemoths.

"What are you thinking?"

"I want to kill one of them and take his weapons," Onnen said calmly. "Our weapons are capable of nothing against the machines, but if we fire their own weapons against them, maybe we have a chance."

It must be a dream. A nightmare. "Onnen, there are thousands of machines. Even if we could destroy one of them, it wouldn't change anything—"

"But if we take one and use it to attack the others . . . that would change things!"

"They're too powerful, Onnen. Destroy one, and a hundred others take its place."

The voice of the chief was suddenly sharp and impatient. "Didn't you say you choose to fight, Cheun?"

Cheun didn't reply.

"Now is our only chance to act," Onnen declared. He put his arm around Cheun's shoulder, and though he could not see it, Cheun imagined that the chief was pointing down to the plain, to the border. "They've taken down the fence that throws lightning bolts, and their machines are far enough apart for a man to slip between them. And look carefully—there is very little light between some of them. We can sneak up under cover of darkness, penetrate the Gray Land, and attack from behind—they won't expect that for sure. We'll wait until one of them is alone and kill him with an arrow."

Cheun had to admit that Onnen had thought this plan through. During the daytime, they had often seen single individuals walking behind the row of mobile machines. The Gray Land offered no hiding places, but that would not be necessary as long as it was dark. The enemies would not be expecting an attack from that direction, and because the machines sat in the pale blue light, it would be possible to see the enemy without being seen themselves.

And it was better to die in battle than on a sickbed.

"I'm with you," said Cheun.

Onnen slapped him on the shoulder, pleased and also relieved. "I knew it."

Now that the daring venture had been decided on, they didn't hesitate for a moment. Onnen gathered the men around him and explained again what they would do. He designated one of the youngest as the sentry who would remain behind. He had them inspect the few weapons they possessed—stone axes, spears, bows and arrows—and then they began their descent to the fields.

Even in the darkness, they found the path. Fingers felt for protruding rocks and the stumps of dead branches, for dusty moss and clefts in the stone. Feet shuffled along, feeling their way across the scree to locate footholds, steps, and rock ledges. Every man knew when he had to duck and where he had to take care not to plunge headlong from the mountain.

Cheun felt violent rage igniting in his heart and stoking his battle lust. He had often suppressed his hate for the enemies because it was so painful to admit his inferiority—his absolute impotence—to himself. Just the idea, that it might be possible to inflict a wound on this vastly superior enemy, opened the floodgates of a lifetime's pent-up hate and filled him with unrelenting energy.

They had come from another world to kill and to destroy, and if there had ever been a reason, it had been forgotten ages ago. And what would happen when they someday completed their senseless work, when they had killed everyone and had covered the whole planet with their gray stone? Maybe, Cheun thought, maybe things would all unfold differently than the legends prophesied. Maybe they had to annihilate their enemies in order to see the stars again.

Finally, he felt the parched grass of the plain against his legs. His mouth was dry, and he knew the others felt the same. Nobody spoke a word.

They marched toward the blue glow—over dry, rustling bunches of grass, through the treacherous snapping of cripplewood thickets, and through fields of new crops that would never ripen. Blackness surrounded them, except in the direction of the dark blue shimmer, which stretched like a seam from one end of the world to the other. Except for the sound of their steps and their breathing, everything was silent. All animals, even the smallest rodents and insects, fled away from the Gray Land border. They alone were marching toward it.

When they had put the fields behind them, Onnen stopped the warrior band.

"We must consider carefully how to proceed," he whispered. "I think it's best to split up into groups of two. Each pair will search out a different gap, and we will meet again over there in the Gray Land. And we'll go in turns, not all at once. Or does anyone have a better suggestion?"

No one spoke. Hands groped through the dark, silently dividing the men into pairs.

"Now—go!" the clan leader rasped.

The first pair slipped away. After a while, the silhouettes of the two young warriors became visible against the border light. In front of the enemy vehicles, they appeared unexpectedly small and fragile, and only now, seeing this contrast, did Cheun realize how enormous the machines were—gigantic, gloomy metal mountains on armored wheels.

Involuntarily he shook his head. The enemies really were servants of the Evil One—yes, and they were more powerful. Their strength was boundless. They were the victors and would remain the victors forever.

No hope remained but for an honorable death. At least that would bring freedom from endless fleeing and hopeless suffering.

Two bangs cut through the frosty night air like cracks of a whip, and the waiting group jumped. Horrified, they watched as the two warriors collapsed, their arms jerking about as they fell.

"Halt!" Onnen called out to stop the second pair that had already headed off.

They stood there motionless and waited. Nothing happened; everything was still.

We have to think of another way," Onnan whispered finally. "There seems to be no way through, even though the fence is gone. We have to think of something else."

Cheun reached out his hand and touched Onnen's arm. "It's no use, Onnen. If we can't penetrate the Gray Land, we can't accomplish anything."

"I refuse to just give up!" Onnen hissed angrily. "We have to think of something—"

Suddenly, the air was filled with a deep, rumbling sound that slowly grew louder, a sound like distant thunder. Cheun spun around once and tried to identify the source of the noise. It sounded dangerous.

"The attack," someone whispered. "It's starting."

"They've never advanced during the night," Onnen insisted stubbornly.

A high-pitched whirring joined in, like a gigantic swarm of insects coming relentlessly closer. Now Cheun was sure that it emanated from the chain of massive vehicles. It grew ever louder and shriller.

"It is!" he said. "It's the machines."

Then light flooded over them, unbearably bright after the total darkness, overwhelming in its reach from horizon to horizon. It struck their unprepared eyes so unexpectedly that it seemed brighter than the sun, brighter than a hundred suns. Cheun pressed his clenched fists to his closed eyes, and light still penetrated his eyelids, as though it were being pressed into his head, and it hurt. Then the ground shook beneath his feet, and he knew what it meant: the enemy's machines had begun their onslaught, rolling toward them, unstoppable.

"Retreat!" he screamed, and stumbled back, still with closed, tear-filled eyes in which the light burned like fire. The dull growling of the gray colossi filled the air, the screeching, grinding crunch of their wheels and the explosions of rock and tree beneath them. All at once it was so loud, he could no longer hear the others.

Then sharp popping sounds came again, followed each time by the screams of his comrades. Cheun ran, ran for his life and for the life of his tribe. The rage and fear inside him gave wings to his feet. Fight. This could be fighting, too. Sometimes fighting meant running, running away from a superior foe and doing whatever it took to escape.

Again a blast like the crack of a whip far behind him, and this one was meant for him. He felt the sudden pain inside himself like a lightning bolt that passed through his whole body and flung him forward like an unexpected blow to the back. Without thinking and without slowing his dash, he grabbed at the place where the pain began, and through the tears in his eyes, he saw blood on his hand. A lot of blood.

The enemy had hit him, but he was still alive. Don't give up. Keep running. The enemy made a mistake. Even the enemy can make a mistake. Even these monstrous machines were not all-powerful. He had been far enough away to be able to escape. He would escape. He would make it. He was bleeding, yes, but that didn't mean anything. He struggled. Run. Run farther and farther. He always chose to fight. The challenge. He, the warrior. He, Cheun of the clan of the Oneuns. He made it to the foot of the mountains, even made it partway up the path, now brightly lit, before he collapsed.

But now, finally, the time had come. Cheun lay on his back—eyes closed, hands pressed to his wound—and felt life drain from him. With unexpected clarity, he knew he would die, and he only regretted it for the sake of the tribe: now they had to flee without their warriors into a hostile, lifeless expanse where they would all die.

He listened to the sounds of the advancing enemies, felt the uncontrollable quaking of the earth against his back, and heard the thousandfold crackling and snapping of trees being crushed. His breathing was labored. So this is what it is like, the end. His end. At least he would bleed to death, long before the machines began to scale the mountains. He considered whether there was anyone he wished to have here with him, but he could think of no one. This was what his end was like: wretched.

Then it was suddenly quiet, and no light penetrated his eyelids. Cheun opened his eyes. Above him, in the boundless night sky, he saw the stars.

····· XVI ·····

The Return

WHAT GOOD DID ALL this do? He didn't know. After all the years, all the grizzly discoveries and bloody incidents, after all the nightmares . . .

"Captain Wasra?"

He looked up reluctantly. It was Jegulkin, the Navigator, and it was clear that he regretted having to disturb him.

"Yes?"

"We're approaching Planet G-101/2. Do you have special instructions?

Wasra needed no time to think it over. He had visited so many planets like this in the past months, had proclaimed the end of the Empire so often that he sometimes felt he was in a never-ending nightmare, condemned to say the same things and make the same hand gestures forever. No, it occurred to him, this time it was different; he had a special mission on this planet. But that didn't make it any easier.

"No special instructions. We'll look for the spaceport and land there."

"Yes, Captain."

Wasra stared at the large main screen, which showed the universe as the naked eye would have seen it. A small, dully glowing dot came closer: the second planet of Sun G-101. Here, too, lived hair-carpet makers, just as on thousands of other planets—planets that all seemed the same.

And behind it, the stars glimmered cold and rigid, each one a different sun or a different galaxy. Wasra wondered grimly whether they would ever succeed in finally putting the Empire behind them, in finally ridding themselves of the Emperor's heritage. It seemed so futile to him. Who would ever be able to say definitively that there was not another undiscovered part of the Empire hidden behind one of these rigid points of light, or that there was not another door waiting to reveal another terrible secret?

He saw his reflection in one of the instrument covers and was surprised—as so often in past weeks—that his face still looked so young. The gray captain's uniform seemed made of heavier material than the uniforms he had previously worn, and the badge of his rank seemed to weigh more as each day passed. When he joined the expedition under General Karswant, he had just reached the age of majority—a young soldier looking for excitement and wanting to prove himself. And today, after only three years in this gigantic province, he felt ancient, as old as the Emperor himself, and couldn't understand why it didn't show on his face.

They had made thousands of landings like this one, it seemed, and there was no end in sight.

But . . . no—this planet really was different. In a certain sense, everything had started here. Supplied with bad, outdated maps, the

Salkantar had visited this planet once before on an arduous, wandering journey that took weeks. He was just a regular crewman then, and nobody anticipated the bloody battles ahead against Imperial Troops who didn't know that the Emperor was dead and that the Empire had been defeated. At that time, it seemed the expedition was as good as completed. They were getting ready to return home, making careful preparations for the great leap through empty space between the galaxies. Wasra was directing cleanup work on the third deck, and if anyone had told him he would be captain of the *Salkantar* two years later, he would have laughed. But that is exactly what happened, and these two years had mercilessly made a man out of the boy he had once been. And everything started here on this planet, whose bright, desolate, sandy-brown disk was growing slowly larger and rounder and on whose surface they could make out the first features.

Wasra remembered a conversation with General Karswant as though it had been yesterday instead of weeks ago. The bearish old man that everyone feared, but loved nonetheless, had shown him a photograph. "Nillian Jegetar Cuain," he said, and there was an unexplained sadness in his voice. "If it weren't for this man, we would have been home almost three years ago. I want you to find out what happened to him."

This man had landed on G-101/2, despite explicit instructions to the contrary, and had discovered the hair carpets. At first, Wasra couldn't believe the rumors that trickled down to the crew quarters, they seemed so absurd. But then Nillian's report was verified in every detail. The expedition leadership announced that hair carpets were extremely lavish knotwork rugs made of human hair. So lavishly time consuming, in fact, that a carpet maker completed only one carpet in his entire lifetime. But all that would have been just a notation in the expedition log, had it not been for the unexpected explanation: these carpets, so the carpet makers claimed, were destined for the Palace of the Emperor, and their production was a sacred duty. That caused a stir—because everyone who had ever been in the Imperial Palace could attest that it contained the most remarkable things, but certainly no hair carpets.

The expedition fleet began surveillance operations, and in fact, within a few months, a large transport ship in miserable disrepair landed on the planet and departed again after about two weeks. They followed the ship and lost it, but they stumbled onto a second planet where hair carpets were tied with the same religious justification. Then they found another and another still . . . quickly there were dozens and soon hundreds. After expedition ships had swarmed out and found more and ever more worlds making these carpets, hordes of automated reconnaissance robots were sent off with the same result. When ten thousand such planets had been discovered, the search was called off, despite the assumption that there must yet be others. . . .

The engines went into action, and their dull thundering made the floor vibrate beneath their feet. Wasra reached for the logbook microphone. "We are about to land on the second planet of Sun G-101 in Planet Quadrant 2014-BQA-57, Sector 36-01. Our standard time is 9-1-178005, last calibration 2-12. Light Cruiser *Salkantar*, Captain Jenokur Taban Wasra."

The landing platform came into view, a gigantic, paved surface that was scarred and burned by dilapidated spaceship engines. An old spaceport, thousands of years old. Every one of these planets had just such a spaceport, and all of them looked the same. A large, old city always extended out around the landing platform, and all the roads on the planet seemed to come from every direction to converge there. As they had learned by now, that perception was correct.

The noise of the engines shifted. "Final landing preparations," the pilot announced. The *Salkantar* touched down with a resounding boom that frightened every new spaceship passenger to death. But the men and women on board had experienced too much to even notice the sound.

. . . .

The bulkheads of the large main airlocks opened slowly before them, and the loading ramp lowered with a humming sound onto the furrowed surface. Smells rushed inside: heavy, nauseating odors of excrement and decay, of dust and sweat and poverty, which seemed to leave a fuzzy coating inside the nostrils. While adjusting the tiny microphone over his larynx, Wasra wondered why all these worlds smelled the same, a question that occurred to him at every landing. There seemed to be no answers anywhere in this godforsaken galaxy—only questions.

It was hot. The glow of the pallid sun shimmered over the broad, dusty-gray landing field, and a group of old men approached from the direction of the city; they walked quickly and at the same time with an oddly deferential gait. They wore heavy, dark robes, which must have been torture in this heat. Wasra stepped out through the opening in the airlock and waited until the men reached the lower end of the ramp.

He noticed how they had scrutinized the ship as they approached—a ship that looked so very different from all the ships they had ever seen. Now they scrutinized him, timidly and unsure, and finally one of the men bowed and said, "Greetings to you, Shipsmen. We had expected you earlier, if you will pardon us for mentioning it. . . ."

Always the same anxiety. Wherever they went, they found the same unacknowledged distress, because the transporting of hair carpets that had functioned trouble-free for thousands of years had begun to falter. Even this greeting was tiresomely similar.

Everything was so similar: the great, dilapidated spaceports, the broken-down, poverty-filled, stinking cities around them, and the old men in their somber, shabby robes, who refused to comprehend. They told tales about the Emperor, about his realm, and about other planets on which wine was fermented for the Imperial Table or bread was baked . . . about planets that wove clothing for him, raised flowers, or trained songbirds for his gardens. But they had found none of those things, nothing but thousands of worlds on which hair carpets were knotted—nothing but hair carpets—a vast, unstoppable river of carpets made of human hair that had flowed through this galaxy for millennia. . . .

Wasra switched on the microphone, which amplified his voice and transmitted it over the external speakers. "You have been expecting the Imperial Shipsmen," he explained as he had done so often in words that had proved reliable. "We are not the ship you have been waiting for. We have come to tell you that there are no more Imperial Transport Ships, that there is no longer an emperor, and that you can stop making hair carpets." He slipped effortlessly into the language rhythm of Old Paisi, which was spoken on all planets in this galaxy, and sometimes this ease with the archaic language took him by surprise. Their speech would probably bring some odd looks when they returned home.

The men, all of them high dignitaries of the Guild of Carpet

Makers, stared at him in horror. Wasra nodded to the director of the Reeducation Team, and immediately, men and women marched down the ramp carrying dog-eared folders filled with photographs or well-used film players. They looked exhausted, like sleepwalkers. The captain knew they were trying not to think about how many more such planets lay ahead of them.

Reactions to the news of the end of the Empire had been wildly divergent—which provided at least some distraction from the monotony of their task. On some planets, people were happy to be able to discard the feudal drudgery of knotting hair carpets. On others, however, they had been denounced as heretics, insulted, and stoned. They had come across Guild Elders who already knew of the Emperor's death from mysterious sources, but who begged them not to announce it to the populace for fear of losing their status in society. Wasra realized that, in the end, they had no control over what actually happened after they left. On many worlds, centuries might pass before the old ways would really come to an end.

He thought again about his mission for the general. He growled at himself in irritation, because it had almost slipped his mind, and he pulled out his communicator. "Captain here. Chief Officer Stribat, report to me in the ground-level airlock."

Just moments later, a tall, lean soldier stepped through a door and drew himself up to give a casual salute. "Captain?"

Wasra looked up in annoyance. "Forget that nonsense," he grumbled. Stribat and he had started their service on board the *Salkantar* together. Stribat now commanded the land vehicles and foot soldiers. Not much of a career. But brilliant careers are only for fools, he thought darkly.

"Do you remember that we've already been on this planet?"

Stribat opened his eyes in surprise. "Really? For weeks I've had the suspicion that we're just landing on the same planet again and again."

"Nonsense. We were here, but it was three years ago. The *Salkantar* was assigned a search mission to find one of the *Kalyt* boats that got into trouble."

"And because we had no transfer coordinates, we jumped about for weeks from one sun to the next until we found the right one." Stribat nodded as he remembered. "I'll never forget how sick I was then from all the trans-light-speed flights one after another. . . . Nillian, that was his name, right? One of the pilots of the *Kalyt* boat. He landed, discovered the hair carpets, and then disappeared without a trace. Oh? . . ."

Wasra saw comprehension flash in the other man's eyes and simply nodded. "We're supposed to find out what happened to him. Man the armored vehicles; we're going into the city to the Guild Hall."

. . . .

Soon three heavily armored vehicles rattled into the airlock on their caterpillar tread. Their motors emitted a powerful, low thrum, and standing next to them for more than a few moments caused pain in the pit of the stomach.

The side door of the front vehicle opened, and Wasra got in. The guild elders on the landing platform respectfully made room as the three tanks rolled down the ramp, one after the other.

"That's the difference," said Wasra. He said it to Stribat, but, in reality, it was directed to nobody in particular. "A life meant nothing to the Emperor, less than nothing. And now? General Karswant is waiting on board the *Trikood*. . . everything is already prepared for the return flight to present our expedition report to the Council—but he doesn't want to leave without knowing what happened to this one man, this Nillian. Knowing that gives me a good feeling. Somehow it makes me . . ." He fumbled the right word.

"Proud," Stribat suggested.

"Proud, yes. It makes me proud."

When they were on the ground, the captain ordered a short stop. "We'll take one of the elders along; he can direct us to the Guild Hall." He pushed open the side door and waved to one of the old men who happened to be nearby. The Guild Elder approached without hesitation and willingly got in.

"I am so happy you've finally come," he began to chatter as the column got under way. "It's very unpleasant for us when the Emperor's transport ships don't arrive at the appointed time, because then our warehouses overflow with hair carpets. . . . Oh, that happened once before, I remember—I was still a child. It was four years before the Imperial Shipsmen returned. That was bad . . . a real trial for us. And back then, the Guild had bigger warehouses than today, you know. Today, everything's more difficult than it used to be. . . ."

Wasra stared at the stooped old man in his torn cloak, who was looking around the interior of the vehicle with his silvery, almost blind eyes and was babbling away like an excited child.

"Tell me," the captain interrupted him, "what's your name?"

The old man made a trace of a bow. "My name is Lenteiman, Shipsman."

"Lenteiman, did you hear what my crew were explaining to you back there?"

The Guild Elder raised his brow, and his eyes sought uncertainly for the direction from which the commander was speaking. His mouth gaped open carelessly, exposing a row of black tooth stumps. It appeared that he didn't even grasp what Wasra was talking about.

"Lenteiman, we are not the shipsmen of the Emperor. And you don't need to expect the transport ships anymore, because they will never come again—not in four and not in four hundred years." Even though I can't really be sure of that, Wasra thought to himself. "You don't need to tie any more hair carpets for the Emperor, because the Emperor is dead. The Empire no longer exists."

The old man was silent for a moment, as though he had to let the sound of the words run through his mind. Then a giggle bubbled up and burst from his throat. He raised his head toward the pallid glow of the sun.

"But the sun is still shining, isn't it? You shipsmen are a strange bunch and have strange ways. What you're saying would be heresy here. You'd better tell your men to watch their tongues when they go into town. Even though people will put up with a lot from you, of course, because everybody is so happy that you've finally come." He chuckled again.

Wasra and Stribat exchanged astonished glances.

"Sometimes I have the feeling," Stribat muttered, "that Denkalsar was an optimist." Denkalsar was an almost mythical figure; it was said that, several hundred years ago, a man by that name had actually lived and written the book whose title gave the rebel movement its name: *The Silent Wind.* Since the fall of the Emperor, however, reading Denkalsar had fallen out of fashion, and Wasra was surprised that Stribat even knew him.

"Lenteiman," he asked, "what do you usually do with heretics?"

The old man made a vague, broad gesture with his clawlike hands. "We hang them, of course, as the Law commands."

"Do you ever just put them in prison?"

"In cases of minor heresy, sure. But seldom."

"And are records kept of the trials and the hangings?"

"What a question! Naturally, and all the books are kept, just as the Law of the Emperor requires."

"In the Guild Hall?"

"Yes."

Satisfied, Wasra nodded. He began to enjoy the growling and vibrating of the tank engines that shook every fiber of his body; it seemed to him to be a sensation of superior, unassailable power. He was arriving with three armored tanks, with soldiers and with weapons that were immeasurably superior to anything on this planet. Without opposition, he would enter the building that represented the core of this society, and he would do whatever he wanted there. He liked this idea. His gaze turned to the light brown row of huts and low houses toward which they were headed, and he enjoyed the sensation of being a victor.

. . . .

They reached the Guild Hall, which stood massive and awe-inspiring before them. Its gray-brown exterior walls sloped out like the walls of a bunker and had no windows, just narrow openings like defensive embrasures. In the shadow of the building was a large square that presented a remarkable sight: it looked as though a fair had been set up and had been waiting in vain for months for visitors, while all the exhibitors had slipped into a state of half-sleep. Carts of all descriptions

stood wedged in at every angle—large, small, sumptuously orna-
mented and dilapidated, ugly armored wagons and open market carts.
Large, shaggy draft animals huddled together everywhere and stared
stupidly ahead while the drivers dozed on their coach-boxes. These
were the caravans of the hair-carpet traders, gathered here to deliver
the carpets to the Guild. Naturally, the arrival of the tanks brought
movement to the tableau. Heads jerked up, whips were wielded, and
bit by bit the wagons that had blocked the portal of the Guild Hall
were rolled aside.

The portal doors stood wide open. Nevertheless, Wasra commanded that they stop outside the gate. He and Stribat would enter
with the guild elder and a troop of armed men, while the other soldiers stood guard at the vehicles.

"It's a wise decision to stop here," croaked Lenteiman, "because
there's no more room in the courtyard—you know . . . the carpets . . ."

"Lenteiman, take us to the Guild High Priest," Wasra demanded.

The old man nodded agreeably. "I am sure he's eagerly waiting for
you, Shipsman."

Someone shoved open the door of the tank, and an almost unbear-
able stench of animal excrement assailed them. Wasra waited until the
escort troops had taken position before leaving the vehicle. When he
stepped onto the dusty ground of the square—the first time he had
actually set foot on the planet—he could almost physically sense the
eyes of the people on him. He avoided looking around. Stribat
stepped up beside him, and then came the old man. With a nod, the
captain ordered the escort to move ahead.

They passed through the gate. All around was an unnatural, frightening quiet. Wasra thought he heard someone in the crowd whispering

that they didn't look like Imperial Shipsmen. No matter how slow-witted the old men of the Guild might be and how much they might resist the truth with every fiber of their being, the common people always suspected exactly what was afoot and what their arrival portended.

Behind the gate was a small courtyard. It is probably called the Counting Court here, too, Wasra thought, as he saw an armored transport wagon being unloaded by several men. Reverently, they removed one hair carpet after another and stacked them in front of a man wearing the garb of a guildmaster, who compared each piece to the lading records with a snobbish air of precision. He gave only a cursory, dismissive glance at the approaching soldiers; then he noticed Lenteiman and hastened to bow deeply, along with his assistants. Only the trader, a massive man who was watching the whole procedure with a dull stare, remained unmoved.

The sight of the knee-high stack of hair carpets made Wasra shudder. Seeing a single hair carpet was positively distressing when one understood how it was made: that a carpetmaker had worked on it for his entire lifetime, using exclusively the hair of his wives and daughters; that he had spent his entire youth weaving the carpet backing and designing the pattern whose completion would cost him the rest of his life; that he had first knotted the outlines of the design, whose color was determined by the hair of his headwife, so that later, if he had daughters or subwives, he could fill in the various color fields in the design; and that finally—with bent back, gouty fingers, and nearly blind eyes—he would bind the entire carpet with a border of the curly hair he cut from his wives' armpits. . . .

A single hair carpet was an awe-inspiring sight. A whole stack of carpets, on the other hand, was a monstrosity.

Another gate, and behind it a short, dark passageway, so broad that it seemed like a room. The escort soldiers scanned about suspiciously, and Wasra noted their conduct with satisfaction.

They reached the inner courtyard, and now it was clear why it had been so dark in the passageway. In the courtyard, great mountains of carpets were stacked everywhere. Wasra had expected a sight like this, but it still took his breath away. Neatly piled, layer upon layer, the stacks rose taller than a man. And side by side, these carpet towers filled the courtyard from one corner to the other. The plunder of a planet for the last three years. Pondering the implications could make a man lose his senses.

He stepped up to one of the towers and tried to count. There must have been at least two hundred carpets in every stack. He guessed the area of the courtyard and calculated in his head. Fifty thousand hair carpets. He felt sick inside; a sort of panic welled up and threatened to overwhelm him.

"Where's the high priest?" he barked at the elder, sounding louder and more threatening than he had intended. "Where can we find him?"

"Come with me, Shipsmen."

With surprising nimbleness, Lenteiman slipped through the gaps between the piles of rugs and the courtyard wall. Wasra signaled the escort to bring up the rear and followed the old man. He felt an almost overpowering impulse to strike out, to knock over the carpets piled up higher than his head, and to flog the Guild Elder. Insanity—all of it, insanity. They had fought and won, they had destroyed everything that could be destroyed of the Emperor's realm, and still there was no end. . . . It just went on and on. For every step he took, a completed hair carpet was cut from its frame somewhere in this galaxy—

even now. For every breath he drew, a newborn male child was slaughtered because a carpet maker was allowed to have only one son—maybe on one of the numberless planets they had not yet visited, or even on one of the planets they had visited without being believed. It seemed impossible to stop the flood of carpets.

The farther they went, the more pervasive the odor emanating from the hair carpets was—a heavy, rancid smell reminiscent of spoiled fat and fermenting trash. Wasra knew it was not the hair that stank so, but the impregnating agent, which preserved the rugs for an astonishingly long time.

Finally, they reached another gloomy opening in the wall. A short stairway led upward. Lenteiman gestured for quiet and led the way, reverently, as though he were treading on holy ground.

The room into which he led them was large and dark, lighted only by the red glow of a fire burning in a metal bowl in the center of the room. The low ceiling forced them to stand with humbly bowed heads, but the oppressive heat and acrid smoke brought out pearls of sweat on their foreheads. Wasra reached nervously for the weapon on his belt, just to reassure himself that it was there.

Lenteiman bowed in the direction of the weakly glowing fire. "Venerable Master. It is Lenteiman who offers you greetings. I bring you the captain of the Imperial Shipsmen, who desires to speak with you."

The response was a rustling and an indistinct movement in the vicinity of the fire. Only now did Wasra perceive next to the metal firestand a couch, not unlike a child's cradle, and among the blankets and furs appeared the skull-like head and the right arm of an ancient man. When he opened his eyes, Wasra saw blind, silvery pupils reflecting the glow of the fire.

"What a rare honor . . . ," the old man whispered. His voice sounded frail and distant, as though he were addressing them from another world. "Greetings to you, Shipsmen of the Emperor. My name is Ouam. We've been waiting for you for a long time."

Wasra exchanged nervous glances with Stribat. He decided to waste no time explaining to the Guild High Priest that they were by no means shipsmen of the Emperor, but rebels. At least not until they had concluded their mission. He cleared his throat.

"Greetings, Venerable Ouam. My name is Wasra. I asked to speak with you because I have an important question."

Ouam seemed to be paying more attention to the sound of the foreign voice than to the meaning of the words. "Ask."

"I seek a man named Nillian. I want to know from you, whether a man by this name was charged with heresy or executed in the past three years."

"Nillian?" The high priest rocked his desiccated skull back and forth in thought. "I have to consult the books. Dinio?"

Wasra was beginning to wonder how this blind old man could manage to consult any books at all, when another face appeared out of the shadow of the couch. It was the face of a youth, who looked at the visitors with cool disdain before bending down to the old man to hear instructions whispered in his ear. He nodded assiduously, almost like an eager dog, and jumped up, disappearing through a door somewhere at the rear of the room.

He returned right away with a thick tome under his arm and squatted down on the floor next to the firestand to examine the entries. It didn't take long. Again he bent over the couch to exchange whispers with the old man. Ouam's smile was the ghostly grin of a death's-head.

"We have no record of this name," he declared.

"His full name is Nillian Jegetar Cuain," said Wasra. "Maybe he's listed by a different name."

The Guild Elder raised his eyebrows. "Three names?"

"Yes."

"A peculiar man. I should surely remember that. Dinio?"

The boy again consulted the register. This time when he whispered, he seemed to have more to say.

"There is likewise no record of the other two names," Ouam noted. "In the past three years, there was only one single execution for sacrilege."

"And what was that name?"

"It was a woman."

Wasra considered this. "Do you receive reports, when someone is executed for sacrilege or heresy in some other city?"

"Sometimes. Not always."

"What about your dungeons? Do you have any prisoners?"

Ouam nodded. "Yes, one."

"A man?"

"Yes."

"I want to see him," demanded Wasra. He felt like adding that he was prepared to reduce the entire Guild Hall to rubble and ashes to get what he wanted.

But there was no need to threaten. Ouam nodded agreeably and said, "Dinio will take you."

The dungeons were located in the most distant part of the Guild Hall. Dinio led them down decrepit, narrow stairways, holding the book containing records of executions and imprisonments tightly to him like a valuable treasure. Brown-stained plaster crumbled from the walls, and the deeper they went, the more acute became the stink of urine and rot and disease. At some point, the boy picked up a torch and lit it, and Stribad switched on the lamp he wore on his chest.

Finally they reached the first prison bars, a large gate guarded by a pale, bloated jailer. He gave them a dull stare, and if the large number of visitors surprised him, he didn't show it.

Dinio ordered him to unlock the access to the dungeon, and Wasra left two of the escort soldiers as guards at the open gate.

The gloomy gallery was lighted only by torches burning in the entryway. On the right and left, the doors of unoccupied cells stood open. Stribat examined the area with his lamp. In every cell hung a large, colored picture of the Emperor. The prisoners had always been chained to the opposite wall, out of reach of the picture; the mercy of total darkness had been denied them—the barred ventilation shaft above them provided enough light that they were forced to stare at the Emperor's image.

Dinio and the fat jailer, whose stench was even more disagreeable than that of the rotten straw covering the floor, stopped in front of the only occupied cell. Stribat shined his light through the gap in the door. They saw a dark figure with long hair lying curled up on the floor, arms chained to the wall.

"Unlock it," Wasra commanded fiercely. "And unchain him."

The man woke up at the sound of the key turning in the lock. When the door swung wide, he was already sitting up, watching them calmly. His hair shone white like silver, and Stribat's lamp revealed that the prisoner was much too old to be Nillian.

"Unchain him," Wasra repeated. The jailer hesitated. Only when

Dinio nodded did he pull out his keys and remove the old man's manacles.

"Who are you?" Wasra asked.

The man stared. Despite his squalor, he radiated dignity and serenity. He tried to begin several times before he was able to form words. It seemed he had not spoken for years. "My name is Opur," he said. "I was once a flutemaster."

With that he looked sadly down at his hands that appeared grotesquely mutilated. At one time or another, every one of his fingers must have been broken, and all the breaks had somehow grown back together without splints and without treatment.

"What did he do?" Wasra demanded.

As he spoke, he turned to the jailer who stared back stupidly. Answering for him, the boy responded with cold condescension: "He gave refuge in his house to a deserter."

"A deserter?"

"An Imperial Shipsman. A cargo loader from the *Kara*, the last ship to land here."

That must have been the first ship they pursued three years ago. Only to lose it and to discover another planet on which the inhabitants tied hair carpets and believed themselves to be the only ones. "What happened to the deserter?"

Dinio's expression remained chilly. "He's still on the run."

Wasra watched the boy for moment, trying to imagine what position he held. Then he decided it didn't really interest him and turned to the prisoner. He and Stribat helped him to his feet, and he told him, "You're free."

"No, he is not!" Dinio protested in a rage.

"He is free!" Wasra repeated sharply, giving the boy such a threatening look that he shrank back. "One more word about it, and I'll lay you over my knee and thrash you black and blue."

He handed Opur over to two soldiers from his escort with the instructions to get him to the ship for medical treatment and then to take him wherever he wanted to go. If he didn't feel safe on this planet, Wasra was determined to take him with them to the next world of carpet makers they visited.

Sniffing angrily, Dinio watched the departure of the soldiers and the flutemaster but dared say nothing more. Instead, he shifted his book from arm to arm and finally pressed it to his chest like a shield. As he did this, a small white something slipped from between the pages and floated gently to the floor.

Wasra noticed it and picked it up. It was a photograph of the Emperor.

The *dead* Emperor.

The commandant stared at the picture in amazement. He knew the picture. He carried exactly the same one in his pocket. Every member of the rebel fleet carried a photograph of the dead Emperor, just in case he were ever in a situation where he needed to prove that the Emperor really had been defeated and was dead.

"Where did you get that?" he asked the boy.

Dinio pouted obstinately, embraced his book still tighter, and said nothing.

"That must have belonged to Nillian," Wasra suggested to Stribat. He held the white backside of the photo up to the circle of light from Stribat's chestlamp. "It really did. Do you see that?"

The writing on the back of the picture was worn and smeared and so faded that it had almost disappeared. But at one spot there was a suggestion of the syllable *Nill.* Wasra's look at Dinio seemed capable of felling trees and splitting open children's skulls. "Where did this picture come from?"

Dinio swallowed nervously and finally grunted, "I don't know. It belongs to Ouam."

"Ouam surely didn't bring it back from some long trek."

"I don't know where he got it."

Wasra and Stribat exchanged glances, and it almost felt like old times when they each understood what the other was thinking.

"I would be interested," the captain suggested, "in what Ouam can tell us about this."

On the way back they back, they heard strange, keening sounds echoing through the dim halls of the Guild Hall, and they automatically quickened their pace. When they climbed the stair to the high priest's rooms—rapidly this time, not reverently—they were not met by smoke and the red twilight from glowing embers, but by radiant light and fresh air.

The room was transformed. A man walked slowly from window to window, throwing them open, admitting ever more cascades of blindingly bright light. Outside the open windows, the hair carpets looked like the billows of a sea, breaking against the windowsill.

The fire in the metal tripod had been extinguished, and Ouam lay dead on his couch, his blind eyes closed, his shriveled hands folded over his chest. The couch was smaller than it seemed in Wasra's memory, but, in spite of that, the corpse of the high priest in it seemed no larger than a child.

Guildsmen shuffled up the steps behind the space visitors. Paying no attention to the two strangers, they passed them by and sat down by the couch of the dead man and intoned a subdued lament. An echo of their dirge came in through the windows, and it spread through the whole Guild Hall and throughout the city. The man who had opened the window shutters and expelled what must have been years of smoke and stench now also joined the mourners; he presented the rebels with a memorable performance when his manner was transformed in a heartbeat from bustling efficiency to inconsolable grief.

At the sound of wild, hurried steps, Wasra swung about in surprise. Dinio was running breathlessly up the stairway, beside himself with despair. Without a sideways glance, he rushed to the dead high priest's couch, threw himself on the floor in front of it, and shed bitter tears. His was the only lamentation in the room that sounded sincere.

Wasra looked again at the photograph in his hand and shoved it into his pocket. He caught Stribat's eye, and again they understood one another without words.

. . . .

By the time they were outside the Guild House gates once more, the sun was setting, glowing red like melted metal. The two armored tanks on the square glittered like precious gems in this light. The ritual singsong of the wailing and mourning guildmasters lent the scene the fantastic atmosphere of a dream.

"That picture was Nillian's, wasn't it?" Stribat asked.

"Yes."

"That means that he was here."

Wasra watched the merchants, who had closed their stands for the night and were directing occasional questioning glances toward the Guild Hall. "I'm not sure if that's what it means."

"Maybe he escaped, met a nice woman, and has been living happily somewhere on this planet ever since," Stribat thought aloud.

"Yes, maybe."

"Three years . . . He might have two children in the meantime. Who knows, maybe he's begun to make a hair carpet himself?"

He's dead, Wasra thought, don't pretend anything else. They killed and buried him, because he said something against the Emperor. The immortal Emperor. Damn him. It took only one day to overthrow him, but for the twenty years since then, they had had to fight again every day to try to defeat him, as well.

"The landing craft!" Stribat burst out suddenly, and pulled excitedly at Wasra's sleeve. "Wasra! What about the landing craft?"

"What landing craft?"

"This guy Nillian must have come to the surface in an airboat. We could track that down!"

"They found that long ago," Wasra explained. "And they sent out disguised scouts who put their ear to the ground. Nillian had been arrested for heresy, and a carpet trader took him away to the Port City. Based on that, they looked around in the city, but Nillian never arrived here." Wasra had studied the old reports. The reports had not been especially thorough—it would have required considerable effort, for example, just to find the city near which Nillian had landed—and they didn't contain much helpful information. The hair carpets had been viewed back then as a quaint curiosity, and besides, everyone already had his mind on the trip back home. The attitude had been, He was commanded not to land, and he landed anyway—that's what he gets.

"Wouldn't it have made sense to have Nillian's partner accompany us?"

"Sure." Wasra nodded. He felt a wave of exhaustion spreading through his body, and he knew that it was more than a physical reaction. It never ended. Nothing ever ended. "Unfortunately, he's dead. He was with the volunteers who made the first assault on the Portal Station, and one of those flying battle robots got him."

Stribat emitted an inarticulate sound, probably meant to express something like amazement. "Why would a *Kalyt* pilot volunteer for a battle assignment?" When Wasra didn't answer, he continued grunting as he sometimes did when thinking. "And why would the general accept him?"

Wasra wasn't paying attention to his mumbling. Oblivious, he stared at the massive body of the *Salkantar,* a powerful presence rising into the sky in the distance, a dark silhouette against the setting sun, its outline shimmering like silver. Like all spaceships, it belonged in space; on the surface of a planet, it looked like a foreign body.

But the *Salkantar* would be sitting here for a long time, the captain thought unhappily. General Karswant would not set off for the Central World until he had learned Nillian's fate. And until the general reported to the Council of Rebels, they could not decide what should be done. And until the Council made a decision, the flood of hair carpets would continue, and they would have to see these obscene stacks, these mountains, these unspeakable piles of hair carpets everywhere.

"Does that mean we're supposed to scour the whole planet?" Stribat surmised.

"Do you have a better idea?"

"No, but can that time and effort be justified? I mean, suppose

Nillian is alive—then he would surely have made his way here to the Port City. This is where the spaceport is located; his chances of being found would be better here than anywhere else. The other possibility is that he's dead; if so, he isn't the only victim this expedition has to mourn."

"But he discovered the whole phenomenon of the hair carpets."

"So what?" Stribat peered quickly at the captain from the corner of his eye, as though he wanted to be sure he dared tell him what he had to say. "I don't want to rob you of the pride you feel about General Karswant, Wasra, but could it possibly be that his motives are not quite as noble as you want to believe?"

Wasra pricked up his ears. "What do you mean?"

"Maybe he wants, more than anything else, to do a favor for a certain member of the Council?"

"A certain member of the Council?"

"Councilor Berenko Kebar Jubad."

Wasra studied his comrade while giving serious thought to what he was trying to tell him. It had been Jubad who cornered the Emperor during the storming of the Star Palace and shot him single-handedly. Since that time, he had enjoyed a positively legendary reputation.

"What does Jubad have to do with this?"

"Jubad's father," Stribat said slowly, "was named Uban Jegetar Berenko."

The words hit Wasra like a slap in the face. His lower jaw dropped open. "Jegetar!" he repeated with effort. "Nillian Jegetar Cuain. They're related—"

"It would seem."

"And you think *that's* the reason Karswant is waiting?"

Stribat just shrugged his shoulders.

Wasra raised his head, stared into the darkening sky, where the first stars were appearing at its zenith. The Emperor's stars. It never ended. Was the Emperor dead? Or had it reached the point, where they were making his vanquisher into the next emperor?

"We're returning to the ship," he finally blurted out. He suddenly had the feeling he could not stay here one moment longer, especially not here at the gate to the Counting Court. "Immediately."

Stribat gave the escort soldiers a hasty signal, and the rumbling, bone-rattling motors of the two tanks started at once. The draft animals, already unharnessed and bedded down together for the night, raised their startled heads and stared vacantly toward the sound.

Everyone on the square moved obligingly aside when they headed off. They followed the tracks of the third tank, which had gone ahead with the man they had freed. *The flutemaster*—for a while Wasra pondered this word and tried to imagine what it meant. Then, as the vibration of the seat spread through his body, he recalled his feelings during the drive toward the Guild Hall: he had felt powerful and superior and had enjoyed it. The seductiveness of power—even after 250,000 years of the Empire, it seemed no one would ever learn!

He bent down, grasped the microphone of the communication unit. When he reached the broadcast operator on duty, he ordered: "Send a multiformat message to the Trikood, to Gen. Jerom Karswant. Text: Confirm with almost total certainty that Nillian Jegetar Cuain is dead. All indications are that he was the victim of lynch-mob justice by religious zealots. I wish you a good flight home and send my best regards to the Central World. Signed, Captain Wasra . . . and so on."

"Immediately?" the operator asked.

"Yes, immediately."

When he leaned back, he felt defiant and headstrong, and it felt good, like cold fire in his veins. Tomorrow he would send the Reeducation Team swarming throughout the city to tell everyone they could find what was going on in the galaxy. And that the Emperor was dead. Heavens, he could hardly wait to land on the next one of these hair-carpet planets to hurl the truth into the people's faces.

He noticed Stribat watching him from the corner of his eye with a smile that slowly spread across his lips. Maybe this Nillian really would show up someday, who could know for sure? But what counted right now was that Karswant would finally head back to the Central World to make his report to the Council—and that would finally get things moving. If someday they demoted him from the rank of captain, that would not change the fact that he had done what he thought was right.

Wasra smiled; it was the smile of a free man.

· · · · · XVII · · · · ·

Vengeance Is Eternal

THERE WERE SEVEN MOONS in the sky. The night was clear and cloudless, and looking like a deep blue crystal, the heavens arched above a surreal landscape.

It was hard to imagine that this entire world once had served no other purpose than to provide for the pleasure and entertainment of one single man! With the exception, of course, of the vast underground dungeons and defenses. Lamita often stood here on the small balcony of her room in the evening and tried to comprehend it.

Beyond the palace walls stretched the sea, calm and silvery in the moonlight. On the horizon rose gentle, forested hills, so distant that the line separating water and land was impossible to see at night. The entire planet was a single, artfully designed park. She knew that there were countless smaller castles and other country estates, in addition to the Palace, where the Emperor had indulged his pleasures.

All that was long in the past, of course. Now, the Council of Rebels met in the great throne room, and innumerable aides to the Provisional Government inhabited the gigantic Star Palace. Having the government located here on the former Central World of the Empire was not without controversy. In these paradisiacal surroundings, it was argued, the members would be too distant from the real problems of people on other worlds to make sensible decisions. However, basing the Provisional Council here for the time being had come about for practical reasons: all communications systems intersected here in an incomparable way.

A pleasant bell-tone sounded. That was the long-distance connection she was expecting. Lamita hurried in from the balcony and went to the multipurpose unit by her bed. The intergalactic network glyph was illuminated on the visual monitor.

"Speech connection established to Itkatan," a mellifluous but obviously artificial voice informed her. "Your communication partner is Pheera Dor Terget."

She pressed the appropriate button. "Hello, Mother. It's your daughter Lamita."

The screen remained dark. No video connection again. Recently, video seemed to function only for calls to other galaxies.

"Lamita, darling!" The voice of her mother had an unpleasant metallic overtone. "How are you doing?"

"Well, how would you expect things to be here? I'm doing fine, of course."

"Oh, yes, you people on your island of happiness. Here we're just relieved that the water system's functioning again and that the battles have died down in the North Sector. Maybe they've finally done one another in there; nobody would really regret that."

"Anything new about father?"

"He's doing fine. We got some medication again, and his condition has stabilized. If he were five years younger, they could operate, the doctor said. But now things just have to run their course...." She sighed. A sigh from thirty thousand light-years away. "Tell me about yourself, child. What's new?"

Lamita shrugged her shoulders. "I've been invited to take part in a general session of the Council tomorrow. As an observer. The commander of the Gheera expedition has returned and will present his report."

"Gheera? Isn't that the Imperial province no one even knew existed?"

"Yes. It disappeared for eighty thousand years, and the people there apparently did nothing for that entire time but produce carpets out of women's hair," Lamita said, and added sarcastically, "and whatever new oddities the expedition may have discovered, they'll expect *me* to find out what they mean."

"Aren't you still working with Rhuna?"

"Rhuna is being made the new governor of Lukdaria. She flew out yesterday. Now I'm in charge of the Imperial Archive by myself."

"Governor?" There was an obvious undertone of jealousy in her mother's voice. "Unbelievable. Back when we stormed the Imperial Palace, she was just learning to walk, I think. And now she's already made a big career for herself."

Lamita took a deep breath. "Mother, you could say the same about me. I was only four then." The old rebels seemed to have a hard time getting used to the idea that a new generation would constantly replace the old one, now that the immortal Emperor's reign had been ended.

Interstellar silence. Every second cost a small fortune. "Yes, I guess that's the way things go," her mother finally sighed. "So now you're all alone in your museum."

"It's not a museum. It's an archive," Lamita corrected. She sensed the unstated condescension in her mother's words and felt annoyed, even though she had promised herself not to be provoked. "But it really is a ridiculous situation. A quarter million years of Imperial history, and I'm all alone in the middle of it . . . and it would be possible to find answers in the Archive to questions we haven't even asked yet, if only . . ."

Why could her mother make her livid by hearing just half of what she said? "And outside work? You're still alone outside work, too?"

"Mother!" This same old tune again. A million years from now, parents would probably still patronize their children.

"I'm just asking. . . ."

"And you know my answer. You'll be told if I have a child someday. Until then, my relationships with men are nobody's business but mine—okay?"

"Child, of course I don't want to interfere in your life; it would just make me worry less to know that you aren't alone."

"Mother? Can we change the subject?"

. . . .

The Provisional Council had invited an unusually large group of observers to this session. That had been expected—after all, it would be the first report of the findings of a sensational mission to a rediscovered province of the Empire. And it presented no real problem, because the Council met in the former throne room, a hall whose size and appointment were breathtaking, as had befitted the ceremonial center of the Empire.

Lamita slipped between two old councilors into the hall in search of her assigned seat. Surely in one of the back rows. Fragments of sentences reached her and gave her a feel for the mood around her.

"... really have more pressing worries at the moment than an obscure cult in a lost galaxy."

"I think it's a maneuver by Jubad and Karswant, so that their influence in the Council..."

There was no seat for her in the back rows. She clasped her invitation tightly and was annoyed at her insecurity among all these old heroes of the Rebellion.

To her dismay, she found her nameplate at the very front, directly behind the semicircle of tables for the councilors. Apparently, they really did expect her to form an opinion. She took her seat discreetly and looked around. In the middle of the semicircle stood a large table in front of the projector. Diagonally across from her, she discovered Borlid Ewo Kenneken, with whom she had been working on Gheera matters for some time. He was a member of the Administrative Committee for the Imperial Estate, and therefore, in some matters relating to the Archive, he was her superior. He nodded at her with a smile, and Lamita noticed once again how his gaze lingered on her figure.

The imminent start of the session was announced by the sound of a gong. The luxuriously decorated instrument, taller than a man, fascinated Lamita. Someday, the seat of government would be someplace else, and the old Imperial Palace would be a museum, the most fascinating museum in the universe.

She spotted the thickset figure of a general in full uniform accompanied by several officers, just entering the hall. He gave the appearance of a gruff, bullish man with unshakable self-confidence. That must be Jerom Karswant, who had commanded the Gheera expedition. He placed a handful of data-units on the small table next to the projector, organized them carefully, and took his seat.

The second gong. Lamita noticed that Borlid was looking at her again. Now she regretted wearing a dress that emphasized her breasts. Fortunately, the chairman of the Provisional Council rose to open the session and to give the floor to General Karswant, so Borlid's gaze shifted to the center of attention in the room.

Karswant stood up. Within the grim set of his face, his eyes sparkled with alertness.

"First I want to show you what we're talking about," he began, and signaled to two of his aides. They lifted a roll, as long as a man, from the floor to the table and spread it out carefully.

"Honored councilors, ladies and gentlemen—a hair carpet!"

All heads jerked forward.

"Maybe it's best if each of you simply comes to the table for a moment for a close look at this astonishing work of art. The whole carpet is knotted entirely of human hair, and the knotwork is so incredibly dense and tight, that producing it requires the labor of an entire human lifetime."

Hesitantly, a few of the session participants stood up and headed up the aisles to inspect the carpet and, finally, to touch it gently. A general shuffling of chairs followed, as everyone else followed their lead, and in no time at all the session had dissolved into an excited jumble.

Lamita was awestruck when she managed to run her hand across the surface of the hair carpet. At first glance, it appeared to be fur, but a touch revealed that the hair was more closely spaced, far denser.

Black, blond, brown, and red hairs were worked in this carpet into a complex geometric pattern. She had seen photos of hair carpets in expedition reports, but having such a carpet right in front of her was an overwhelming experience. One could almost feel the profound devotion and effort expended on this unimaginable work of art.

In the general press of the crowd, Borlid was suddenly standing next to her, as though by chance. He seemed to have little interest in the hair carpet.

"When all this is over," he whispered to her, "may I invite you to dinner?"

Lamita breathed in once and then out again. "Borlid, I'm sorry. I'm not in the mood to talk with you about that at the moment."

"And after the session? Will you be in the mood then?"

"I don't know. Probably not. Besides, I'm sure I would have a guilty conscience if I accepted an invitation from you, because I know it would give you false hopes."

"Oh?" he responded with mock surprise. "Did I express myself unclearly? I wasn't proposing marriage, just a simple dinner—"

"Borlid, not now, please!" she admonished him, and returned to her seat.

How could he be so cocksure? She had found him pleasant as a coworker up to now, but when he thought he was being irresistible, he was just silly and boorish. He couldn't seem to accept the fact that she wasn't interested in him. His behavior seemed so immature to her that she would have felt like a child molester.

Gradually the auditorium calmed down again. After everyone had again taken a seat, the general continued with his presentation. Lamita was not paying close attention. She already knew most of what he was explaining—how the hair carpets had been discovered, details about the carpet cult on the planets of Gheera, about the trade routes, and about the spaceships that took the carpets on board to transport them to an initially unknown destination.

"We were able to follow the trail of the hair carpets to a large space station orbiting a double star, which consisted of a red giant sun and a black hole. According to our observations—which were later confirmed—the space station was a kind of transfer point for the carpets. When we approached the station, however, we came under such fierce and unexpected attack that we had to withdraw for the time being."

Of course Borlid was attractive by the usual standards. And the rumors suggested he didn't pass up many opportunities with the female members of the palace administration. Lamita carefully examined her motives. That was not really the reason she was turning him down, however. It was more . . . his immaturity. Yes—as a man, she found him shallow, immature, uninteresting.

"You must remember that up to that time, we were only a small expedition fleet: one heavy and three light cruisers, along with twenty-five expedition boats. So we waited for the arrival of the battle units approved by the Council; we attacked the station and finally occupied it with relatively minor casualties. It turned out that the black hole was actually the portal field of an enormous transdimension tunnel, large enough to accommodate oversize transport ships. For tens of thousands of years, every one of the hair carpets produced in the Gheera galaxy had gone into that tunnel."

Lamita knew that she was good-looking; she was slender, with long, blond hair and incredibly long legs. There was not a man who didn't turn his head when she walked by. Her appearance couldn't be the reason she had been alone so long. She wondered what it was that was wrong with her.

"We seized a transport ship returning from the tunnel. It was loaded with empty containers, apparently intended for hair carpets. After careful study and consideration, we decided to risk a flight through the dimension tunnel with a complete battle unit. And we discovered a solar system everyone believed no longer existed, because it couldn't be found where the star maps indicated it should be. We found the planet Gheerh."

Borlid was completely forgotten. Now the story was riveting. Gheerh had presumably once been the center of a great realm, the Kingdom of Gheera, before the Emperor's fleets attacked and conquered it . . . in order to incorporate it into the Empire . . . but then, inexplicably, to isolate it from the rest of the Empire and forget it again.

"The solar system was located in an immense bubble, a dimension chamber, and the tunnel we used was the only access. That was why we didn't find Gheerh at the location indicated on the star maps. We believed it had been destroyed, when, in fact, it had been removed from our universe into a bubble in another dimension. You could say that it had been encapsulated in its own little universe, in which there were no other stars but Gheerh's own sun. This bubble was maintained by control stations on the planet closest to that sun; they tapped the sun itself as the source for their enormous energy requirements. These stations were guarded by heavily armed and extremely maneuverable battleships, which attacked us as soon as we entered the bubble. Since they cut off our retreat, we responded with attacks on the bubble stabilization units of the control stations and destroyed so many of them that the solar system tumbled back into our common universe. It returned to its original location, and when the rest of our battle units came to our aid, we finally succeeded in neutralizing the enemy forces and occupying the planet Gheerh."

Karswant paused. For the first time, he seemed to grasp about for the appropriate words.

"I have seen many curious things in my life," he continued haltingly, "and most people who know me say I am not easily rattled. But Gheerh . . ."

The projector image showed a largely monochrome gray planet, on which there were almost no oceans. Only in the vicinity of the poles could slight color variations be detected.

"We found several million aboriginal inhabitants eking out a primitive life under pitiful conditions. And we found several hundred thousand men, who believed they were Imperial Troops, waging a merciless genocidal war against those people. Step by step, they were working their way forward—killing, burning, and butchering—and inexorably extending their borderline. Somewhat less than one fourth of the planet surface is still inhabited by the natives, and that area is mostly in the desolate inhospitable polar regions."

"We would hope you've put an end to this ruthless war!" one of the councilors thundered.

"Of course," the general replied. "We were able to halt an assault that had just begun."

One councilor raised her hand. "General, you stated that the native inhabitants had been driven together over the course of time onto one fourth of the planet's surface. What about the other three quarters?"

Karswant nodded. "The area emancipated from the troops, so to speak, amounts to approximately two thirds of the land mass of the planet, and . . ."

He paused again and looked slowly around the hall, as though he were seeking help from some quarter. When he finally began to speak again, his voice had lost its usual military edge; it seemed as though Jerom Karswant, the man, was now speaking.

"I admit that I have dreaded this moment. How in the world can I describe what we saw? How can I describe it so that you will believe me? I didn't even believe my commanding officers, men to whom I would entrust my life without hesitation. Instead, I had to land there to see it for myself. And even then, I didn't want to believe what my own eyes were witnessing."

He made a vague hand gesture. "During the entire return trip from Gheera, we sat together and went over every detail time and time again, but we were still unable to reach a conclusion. If the whole thing makes any sense, I beg to be initiated into the secret. That is all I really still desire in life—an explanation, a reason for the planet Gheerh." With that he turned the projector back on, and a film presentation began.

"Every foot of ground won through slaughter or expulsion of the native inhabitants was promptly leveled and paved over by the engineering personnel, which numbered nearly five hundred thousand men. After the fighting forces had moved on, the surface created in this manner was covered with hair carpets. In the course of many millennia, the Emperor's men had covered two thirds of the entire planet's surface with hair carpets."

One of the councilors broke the bewildered silence; he cleared his throat and asked, "Are you suggesting, General, that the hair carpets were all produced, in order to cover a *planet* with them?"

"That is what one sees on an overflight of Gheerh. Wherever one goes, hair carpets, edge to edge, with no visible trace of the original ground beneath them. Broad plains, deep valleys, high mountains, coastlines, hills, slopes—everything, everything covered with carpets."

The assembly watched the projected images, which confirmed the general's statements, with fascination.

"But that's insane," someone finally said. "What purpose could something like that serve?"

Karswant shrugged his shoulders in a helpless gesture. "We don't know. And we can't imagine any possible rationale for it."

Animated discussions erupted among the session participants, which the chairman of the Provisional Council brought under control with a commanding wave of the hand. "You are right, General Karswant. It certainly is difficult to believe," he declared. "It's surely the most unbelievable thing I've ever heard." He paused for a moment. It was apparent that he was having difficulty getting a grasp on what he wanted to say. "We cannot possibly all fly to Gheera, even though I, quite honestly, feel the need to do so. We will simply try to believe you, General."

He seemed positively stunned as he abruptly fell silent again and looked aimlessly about. Everyone in the hall seemed dazed.

"Whatever the explanation for all of this may be," he continued, obviously trying to take charge of the situation again, "we will find it in the historical records. I am pleased that our charming Lamita Terget Utmanasalen is present today—one of the best historians we have. She administers the Imperial Archive, and perhaps she understands this better than we do?"

At that, Lamita stood and turned in all directions, nervous to be the center of attention so unexpectedly. "I'm sorry that I'm unable to say anything about the matter," she responded after the chairman nodded to her. "No references to the hair carpets have yet been found in the Archive. That doesn't mean that they do not exist. The organizational system is still something of a mystery. And the Archive encompasses the entire Imperial Age, and so, of course, it is enormous. . . ."

"Lamita, you are relieved of all other responsibilities," the chairman interrupted. "For the time being, concern yourself with nothing but this matter."

Thanks a lot, Lamita thought with annoyance as she took her seat again. Alone. Just me and the Archive. He should have given me a staff.

"Our deliberations," the old councilor quickly continued, "should be concerned with the present and the future. The inhabitants of Gheera must be educated, faith in the Emperor must be eliminated, and a new political order must be established. I could imagine a successful transformation of Gheera into an independent federation by using the model of the provinces of Baquion and Tempesh-Kutaraan."

Lamita barely paid attention to the subsequent political discussion. The politics of the day didn't interest her. What captivated her were historical events and developments and the millennia that preceded them. In her thoughts, she was searching through the Archive again and trying for the thousandth time to unlock the secret of its organization, but she came up with nothing new. She was relieved when the meeting finally closed.

Borlid caught up with her before she was able to get out of the hall.

"Lamita, I have to speak with you a moment."

She folded her arms, holding her files like a shield in front of her chest. "Yes?"

"You've been avoiding me for weeks. I want to know why."

"Have I?"

"Yes. I ask if you want to have dinner with me, and you just . . ."

She sighed. "Borlid, let's not pretend. You want more from me than eating dinner together. And I am just not interested. So it would be unfair to accept your invitation. And stressful."

"No chance?"

"No." She sensed his injured male pride . . . terrible!

"So there's another man in your life?"

"And even if that were the case, Borlid—it's my life, and it's none of your business."

. . . .

She lay on her back, staring at the painted ceiling over her bed. The wind chime hanging in the open balcony doorway turned gently in the night breeze, and delicate, wistful tones rang out. In the light of the moons, its shadows fell onto the bedcover; other than that, it was dark in the room.

"I turned down one of the most attractive men in the palace," she said loudly. "And now I'm lying alone in my bed and don't know what I want."

A gentle laugh came from seventeen thousand light-years away.

"Since you rejected him, he apparently wasn't attractive enough, Lamita."

"Yes, exactly. I find him childish and shallow."

"But you just said, he's one of the most attractive men—"

"Well, yes. Many women find him appealing."

That laugh again. "It seems to me, dear sister, that you still think the important thing is to become like everybody else. In reality, the important thing is to become *different* from the others, to discover your uniqueness. You're a rebel by birth, but that doesn't mean much. Your own rebellion is still ahead of you."

Lamita wrinkled her nose while she tried to understand what these comments were supposed to mean. Her older sister loved to spout cryptic maxims and then leave it to her conversation partner to make sense of them—or not.

"Sarna, what's wrong with me? Why am I alone?" Lamita pouted.

"What's your problem with being alone?"

"It's boring. Unsatisfying."

"Worrying?" Sarna dug deeper.

"That, too," Lamita had to admit reluctantly.

"How long has it been since you were with a man?"

"Long. It was so long ago, I can hardly remember it. And besides, it was awful. I felt like a nanny caring for a child."

"But because it was so long ago," her sister surmised, "you've had time to forget it. So that can't be the problem. Lamita, which one of the men around you do you find exciting, fascinating?"

"None of them," Lamita shot back.

"Think it over carefully."

Lamita hastily reviewed all the young men who were somewhat tolerable and with whom she had contact. All of them boring. "There's not much to think over. Really, there's nobody."

"I don't buy that. Based on my experience with the effects of our hormones"—Lamita had to admit that her sister's experience in this area was extensive, and was, in fact, the reason she had called her up—"I think that's impossible. I'm convinced there's somebody. There's a man there who fascinates you and whose presence makes you moist between your legs. You just won't admit it to yourself. Maybe he's married, or he's ugly, or there's some other reason—but somehow you've blocked him out of your consciousness. But he's there. And that's why none of the others interest you." Pause. "Well, does that bring anybody to mind?"

Absent-mindedly, Lamita brushed a strand of hair from her forehead. Yes, there was something. She sensed a place in her mind, where there was resistance, a blind spot, a self-made barrier. If she could just put aside all her taboos for a moment, then . . . No. That was out of the question. What would they say about her, if she . . .

What would the others say? There it was! It was an astonishing thought for someone who considered herself a rebel, wasn't it? She almost became angry at herself, but she was still proud of catching herself at her own tricks.

"Actually, there is a man . . . ," she began reluctantly.

"I told you so," Sarna said with great satisfaction.

"But it's still impossible. Not with him."

"Why not?" her sister pried gleefully.

"He is much older than I am."

"It must be a family trait. After all, our father wasn't exactly a boy when he met our mother."

"And he's an incurable devotee of the Emperor."

"That will guarantee some lively discussions," Sarna commented with amusement. "Anything else?"

Lamita mulled it over. "No," she finally sighed. "But now I really don't know what I should do."

"You don't?" her sister was amused. "I'll bet you know exactly."

. . . .

This state of mind was not new to her—this absolute decisiveness, this determination to act, to be courageous, and not to allow obstacles to dissuade her. She also knew that it was important to take advantage of this decisiveness while it lasted.

She couldn't even think about sleep. She dressed quickly and phoned the Imperial Archive. After a brief time, the archivist answered.

"Would you object if I come to the Archive this evening?" she asked.

He raised one eyebrow. "You're the representative of the Council. You may come and go whenever you want."

"Yes," Lamita said nervously. "I just wanted to inform you. I'll be there soon."

The door to the Archive stood open when she arrived. At a loss, Lamita stood for a while in the brightly lit entry hall and looked around. Everything was empty and deserted; there was no one to be seen. Lights also burned in the great domed hall. Lamita entered the main reading room and placed her portfolio on the oval table where the Emperor himself used to sit. The echo of every sound seemed amplified, which only increased the sensation that she was alone.

She walked into one of the radiating aisles and took an old folio volume from a shelf. When she returned with it to the table, she spotted the archivist. As always, he stood in the half-shadow of the columns at the entrance to the reading room, cautious and stock-still.

Lamita lay the thick tome slowly on the table. "I hope I'm not disturbing you," she spoke into the stillness.

"No," said Emparak.

She hesitated. "Where do you actually live?"

If he was surprised by the question, he didn't let it show. "I have a small apartment on the first lower level."

His voice sounded cold. She knew that he had known and worked with the Emperor, and whenever she had had business with the archivist in the past, it had not escaped her, that his attitude toward her and, in general, toward everyone who had anything to do with the Rebellion was antagonistic. He was a short man—hardly taller than she was—with thick, silver-gray hair and a slightly misshapen spine, which forced him to assume a bent posture. Nevertheless, he was an impressive, dignified figure who radiated composure and maturity.

"It must be an odd feeling," she said thoughtfully, "to live here in the midst of tens of thousands of years of momentous history. . . ."

She noticed that Emparak started at these words, and when she looked into his eyes, she saw that he had been taken by surprise.

"When the Empire ended, I was still a child only five or six years old," she continued, and for the first time, she had the feeling that he was actually listening to her. "I grew up in a world in transition. I saw things disintegrating all around me, and I began to wonder how things had been in the past. That was probably why I studied history. And during my entire academic training, it was my dream to be here one day in the Imperial Archive. Excavations, experimentation, field research—none of that attracted me. Out there were only questions—but here, I was convinced, were the answers. And I wasn't interested in looking for questions; I wanted to know the answers." She looked at him. "And now, here I am."

He had moved a step forward out of the shadow, probably without being aware of it. He searched her face as though he were seeing her for the first time, and Lamita waited patiently.

"Why are you telling me this?" he finally asked. His question sounded pained.

Lamita walked cautiously toward him. She inhaled deeply and slowly and tried to feel the determination that had animated her earlier. "I came to figure out what is going on between us," she said softly.

"Between . . . us?"

"Between you, Emparak, and me—there is something. A resonance. A connection. An electrical field. I feel it, and I'm sure you feel it, too." She was standing directly in front of him, and the feeling was powerful. "I noticed you immediately, Emparak, when I saw you standing here by the columns for the first time. I didn't admit it to myself until now, but your presence arouses desire in me, an intense desire I have never felt before. I've come to find out why."

His breath came in gasps, and his eyes darted around the floor and walls, only daring to settle on her for brief seconds at a time.

"I beg you, don't play with me."

"I'm not playing, Emparak."

"You are . . . an exceptionally beautiful woman, Lamita. You can have any man you want. Why would you want to have anything to do with a cripple like me?"

Lamita suddenly felt his anguish as if it were her own. It was a feeling that seemed to come from the region of her heart. "I don't see you as a cripple. I see that you have a misshapen back, but why is that important?"

"I *am* a cripple," he insisted. "And an old man."

"But a man."

He said nothing. With his back to her, he stared at the marble floor.

"I came to find out what you feel, Emparak," Lamita finally said quietly. Maybe it hadn't been a good idea. "If you prefer, I'll leave."

He mumbled something she did not understand.

She reached out her hand and touched his upper arm. "Do you want me to go?" she asked nervously.

His head turned to her. "No, don't go." He still didn't know where he should direct his gaze, but his hand had suddenly reached for hers and clung to it, and his words suddenly gushed out. "I'm an old fool . . . I really am . . . I didn't expect ever again in my life . . . and a woman like you! I have no idea what to do now."

Lamita had to smile. "I bet you know exactly," she said.

She had expected that she would have to battle against a mountain of insecurities built up in him over a lifetime, and she was prepared to do it. But when Emparak took her in his arms and kissed her, it was with a sensitive self-assuredness that surprised her beyond measure. She virtually melted in his embrace. It was as though her body had always been waiting for the touch of this man.

"May I show you where I live?" he finally asked after what seemed to her like hours.

She gave him a dreamy nod. "Yes," she sighed. "Please."

. . . .

"I still can't believe it," Emparak said into the darkness. "And I'm not sure I'll ever believe it."

"Don't worry," Lamita purred sleepily. "I can hardly believe it either."

"Have you had many men?" he asked, and in an almost amusing way, the question sounded jealous.

"Not as many as most people suppose." She smiled. "But enough to know that I am bored by men for whom the most important era of history began with their own birth." She turned over and pressed herself against his chest. "Luckily your experience in this regard seems to far surpass my poor abilities. I bet you have not always lived such a monastic life as your apartment suggests."

Emparak smiled; she could hear it in the sound of his voice. "In the past, my position was influential and that had its rewards. I was discreet, but I think everyone knew that I pursued all the women in the palace. . . . Then came the revolution, and you rebels humbled me severely, showed me your might, and let me know that I had been on the wrong side, the losing side. You stored me away just in case you might need me again someday, but I became nothing more than an old janitor. So since then, I have completely withdrawn."

"I noticed that," Lamita murmured. Something inside her warned that she was heading toward dangerous ground, but she decided she was still prepared for the risk. "I think you are still devoted to the Emperor."

She felt him suddenly pull back.

"And what would that mean to you?" There was unyielding pride in his response. Defiance, but also fear. More than a little fear.

"Just as long as you are devoted to me, too, it's all right," she said softly. A good answer. She felt him relax. In spite of his fear, he would not have been willing to deny his beliefs, not even for her sake. That impressed her.

"Actually I was never a devotee of the Emperor in the usual sense," he said thoughtfully. "The people who venerated and worshipped him didn't know him; they only knew the image they had created of him.

But I knew him, face-to-face." He was silent for a moment, and Lamita could virtually feel the memories awakening inside him. "His presence was even more overwhelming than all the legends his priests were able to concoct. He was an unimaginably charismatic personality. You rebels try to get off too easy with your simple view of him. He was beyond the scale of human measurement; the measures for assessing natural phenomena would be more appropriate. Don't forget, he was immortal, nearly a hundred thousand years old—no one comprehends the meaning of that. No, I'm no blind worshipper—I'm a scholar. I try to understand, and I despise cheap, quick, ready-made answers."

Lamita had sat up and turned on the light next to the bed. She looked at Emparak as though she were seeing him for the first time, and in some sense that was true. The scowling, venomous old man had disappeared. The man lying next to her was alert and lively and was turning out to be a closer kindred spirit than anyone else she knew.

"That's exactly the way I feel," she said, and she suddenly felt like seducing him a second time on the spot.

But Emparak threw the blanket aside, stood up, and began to get dressed. "Come with me," he said. "I want to show you something."

. . . .

"The Archive is as old as the Empire, and over the course of time, there have been far more than a thousand changes in the organizational systems. That's the reason the current system is so complicated. For someone who doesn't know that, it's utterly impossible to comprehend." Emparak's voice echoed back from the low, dark, side aisles, as they descended from one level to another farther down into the mysterious depths of the Archive. Down here, there was dim illumination only in the main hallways, and all the things that were hidden in the shadows cast by the cabinets, cases, and baffling bits of plunder were left to the imagination. At some point, Lamita had grabbed the archivist's hand and didn't let go.

"Level two," Emparak said, after they descended another broad stone staircase. He pointed to an inconspicuous little wall plate on which the number was painted in an ancient script.

"Is that the second level from the bottom?" Lamita asked.

"No. There's no correlation. The Archive was extended, reconstructed, enlarged, and reorganized countless times." He gave a scoffing laugh. "Below us are still four hundred additional levels. No rebel has ever been that far down."

They walked down a broad hallway. At a sign bearing the letter *L* in a form that was in use in the days of the third Emperor, they turned into a narrower side gallery. And then they began to walk past archive cabinets and mysterious artifacts, implements and works of art, which seemed absolutely endless to Lamita. The numerical symbols on the signs illustrated the semiotic changes in the Empire's writing for a period of a hundred thousand years before they reached the number *967*, written in a script that was common eighty thousand years ago.

Emparak opened the single door panel of a large cabinet. He swung back the door as far as possible and then switched on the ceiling light.

On the inside of the cabinet door hung a hair carpet.

Lamita noticed after a while that her mouth was agape, and she closed it again.

"So it's true," she said. "The Archive does know something about hair carpets."

"The Archive knows *everything* about hair carpets."

"And you've withheld that the whole time."

"Yes."

Lamita felt a giddy chuckle gurgling up inside her like a bubble in water that's finally just about to boil, and she didn't hold it back. She threw back her head, and her laugh echoed back from all directions. Through a fog of tears, she saw that Emparak was watching her with a grin.

"Archivist," she huffed in an unsuccessful attempt to sound stern after she had caught her breath, "you will immediately reveal to me everything you know about this matter. Otherwise I will chain you to the bed, and I won't finish with you until you talk."

"Oh," Emparak mugged. "I was actually about to tell you the whole story, but now you are tempting me to hold my tongue."

He pulled out a large star map embedded in transparent archival sheeting. "Gheera was once a flourishing kingdom, whose origin, as is the case with nearly all the old realms of human history, is lost in the dark ages of prehistory. This kingdom was discovered and attacked by the tenth emperor, the predecessor of the last emperor—for no other reason than the fact that it existed and the Emperor wanted to dominate it. A long war with many victims ensued, in which, however, Gheera never really stood a chance against the Imperial Battle Fleet and was therefore finally defeated."

He pointed to a series of old-fashioned image recorders. "The king of Gheera was named Pantap. He and the Emperor first met face-to-face on Gheerh after the kingdom had been defeated. The Emperor demanded a solemn, public display of submission by Pantap." Emparak looked at Lamita. "Do you want to take the material upstairs with us?"

"What? Oh, yes"—she nodded—"yes, of course."

Emparak disappeared into a nearby side hall and returned with a lightweight wire container on wheels. He put the star map and the image recorders inside.

"Gheerh must have been an incredibly beautiful, vital world at that time," he continued and pulled out an ancient binder. "This report gives a description of Gheerh. It calls the planet the gem of the universe and praises its innumerable artistic treasures, the sagacious lifestyle of the inhabitants, and its natural beauty."

Lamita took the binder carefully and placed it, too, into the wire cart.

"Did you know the tenth emperor was bald his entire life?" Emparak asked.

Lamita raised her eyebrows in surprise. "Then I must have seen the wrong photographs."

"Of course he had hair implants, but these had to be replaced every few months because his body rejected them. It was an allergic reaction that stayed with him his entire long life—it's possible that it was connected to the treatments that extended his life.... No one knows. What is known is that he considered this physical flaw a humiliation, an insult of fate—a blemish that kept him from achieving the perfection he so desired."

Lamita inhaled audibly. "Oh!" her sigh implied that a vague suspicion about the connections was beginning to form inside her.

"King Pantap's spies had learned about this sensitive spot in the Emperor's character," Emparak continued, "and Pantap was apparently a proud, angry man. He decided, for reasons that seem incomprehensible, that it would serve his interests to strike this sore spot with all his remaining strength. When the Emperor arrived to accept the surrender, Pantap, who had a magnificent beard and head of hair, said verbatim, 'Your power may be great enough to force our submission, bald Emperor, but it is not great enough to cause hair to grow on your own scalp.'"

"That doesn't sound like a good idea."

"No. It was probably the worst idea any man ever had."

"What happened?"

"The tenth emperor was generally known to be quick-tempered and vengeful. When he heard that, he was enraged. He swore to Pantap that he would regret those words as no one had ever regretted any calumny. He said, 'My power is great enough to cause this entire planet to be covered with the hair of your subjects, and I will force you to watch it happen!'"

Lamita stared at the old archivist in horror. She felt as though a chasm were suddenly gaping below her.

"Do you mean that the history of the hair carpets . . . is the history of an act of revenge?"

"Yes. Nothing more."

She clapped her hand to her mouth. "But that's sheer insanity!"

Emparak nodded. "Yes. But the real insanity is not so much the idea itself, but the merciless determination with which it was put into effect. As usual, the Emperor sent out his priests to spread the God-Emperor cult and overcome all resistance to it. At the same time, he had the hair-carpet cult set up—the complete, complex logistical plan, the caste structure, the tax system, and so on. From the remnants of the armed forces of Gheera, the Shipsmen were recruited to transport the hair carpets from the individual planets to Gheerh. In order to make any escape and any outside interference impossible, Gheerh itself, the entire solar system, was encapsulated within a dimension bubble, and thus artificially removed from the normal universe. Specially selected and particularly ruthless troops bombed the culture of Gheerh's inhabitants into a primitive state and undertook an agonizingly slow military campaign of extermination. All around the royal palace, they began to pave over the land and lay the first hair carpets."

"And the king?" Lamita asked. "What happened to Pantap?"

"On the order of the Emperor, Pantap was chained fast to his throne and attached to a life-support system that must have kept him alive for several thousands of years. The Emperor wanted Pantap to watch helplessly what was happening to his people. At first, Pantap probably had to watch through the throne room windows as the capital city was leveled street by street and the resulting surface was covered with carpets. At some point the teams switched over to filming all their activities—their murderous conquests and their demolition work—and they broadcast it all onto screens set up in front of the defenseless king."

Lamita was horrified. "Does that mean that Pantap may still be alive?"

"It can't be ruled out," the archivist admitted, "although I don't believe so, because life-support technology was not as advanced as it is today. The palace must be there, however—somewhere on Gheerh, probably in the middle of a very large region where the very first hair carpets have surely turned to dust long ago. Obviously, the Gheera Expedition didn't find it . . . otherwise they would have discovered Pantap or his remains."

The young historian shook her head. "That has to be resolved. The

Council has to be told; it must send someone back. . . ." She looked at Emparak. "And all this has continued the whole time since then?"

"The Emperor died soon after the hair-carpet system was set up. His successor, the eleventh and last emperor, made only one brief visit to Gheera. Some notes seem to indicate that he was disgusted, but couldn't bring himself to put a stop to the whole thing—probably out of loyalty to the earlier emperors. After his return, he had the province removed from all star maps and deleted from all data recorders, and he just left them to themselves. And since then, the machinery has ground on, from millennium to millennium."

Silence settled on the oddly matched couple.

"So that is the history of the hair carpets," Lamita whispered in shock.

Emparak nodded. Then he locked the cabinet again.

Lamita looked about, still numb from what she had heard. Her gaze passed along the hallways and side aisles over countless other cabinets like this one . . . on and on with no end to them in sight.

"All these other cabinets," she asked quietly, "what do they contain?"

The archivist looked at her, and eternity shimmered in his eyes. "Other histories," he said.

Epilogue

Knot after knot, always the same hand movements, always looping the same knots in the fine hair, infinitely fine and tiny, with cramped hands and red-rimmed eyes—and still he made almost no headway, no matter how he slaved and rushed. So he squatted every waking hour before the creaking carpet frame where his father had sat and, before him, his father's father and grandfather, stooped and attentive, with the old, filmy magnifying lens before his eyes, his arms propped against the breastboard, moving the knotting needle with only the trembling tips of his fingers. He tied knot upon knot in feverish haste, as though driven and fighting for his life; his back hurt up to his neck and an excruciating headache pounded behind his forehead, pressing on his eyes until he sometimes could no longer see the knotting needle. He tried not to listen to the new sounds that filled the house—the loud disruptive arguing of his wives and daughters below in the kitchen, and, above all, the voice ringing out of the apparatus they had installed there, which constantly spewed out blasphemies.

Heavy footfalls creaked up the stairs to the carpet-knotting room. They couldn't leave him in peace. Instead of going about their God-given duties, they sat around the whole day and parroted this stupid empty prattle about a *new time*, and there was an endless stream of visitors joining in the ceaseless drivel. He snorted and tightened the knot on which he was working. Without removing the magnifying lens, he reached for the next hair from among those he had spread out on a pillow beside him, all neatly brushed and individually cut to the proper length.

"Ostvan . . ."

It was Garliad. He clenched his jaws until his teeth ached, but he didn't turn around.

"Ostvan, my son . . ."

Furiously, he tore the headband of the old lens from his forehead and spun around. "Can't you leave me in peace, all of you?" he screamed, his face red with anger. "Can't you just leave me alone? How long are you going to continue to neglect your responsibilities and constantly interrupt me at my work?"

Garliad stood there with her long, snow-white hair and just looked at him. This solicitous, pitying look from her clear eyes enraged him. "What do you want?" he spat.

"Ostvan," she said gently, "won't you please finally stop?"

"Don't bring that up again!" he shouted, and turned away from her, fumbling with the magnifying lens and getting it only halfway back in position. His fingers reached for the knotting needle and for the next hair.

"Ostvan, it's senseless, what you're doing—"

"I am a carpet maker, just as my father was a carpet maker and his father before him and so on. What else should I do but tie a hair carpet?"

"But nobody will buy your hair carpet anymore. There are no more hair-carpet traders. The Imperial Shipsmen don't come anymore. Everything has changed."

"Lies. All of it, lies—"

"Ostvan . . ."

This motherly tone in her voice! Why couldn't she just leave? Why couldn't she just go back to the kitchen and leave him in peace, leave him in peace to do what he had to do? This was his duty, his duty to God, the purpose of his life—a carpet for the Palace of the Emperor.... He looped the knots hastily, sloppily, distractedly. He would have to cut them all out again later ... later, when he had his peace and quiet again.

"Ostvan, please! I can't stand to watch you do this."

His jaws ached with rage. "You can't stop me. I have a debt to my father. And I will pay that debt!"

He continued working, rushing on feverishly as though he had to finish the entire gigantic carpet today. He looped knot after knot, always the same hand movements, quickly, quickly, always the same knots in the manner passed down for thousands of years, so fine and so tiny, before the creaking carpet frame, his trembling arms propped against the sweat-stained, worn-out breastboard.

She didn't leave. She just remained where she was standing. He could feel her eyes probing into his back like a terrible ache.

His hands began to shake, and he had to interrupt his work. He couldn't work this way. Not while she was standing there. Why wouldn't she just go away? He didn't turn around; he just clutched the knotting needle and waited. His breathing was labored.

"I have a debt to my father, and I will pay that debt!" he insisted.

She was silent.

"And ...," he added, but then he stopped. He began again: "And ..." Nothing more. No, that was beyond the limit of what he could say. He grasped a new hair, tried to find the eye of the needle, but his hands were shaking too violently.

She didn't leave. She stood there, said nothing, just waited.

"I have a debt to my father. And ... and I have a debt to my brother!" It burst from him in a voice like shattering glass.

· · · · · 299 · · · · ·

And then it happened . . . something that should never have happened: his hand slipped with the knotting needle; it slashed into the carpet and cut open the delicate backing fabric . . . a rip as broad as his hand . . . the work of years.

Then, finally, the tears came.